The Champ:
Griffin Cahill

Age: 34
Occupation: Photographer
Height: 6'3"
Weight: 210 lbs.
Weapons: Wit, charm, experience
Record: UNDEFEATED

The Challengers:
Stewart & Robert Cahill
aka the Stewberts

Age: 8 months
Occupation: Cooing & drooling
Height: 30"
Weight: 25 lbs.
Weapons: Big smiles & lethal cuteness
Record: No wins, no losses, no ties

Expert Analysis:

Despite the inexperience of the challengers, the champ is in for a tough one. Griffin Cahill has never met an opponent of this caliber before, and the Stewberts have been well prepared for the big match. Griffin has a chance to win—but only if he manages to convince Heather Delaney to work his corner. He'd better not hold his breath…

Books by Kathleen O'Brien

HARLEQUIN SUPERROMANCE

927—THE REAL FATHER
967—A SELF-MADE MAN
1015—WINTER BABY

Dear Reader,

I'll admit it right up front. I love babies. I'm a hopeless cornball on the subject. Madison Avenue must love me. I'll buy anything if a freckle-faced little boy asks me to. I'm even worse about my own children. Avoid going to lunch with me unless you want to hear every precious word my son uttered this morning. Don't come over unless you're dying to watch the blurry video of my daughter's school play. But here's my other confession. I don't love babies *because* I had two of my own. I love them *in spite* of that.

If you made a list of the pros and cons of having babies, the cons would fill a notebook. They are expensive and exhausting. They're terrible conversationalists. They have shocking table manners. And let's be honest. Sometimes they don't smell quite right. The pros... Well, there's just one, really. One big, wonderful pro. Babies make the world new again.

They put the magic back in the merry-go-round, the sparkle back in snow. They make you believe in fairies and flying elephants and Forever. They cleanse the past of pain and fill the future with promise. Best of all, they remind you that happiness is not complicated.

Griffin and Heather, the hero and heroine of *Babes in Arms*, knew all this once upon a time. But ten years ago they bitterly ended their engagement, and the world hasn't held much magic since. Until the babies come to stay...

I hope you enjoy their story. And if your son said anything precious this morning, remember I'm one of the few cornballs who would really like to hear about it.

Warmly,

Kathleen O'*Brien*

P.O. Box 947633, Maitland, FL 32794-7633 or KOBrien@aol.com

Babes in Arms

Kathleen O'Brien

TORONTO • NEW YORK • LONDON
AMSTERDAM • PARIS • SYDNEY • HAMBURG
STOCKHOLM • ATHENS • TOKYO • MILAN • MADRID
PRAGUE • WARSAW • BUDAPEST • AUCKLAND

ISBN 0-373-71047-X

BABES IN ARMS

This edition published by arrangement with Harlequin Books S.A.

Visit us at www.eHarlequin.com

Printed in U.S.A.

To Mikey, because I'm crazy 'bout you.

CHAPTER ONE

FOR ONE CONFUSED and horrible split second when he first woke up that Monday morning, Griffin Cahill felt—

He couldn't even say it. He stuffed his aching head under his silk-covered pillow to make the word go away. But there it was, darting around his brain like a sniper, eluding every attempt to capture and evict.

Old.

Griffin Cahill felt old.

It didn't last long, of course. Because it was ridiculous. Griffin was only thirty-four. He was mystifyingly healthy, considering how little attention he paid the issue. He was active and fit and, by some lucky combination of mix-and-match genes, the first Cahill since the *Mayflower* who didn't look like a horse.

Definitely not old.

The sniper receded.

Still, if he wasn't old, Griffin wondered as he emerged from the pillow and slid his feet over the edge of the bed, why did he ache all over? He hadn't played tennis yesterday. He hadn't been out fishing yet this year. He hadn't—

And then he remembered. *Miranda.* He was achy

because he'd spent the night with Marvelous Miranda, who got her blue eyes from Bausch & Lomb, her blond hair from L'Oréal, and her high spirits from a bottle of Chivas Regal. But she got her body, and her flair for using it creatively, straight from God.

Griffin ran his fingers through his tangled hair. That proved it, then. Women like Miranda damn sure didn't think he was old. They thought he was a state-of-the-art roller coaster, and one ride was never enough.

So there. *Goodbye, sniper. And good riddance.*

Griffin's housekeeper didn't come until noon on Mondays, so Griffin gathered the sheets off the bed and dropped them into the laundry chute himself. He disliked an unmade bed—especially if it still held a whiff of last night's perfume.

As he always did, he plotted his day while he showered. Coffee and toast, a couple of hours in the darkroom, two interviews with candidates for this year's photography scholarship. Then, at five, that damn city council meeting.

Griffin made a mental note. Never, ever again allow anyone to talk him into sitting on the city council. That was probably why he'd woken up feeling so rotten this morning. The politics of Firefly Glen could make a grumpy old man out of Peter Pan himself.

If they weren't planning to vote on Heather Delaney's rezoning request today, he might have skipped the meeting altogether. Heather needed his vote, though of course she hadn't asked him for help. Griffin was well aware that she'd cut out her tongue with a pair of nail scissors before she'd ask him for anything.

Still, he'd go, and he'd vote for her rezoning. Not to do Heather a favor, but merely because it was fair.

He had finished the *Glen Gazette* and started on the *Wall Street Journal* when the doorbell rang. He was tempted not to answer. It might be Miranda, who had a tendency to think the Griffin Cahill amusement park was open twenty-four hours a day, which it wasn't.

But he put his mug on the butcher-block table and crossed his sunny, two-story great room to reach the door. He knew how to get rid of Miranda, or any other uninvited female. And he knew how to do it with a smile.

He opened the door, letting his eyes and his body language send the required rebuff—what a shame, it would have been delightful, but this simply isn't a good time.

Unfortunately, it wasn't Miranda. It was someone else, someone who didn't give a damn about Griffin's body language. It was Griffin's little brother, Jared.

And in his arms Jared was holding his twin eight-month-old sons, Stewart and Robert.

Jared lived on Long Island. Hours away. Griffin hadn't seen him in months. Jared was a corporate lawyer, a hotshot. He hated small towns, Firefly Glen in particular. And where was Katie, Jared's wife—the one who was officially in charge of those squirming creatures?

For several seconds, Griffin was too surprised to do

anything but stare at the babies stupidly. They stared back, frowning in openmouthed curiosity at this man they probably didn't recognize, though he had met them several times, and each time had brought ridiculously expensive gifts.

"Jared?" Griffin wasn't doing very well verbally, either. He squinted into the spring sun, trying to read his brother's face. "What— Is anything wrong?"

"No. Well, yes." Jared shifted the boys higher on his arms, to balance the burden. "Damn it, Griff. Let me in."

Reluctantly Griffin moved out of the doorway, and Jared lurched in, bumping clumsily into everything with the huge blue-plaid plastic cases he had slung over each shoulder.

Griffin's early detection radar was sending out a signal. This didn't look right. He mustered a smile for the boys, who were starting to get on his nerves. They kept staring with those wide, unblinking eyes. And their little pink pudgy lips were drooling something suspiciously milky in hue.

He managed not to make a sound when Jared jostled the Chihuly bowl that stood on a pedestal by the door. The large green glass rocked precariously. Griffin's heart waited politely, watching Jared steady the bowl with one hip, before resuming its regular beat.

Jared didn't even look alarmed, much less apologetic. He merely scowled at the museum-quality piece and shook his head. "That will have to go."

"Really?" Griffin raised his eyebrows. "And why is that?"

"Because glass is dangerous." Jared scanned the large, simple room with a critical eye. "God, Griffin, why do you have so much glass around here?"

"I like it." Griffin let his voice get chilly. "Frankly, I hadn't noticed it being particularly dangerous. Most of the time it just sits there."

"Well, when you have kids around, it can be lethal."

"Perhaps. But you may remember I don't have children."

Griffin saw the discomfort dig furrows into his brother's face. Jared was obviously miserable. Griffin glanced at the boys, at their overflowing bags of supplies. Then he glanced back at Jared.

"Or do I?" he asked mildly.

Jared sighed, a heavy, helpless sound that came from the depths of his diaphragm. He plopped down onto the large beige sectional sofa, his boys still safely in each arm.

"I'm sorry, Griff," he said. "If there were any other way. If there were anyone else we could ask..." He groaned, obviously reading Griffin's face correctly. "It's only for a few weeks, Griffin. I'll be back in just over three weeks."

Three weeks? Jared must be out of his mind. Griffin subdued a weird impulse to start talking very loudly and very fast, using his hands, like an Italian grandmother, like someone in a panic. Nonsense. Griffin never panicked. Not even at a moment like this.

"There must be someone else, Jared," he said slowly and rationally. "Where's Katie?"

"With her mother in Toledo. Remember her mother is having a hysterectomy? She'll be there for at least three weeks. She just can't handle the boys and her mom, too, so I promised I'd keep them while she was gone."

"If you *promised,* why are you—"

"I can't help it." One of the boys had grabbed Jared's nose, so his answer had a strangely adenoidal quality. "I've got to go to London. Tomorrow. Remember how we thought the Bailey merger had fallen through? No, of course you don't, I probably never even mentioned it. It's on again, and I have to be there for the negotiations."

"But why does it have to be you? Can't you send—"

"No. I can't send anyone. I have to be there, or it won't happen. It's worth millions, Griff. I have to be there."

Jared was beginning to sound a little desperate. Even worse, his tension seemed to communicate itself to the children. One of the babies...the one in red. Griffin couldn't ever remember which one wore red. Robert, maybe? Anyway, one of the boys screwed up his face, as if preparing to let loose a sympathetic wail.

Griffin began mentally scanning the possibilities. There had to be a way to fix this. He had learned in his early years as a photographer that even the trickiest problems had answers, if you just kept trying new ideas. Some small adjustment to an f-stop or the lighting, or the angle or the lens—and suddenly the "impossible" picture was yours for the taking.

"Didn't you have a nanny? An au pair or something?"

"Just for the first six months. She's with a different family now. Griff, relax. It won't be so hard. They're easy kids, really—"

"Doesn't Katie have a sister? I thought I remembered a sister."

Jared frowned at him. "Katie's an only child."

"Then who do you use for a baby-sitter the rest of the time?"

"Teenagers. That's fine for an hour here and there, but Katie would kill me if I left the boys with someone like that for three weeks." Jared leaned his cheek against the downy head of one of the babies. "She's going to kill me anyhow. She's always saying I spend too much time at work. This is just going to prove it."

He lifted his head, and Griffin was shocked by the raw desperation he saw in his brother's face. "Griffin, you've got to help me. You're the only person she'll trust. If it's anyone else, she'll really never forgive me."

Griffin tilted his head. "Come on, Jared. Katie doesn't even like me."

"Yes, she does. Well, she *trusts* you. You knew we'd named you as guardian in our wills. And besides, she's said several times that you'd make a great father."

Griffin merely raised one brow skeptically and waited. His little brother wasn't much of a liar.

"Well, okay, she said something kind of like that. She said it was too bad you were so allergic to commitment because fatherhood would probably be the saving of you." Jared looked sheepish. "But she thinks you're smart, and she knows you're reliable—except with women, of course."

Griffin half smiled. "Of course."

"And most important, she knows you'd never let anything bad happen to your own nephews, your own flesh and blood." Jared's voice deepened. "Griffin, you've got to do this. You've got to help me."

Griffin knew that look, that sad wrinkling of the high, Cahill brow, that twitch under one eye, that pulse just above the jaw. It was the "don't tell Mother I got suspended for fighting" look, the "don't tell Dad I wrecked the car" look. It was the "you're my big brother, and you can fix anything" look. Griffin was helpless against it. He always had been.

"Damn it, Jared," he said softly. "You're a serious pain in the ass, did you know that?"

But apparently Jared knew Griffin's looks, too. He grinned, obviously aware that he had won. "I knew it! I knew you'd say yes."

"I'll bet you did," Griffin said cynically. "I'll bet your car is filled with the tacky, plastic paraphernalia of parenthood. Toys and bottles and—" he closed his eyes ''—and a hundred other items too personal to imagine.''

''Diapers, bro. Zillions of 'em. I even brought you one of those diaper pail deodorizers.''

''How thoughtful,'' Griffin drawled, trying not to imagine the situations that would make such an item necessary. ''You know, Jared, maybe this isn't such—''

But Jared was already on his feet. He handed one of the babies to Griffin—the one in red. Was it Robert? Griffin dimly suspected that he ought to find out before Jared drove away.

Jared took the other one—the one in blue—with him to the car. Griffin eyed his red-clad baby much as he might watch a ticking bomb, waiting for him to start bawling because Daddy had disappeared.

But Robert—or was it Stewart?—showed no signs of distress. He studied his uncle for a few seconds, then, apparently finding him boring, transferred his gaze to Griffin's crisply laundered shirt. He reached out a handful of fat fingers and, as slowly and carefully as the arm of an orbiting space shuttle might lock around a satellite, took hold of Griffin's top button.

The baby crowed softly, pleased at the success, his damp, toothless mouth beaming. Then, without warning and certainly without permission, he bent his wet face into Griffin's chest and began trying to gum the button right off the shirt.

Oh, great. It didn't take a Ph.D. in parenting to know that little hard plastic discs, like buttons, could be swallowed and were therefore *dangerous.* Like bleach and stairs and light sockets. And sea-green Chihuly art glass.

"I'm afraid not, champ," Griffin said softly, prying the button free before any damage could be done. Any damage to the baby, anyhow. His once-pristine shirt was soggy with little bubbles of milk that would undoubtedly dry into nasty, smelly stains.

Jared kept bustling back and forth, bringing in more blue plastic stuff than one car should have been able to hold. A portable playpen, two car seats, five boxes of diapers, a diaper pail, a crate of baby food, dozens of plastic bottles, a mechanical swing, a small plastic circle on wheels that Griffin couldn't figure out to save his life, and more.

And more and more and more. Griffin watched, stupefied, as his sleek, minimalist decor became as junky and cluttered as a carnival midway. God—could it possibly take this much gear to sustain two babies for three weeks? He had photographed whole armies setting out to war with less artillery than this.

"Don't look so shell-shocked." Jared, who was still holding one of his sons while deftly erecting the playpen with one hand and one knee, looked over at Griffin with a smile that struck Griffin as completely patronizing. "You'll get used to it. And maybe you can get someone to help you. Do any of your girlfriends have a secret hankering to be a mommy?"

"I certainly hope not." Griffin shuddered. "It would

mean that my screening process was profoundly flawed.''

Jared laughed. ''You'll never change, will you, Griff?''

''Well, I'm definitely going to have to change my shirt.''

''Don't bother. Not until they're asleep for the night, anyhow.''

With that ominous warning, Jared finished with the playpen, then began digging one-handed through an overstuffed suitcase. He emerged with a pair of small stuffed toys. He handed one to the baby he still held, and then brought the other over to Griffin.

With a bubbling cry of obvious delight, Griffin's baby lurched eagerly toward the toy, a multicolored caterpillar whose eyes had clearly been removed. Griffin had to react quickly to hang on to the boy.

''Say hello to Mr. Giggles, Stewart,'' Jared said, waving the rather nasty toy in front of his son's face.

Ahh. Stewart, then, Griffin noted carefully. This one, the one in red, was Stewart.

Stewart clasped the toy blissfully toward his face, then immediately and, Griffin felt sure, deliberately, dropped it on the floor.

Patiently Griffin retrieved the caterpillar and handed it back to the boy.

''Yes, Stewart,'' he said. ''Say hello to Mr. Giggles.'' He looked impassively over the boy's head at the shambles that once had been his elegant home. ''And goodbye to life as we know it.''

HEATHER DELANEY was so happy it almost frightened her.

As she stood by the fanciful front door to Spring House, she touched her fingers softly to the exquisite cut-glass doorknob. Then she ran them slowly along the cool edge of the beveled rainbow glass.

So lovely. And it all belonged to her. Well, to her and the Firefly Glen Mountain Savings and Trust Company.

She closed her eyes, absorbing through her other senses the happy camaraderie of the workers around her, half-a-dozen men who were whistling, wallpapering, painting, sanding, hammering and laughing.

They thought they were doing an ordinary remodeling job, just a routine cut-and-paste, as the architect had called it. They had no idea they were putting the finishing touches on a dream.

A deep thrill beat fast in her chest, and she took a long breath to slow its pace. But she couldn't help herself. She loved Spring House, this pink-and-white gingerbread Victorian mansion that was one of the Glen's four premiere "season" houses. Really loved it. She always had. She had dreamed of living here, working here, creating a family here, as long as she could remember.

And now, or at least as soon as the city council put their official seal of approval on her zoning variance this afternoon, the dream would come true. The remodeling was almost complete. Next Monday, Tuesday at the latest, she would be able to close up her little office over on Main Street and move her fledgling obstetrical practice here, to the first floor of Spring House.

She rested her forehead against the glass of the door, marveling that she had actually had the courage—or was it the foolishness?—to invest so much, both emotionally and financially, in one grand, outrageous, beautiful plan.

One dream.

Because frankly her track record with dreams was fairly abysmal.

She was thirty-three years old, and in all those years she had allowed herself to want—really, truly, desperately want—only three things. She had wanted to know her mother, who had died when she was three. Much later, she had wanted her father to win his war with cancer. And she had wanted Griffin Cahill to love her.

Yep. Heather Delaney was batting zero in the dream department.

Until today.

"Heather, have you fallen into a trance? We're going to be late. And where's your umbrella? It's raining buckets out there."

Heather smiled at Mary Brady, her bossy young receptionist and good friend. Mary was five years younger than Heather, but she had raised four brothers, and she hadn't been on the job ten minutes before she had begun running Heather's life, too.

"Maybe I *have* fallen into a trance," Heather said softly, transferring her gaze to the window, where she could see one of the dedicated workers kneeling in the mud, trying to get the last of the pansies planted before the rain drove him inside.

"Oh, yeah? Well, snap out of it."

Heather didn't respond. She touched the fine Irish lace curtain that fell like a soft white mist alongside the window. She could hardly bring herself to leave. She wanted to be here to see every minute of the transformation.

She took a deep breath, and the air was full of wonderful smells—wood chips and fresh paint and clean, sweet rain.

"I keep thinking I'm going to wake up and discover that none of this is really happening."

Mary had dug a second umbrella out of the hall stand, and she nudged it against the back of Heather's hand.

"Oh, it's happening all right. But it's going to be happening without you if you don't hurry. It's ten to five already."

Heather took the umbrella and began to open it. Mary was right. She needed to be there when the council took up her request. They might have questions.

With a low cry, Mary leaped to stop her. "Good grief, Doc, what's the matter with you? Do you want to jinx this vote before we ever get to city hall?"

Heather shook her head. "Mary, you know I don't believe in—"

"Well, I do. We've already got the rain. That's bad luck right there. You don't want to go opening any umbrellas indoors, not on a day as important as this."

Heather began to protest again, but somewhere in the back rooms of Spring House a loud bang sounded. A worker cursed, and then something shattered, something heavy and glass and probably dreadfully expensive.

Heather winced, thinking of her tight budget, but a look of true horror spread across Mary Brady's tanned and lovely face.

"Oh, no," she said, wide-eyed. "You don't think that was a mirror, do you?"

"Mary," Heather said sternly. "Stop pretending you're some old-country Irish fishwife. You know perfectly well that superstitions are pure nonsense. The city council has already given tentative approval to this zoning variance. Mayor Millner himself told me to go ahead with the construction. Nothing can happen now to spoil things. Not at this late date. Not even a broken mirror."

Mary returned the glare haughtily. "Tempting fate. Overconfidence. That's as bad as a broken mirror any day."

Groaning, Heather stepped out onto the wide verandah and opened her umbrella. She didn't care what Mary said. She didn't care about rain or mirrors or anything else.

This was her day, the day Dr. Heather Delaney finally caught a dream by the tail and reeled it in. She intended to enjoy every minute of it.

"NO. NO BABIES. NO."

Griffin stared at his housekeeper, wondering what had ever possessed him to hire such a bad-tempered old bat. It was just one hour of baby-sitting. No big deal. You'd think he had asked her to dance naked in the middle of the town square.

"It's just an hour or two. I have to get to the council meeting. I have to go right now, Mrs. Waller. I'm already late. It started five minutes ago."

She folded her arms over her apron and stared at him. "No babies. I took this job, I never said babies."

Griffin cast a desperate glance out the half-open door. It was a monsoon out there. The five-minute ride to city hall would probably take fifteen in this weather. He tried to remember how many other things were on the agenda before Heather's zoning variance came up. Enough, he thought. Enough that he still could get there in time.

If Mrs. Waller would just listen to reason.

"Look, Mrs. Waller, they're both asleep, and I'll be back very soon."

"They'll wake up," she said darkly.

The sad truth was, she was probably right. They hadn't slept more than ten minutes at a time since they'd arrived this morning. But still, this was important. Why couldn't she see that?

"Damn it, Mrs. Waller—"

She scowled fiercely, the lines in her sharp face deepening into troughs of displeasure. "No cursing. No babies, and no cursing."

God. Griffin was ready to tear his hair out. But the

twins had been working on that all day, and his scalp was already sore. What, he wondered, was the diabolical fascination babies had for grabbing things and trying to stick them in their mouths?

As if he didn't have enough to contend with, the telephone took that moment to ring. He picked it up, growling "What?" in a voice that could have etched glass.

"Where the hell are you, Cahill? You need to get down here."

It was Hickory Baxter, one of the other four councilmen. Griffin frowned, wondering why Hickory sounded so tense. He'd been late for meetings before himself. In fact, Hickory had been known to skip a meeting altogether now and then.

"Why? What's going on?"

Hickory lowered his voice to a whisper. "I'm not sure. But I don't like it. Somebody has been stirring things up on the zoning."

Griffin wasn't sure he had heard correctly. "Zoning? You mean Heather's request for a zoning variance?"

"I tell you, I smell something rotten. It may be Millner. You'd better get down here, Cahill. And you'd better hurry, or she may take a fall on this one."

With that cryptic warning, the old man hung up. Griffin replaced the receiver slowly, trying to make sense of it all. How could anything have gone wrong with Heather's zoning variance? The council had given its tentative okay two months ago. The Planning and Zoning Commission committee had unanimously recommended approval. So had the Firefly Glen Chamber of Commerce and the Home Owners' Association.

Heather was no doubt deep in construction on Spring House already.

But Griffin recognized that urgent note in Hickory Baxter's voice. Hickory had been old Doc Delaney's best friend, and he loved Heather like a daughter. He might be mistaken, but Hickory obviously believed that someone was about to hurt Heather.

That meant Griffin couldn't play power games with Mrs. Waller any longer. He knew how to reach her, so he went straight for the kill.

"An extra hundred dollars," he said bluntly. "For one hour. An extra hundred dollars in this week's check."

He saw her eyes light up, and he knew he had hit on the right amount. Though she worked like a Trojan cleaning houses every day of her life, Griffin suspected that Mrs. Waller was probably richer than he was. She loved money, would do almost anything if you offered her enough cash. And, as far as Griffin knew, she had never been seen spending a single cent.

"A hundred and twenty," she said slowly, her narrowed eyes appraising him, estimating the depth of his desperation. "No. One-fifty. Because they will wake up."

He could get her down to one twenty-five, but he didn't have time to haggle. "Done," he said, pulling on his raincoat. "Those boys had better be damn happy when I get back."

"They will be as happy as kings," Mrs. Waller said, smiling for the first time since he had dared to suggest that she might serve as a baby-sitter. She followed him to the door, helping him with his coat, oddly expansive now that she had secured her cash bonus.

She handed him his umbrella. "So, Mr. Cahill. A beautiful woman is making you rush like this and be crazy? This is all because of a woman?"

Griffin paused at the threshold, turning his collar up against the driving rain. He considered trying to explain that, while Mrs. Waller might think he was a good-for-nothing dilettante, he was actually a city councilman, that it was his duty to attend all city council meetings.

But would he really have spent a hundred and fifty dollars, abandoned his innocent nephews and tramped through this rain just to cast a vote on some anonymous businessman's zoning request?

He sighed. Of course not.

"Yeah," he said, glancing back at her sharp, clever face with a rueful smile. "This is all because of a woman."

CHAPTER TWO

HEATHER HAD TO ADMIT, as backstabbing betrayals went, this one was going to be a doozie.

There she was, settled in the front row of the Firefly Glen City Council chambers like the proverbial sitting duck. She had arrived so innocently, in her nice dress, all smiles and eagerness, like a child who is unable to see that she is climbing the stairs to her own execution.

How could she have been such a fool? She should have realized something was wrong in the first five minutes, when the council took up the matter of her zoning variance first, ignoring the printed agenda.

Zoning variance. It sounded like officious bureaucracy and moldy red tape—not real human beings and their hopes and dreams. But it would certainly be easier to cast a no vote against a ''zoning variance'' than to tell Heather Delaney, the daughter of Tim Delaney, who had been Firefly Glen's obstetrician for six decades, that she couldn't work and live under the same roof. That she would probably eventually have to sell her dream house just to make ends meet.

And no was exactly what it appeared they were going to say.

Like an idiot, she hadn't suspected anything. It

wasn't until Mayor Millner had begun talking morosely of "complications," mentioning anonymous "complaints" about the prospect of having a medical clinic in the neighborhood, that she had begun to feel true fear.

Finally, when two other councilmen began to echo the mayor's comments, even Heather, who had been half-blind with excited anticipation, could see what was happening.

She had been set up. When they had given her tentative approval at the last meeting, she had believed them, as trusting as a baby. She had put a team of men to work and spent a fortune. She had, in essence, placed her own head on the block, sparing them the trouble.

Now she was about to get it chopped off.

Her heart had begun to pound again, this time in an extremely disagreeable way. Fight or flight—as a doctor she recognized quite clearly that she was having a primitive reaction to danger.

But she'd be darned if she'd let them see it. She lifted her chin and stared unwaveringly at the four councilmen sitting on the dais, four men who held the executioner's ax in their well-manicured hands.

"Heather." Mary, who was sitting next to her, cast a worried side glance. "What on earth is going on here? This was a done deal. You've already spent thousands—"

Heather didn't take her eyes off the councilmen. "Someone appears to have undone it," she murmured acidly.

And she had a pretty good idea who that "someone" was. Mayor Alton Millner, who even now was smiling down at her from the podium with a smarmy pretense of sympathy.

"It would trouble this council to reverse its position. We are well aware that we granted tentative approval to this zoning variance. But, although we sympathize with Dr. Delaney's dilemma, I believe we cannot in good conscience ignore the concerns of her neighbors. I'm sure Dr. Delaney will understand."

He smiled right at her, the arrogant hypocrite. She knew that smile. Confident, smug. Triumphant.

Her racing heart paused for a blinding moment of painful clarity. Her Spring House clinic was doomed.

And all because she had offended Alton Millner. All because she had dared to give him advice about his daughter Justine. She had known he was offended, had seen it immediately in his arrogant little black-marble eyes. But she had never, ever considered the possibility that he would retaliate by trying to sabotage her here, in the council chambers.

He would never abuse his public powers, she'd thought. Naively, she had assumed that kind of thing might happen in New York or Los Angeles...but certainly not in Firefly Glen.

How stupid of her! Corruption was human nature, not a product of city living. Vindictive, amoral people like Alton Millner probably existed in villages even *National Geographic* hadn't discovered yet.

She felt like getting up and stalking out right now,

right in the middle of the vote, just to show them how disgusted she was. But she wouldn't give them the satisfaction. She sat utterly still as they went through the farce of roll call and vote.

Hickory Baxter.

"Yes." The white-haired old man, who had been Heather's father's best friend, smiled down at her apologetically, as if he knew his one little vote wouldn't make much difference. She smiled back, assuring him that it did. At least her rejection wouldn't be unanimous.

Sylvester Brooks. "Yes."

Heather was surprised. She wouldn't have thought Sylvester had the courage to defy the mayor. But the young man winked over at her and shrugged. The shrug said it all.

Bart Miglin. "Opposed."

Stuart Leith. "Opposed."

So it was a tie.

Mary was twisting her purse strap into knots. She leaned over and whispered furiously. "Where the hell is Griffin Cahill? He didn't even show up? The *coward.*"

But Heather didn't think it was cowardice that had kept Griffin, the fifth councilman, away from today's meeting. He wasn't afraid of Alton Millner or anyone else. It was far more likely to be a woman.

Or sheer, lazy, self-absorbed indifference.

"My God, this is disgusting! I can't *believe* it." Mary was so agitated it was like sitting next to boiling water. ''I mean, Cahill may be a spoiled, rich brat, but still. I just can't *believe* he'd let you down like this.''

But Heather wasn't one bit surprised. Playboy Cahill's record of disappointing her went back approximately twenty years.

He'd been her teenage sweetheart, her first lover, the man she'd planned to marry. But from the beginning she had known that her spoiled, gorgeous fiancé was frivolous and unreliable. For years—through high school, into college and even into the arduous years of medical school—Heather had been too in love to object to the endless string of forgotten promises, careless mistakes, thoughtless betrayals. Some were small and easily overlooked, but eventually they grew profound and painful. By the end, taken together, they had finally been enough to destroy even Heather's blind adoration.

So why should today be any different? He was probably still asleep. Or else he'd seen the rain from the big picture window in his ultramodern bachelor pad and decided it wasn't worth getting his beloved BMW muddy.

She stopped herself, ashamed of this sudden, sharp bitterness. She had thought that her feelings toward Griffin had mellowed.

But she was human, wasn't she? Griffin's vote could have saved her. The variance would have passed three to two. Mayor Millner's scheme would have been thwarted, all by one lazy yes cast by the Glen's golden boy.

If only he'd been able to drag himself out of bed.

Now it was tied, two to two, which was probably just what Alton Millner had been hoping for. In case of a tie, the mayor cast the deciding vote.

"I'm afraid I must vote opposed. The vote is three to two," the mayor intoned gravely. "The variance is denied."

And, just like that, her dream was dead.

"No." Mary made fists in her lap and growled fiercely under her breath. *"No."*

Heather didn't say anything. She felt frozen in her seat.

"My God." Mary's voice was shaking. "Can they do that? Just waltz in here and destroy everything? Just like that?"

Heather nodded. "Yes. Just like that."

"But—" Mary was temporarily incoherent. "But—" She looked at Heather. "Does he have any idea how much money you've already spent?"

Heather watched the mayor pompously shaking hands with his council. "Of course he knows. He loves it."

Mary turned and watched him, too. *"Bastard,"* she hissed heatedly. "Do you think this is all because of Justine? Because of what you said?"

Heather nodded. Her jaw felt so tight she wasn't sure she could speak whole sentences. "Probably."

"Son of a—" Mary held herself back with an obvious effort. "I knew it. I have to tell you, I was afraid something like this would happen. He's a petty bastard, isn't he?"

Heather nodded. She was beginning to feel a little numb, a little distant. Maybe that was a good thing.

"Well, can we sue?"

"I don't know," Heather answered tersely. "We'll look into it."

She was so consumed by her own distress that when her pager went off, just a small vibration at her waist, she felt as if it were a summons from another planet.

She looked down, read the short sentence her service had typed in. Mrs. Mizell wanted an emergency after-hours visit. In less than thirty minutes.

So life went on. Heather automatically pressed in the number for yes.

People needed her. She was going to have to pull out of this quicksand of disappointment somehow and go back to work. Maybe that was a blessing in disguise.

Up on the dais, the meeting was breaking up. Heather didn't think her poise could hold much longer, especially if Alton came over to gloat.

She picked up her raincoat, which was still damp. "Come on. Let's go."

But they were too late. At the front door of city hall, where the rain was beating the newly blooming tulips into the mud, the mayor intercepted their path. He had arranged his round, fleshy face in a show of concern.

"Heather. My dear. I just wanted to say I'm so sorry things didn't work out for your clinic. I would have liked to help. But unfortunately, as I mentioned in the meeting, we received several complaints from your neighbors and..." He shrugged sadly. "We just couldn't ignore their concerns about their property values."

Heather stared coldly into his lying face. He knew darn well there had been no complaints. Long before she had even bought the place, Heather had consulted each and every one of the Spring House neighbors, exploring their feelings about her idea to turn the first floor of the lovely old Victorian gingerbread house into a clinic. Not one of them had been opposed.

Including Mayor Millner, who lived four houses down from Spring House.

But she wasn't going to brawl with him about it now, not out here on the City Hall steps, where everyone could see them.

Mary obviously had no such inhibitions. She would have wrestled the mayor to the mud if Heather hadn't put a restraining hand on her arm.

She settled for scowling at him under her rain hood. "Tell me, Mayor," Mary said acidly. "Why was no one concerned about their property values when *your wife* turned your carriage house into an antique shop?"

Mayor Millner's lips tightened. "That was quite different."

"Oh, yeah? How? And what about Ginger Jackson's preschool? Or Parker Tremaine's new law offices? Or Mrs. Bry—"

"Mary." Heather glanced quellingly at her friend. The list could have gone on forever. Spring House was on Old Pine Barren Road, which was so close to the center of town that most of the fine old houses there had already been converted to retail or professional uses.

In typical Firefly Glen fashion, rather than rezoning the entire street—which would have felt sweeping and impersonal—they granted the zoning variances one at a time.

Still, no one had ever been turned down. Until today.

"Mary," she said again.

"What?" Mary looked over at Heather mutinously. She wasn't the type to give up without a fight. "It's true. You know it is. This is so unfair."

Heather turned her even gaze toward the mayor. "There's really no need to explain, Alton," she said calmly. "I fully understand your motives."

He flushed, narrowing his beady eyes, but Heather found an extra measure of strength from somewhere, and she didn't allow the ugly expression to ruffle her. She smiled slightly, raising her eyebrows in polite inquiry. "By the way. How is Justine?"

The mayor's face purpled, and Heather wondered whether someday soon his nasty temper was going to give him a stroke. As a doctor, she cared. But as a woman, and as the victim of his latest dirty trick, she thought maybe he had it coming.

"Dr. Delaney," he said darkly, with a sarcastic emphasis on the "doctor" part. "My daughter is no longer your patient. Maybe you should keep your nose out of my family's private business."

"I'd be glad to," she said smoothly, fastening the

top button of her raincoat with steady fingers. "If you'd stay out of mine."

She snapped open her dark green umbrella so quickly that he had to duck to avoid being hit by the spokes. Beside her, Mary opened her own, the sound echoing hers like a crisp salute.

Without bothering to say goodbye to the silently fuming mayor, Heather turned toward the parking lot. Mary was right behind her, their footsteps splashing in unison down the City Hall steps and across the sodden green. Cold mud sprayed up against Heather's hem and worked its way inside her shoes.

God, she hated April.

Mary had driven separately, so when they reached her little sedan she waved a quick goodbye without standing to chat. Heather understood. The disappointment was too fresh, the blow too stunning. There would be plenty of time tomorrow to rehash and analyze the council's ambush—and to decide how to respond. Right now Heather wanted a warm shower and a hot bowl of soup more than anything on earth, even more than she wanted justice.

Or revenge.

Of course, she couldn't have either one. She had to go back to the office, and she had to calm Anna Mizell down one more time.

She huddled at her car door, her small umbrella propped on her shoulder and funneling rain onto her head, then down the back of her coat, while she fumbled through her purse, looking for her keys.

Suddenly, above the rain, she heard a new sound. She lifted her head to see a small, gleaming ice-blue BMW come purring into the empty space next to her.

No. She shut her eyes, refusing to believe her luck could be this bad. It couldn't be.

But it was. The BMW's tinted window hummed down, revealing Griffin Cahill.

The sight of him, handsome as sin, as beautifully tailored as if he'd just stepped out of a magazine, brought all her repressed anger suddenly surging to the surface.

It was unfair, she knew that. It wasn't his fault he looked so glamorous when she looked so soggy, that he looked so confident when she felt so defeated.

This was just pure, everyday Playboy Cahill. The last time she'd seen a single golden strand of hair out of place on his elegant head, he had been seventeen years old. Just seventeen—sexy, sweaty, tousled and panting…and locked in her trembling arms.

She blinked away the image, as she had done a million times through the years. It wasn't his fault she couldn't forget.

But it was his fault she'd lost the vote today.

"Heather?" He peered up at her through the window. "Oh, hell. I haven't missed the meeting, have I?"

She knew how she must look, with her hair soaked to the scalp, and rain dripping off her chin. She used her hand to wipe her cheeks, just in case mascara had begun to run. But it was hopeless. Her fingers were as wet as her face.

"Yes," she said succinctly. "You missed it."

"What's wrong, Heather?" But before she could answer, his eyes tightened. "You lost, didn't you?"

For the first time, she felt the threat of tears. She didn't want to talk to him about this. She didn't want to talk to anyone. Not yet.

"Yes," she said. "I lost."

He said something then, but the rain was drumming loudly on the fabric of her umbrella, and she couldn't make out the words.

"What?"

"Nothing." He shook his head. "I just said I'm sorry I didn't get here in time. I could have helped."

She held herself stiffly, hoping the dignity she'd clung to since the vote wouldn't desert her now. But it was true, and she couldn't help feeling bitter. He could have changed everything. And not just with his vote. He could conceivably have talked the others into supporting her, too.

Everyone in town listened to Griffin, though Heather wasn't exactly sure why. He was frivolous and sardonic, lazy and self-absorbed. But he was also young and handsome, smart and rich and fiercely admired, by women who wanted to bed him, and by men who wanted to be him.

If Griffin had been there, if he had argued passionately for her case, perhaps he could have swayed the other councilmen, and thwarted the mayor completely.

Their fear of Alton Millner's bludgeoning anger was

strong. But perhaps their desire for Griffin Cahill's lazy approval was even stronger.

It was possible.

But who was she kidding? Griffin never argued passionately for anything or anybody. He simply couldn't be bothered. Just look at him now. He hadn't even been able to bestir himself to get to the meeting on time.

"Heather." He leaned over and shoved open the passenger door. "You're drenched. Get in and tell me exactly what happened. Maybe I can think of some way to fix it."

She looked into the little car, at the rain spattering against its silver leather seats. The seats hadn't been leather, back when Griffin was a teenager. They had been nubby, tattered black cloth that scratched her shoulders and left small red burns against her bare skin.

"No," she said, pushing the door shut quickly, so that the rain wouldn't ruin those expensive seats. "I mean, thanks anyway. But I don't need your help. And I have to get back to work."

"Heather, we should talk—"

But the afternoon's disappointments had finally gotten the better of her. She let loose a jagged laugh.

"Don't be absurd, Griffin. We haven't talked in ten years, and I don't intend to start now. If you had anything to say, you should have said it in there. With your *vote*."

He took her anger with a small smile, as he took everything. He was impenetrable, she thought, watching the corners of his mouth turn up in that old, familiar way. Nothing ever hurt him, did it?

Because nothing mattered to him.

"I really did mean to be there, Heather," he said softly. "Something important came up."

She looked at him, unable to form a reply. Did he even remember how often, in their long, lost past, he had come to her with those very words? *Something came up.* But some*thing* always turned out to be some-*one.* A blonde, a brunette, whatever. Any great body and empty head that wanted to party instead of study, idolize instead of criticize. Any girl who wouldn't require him to be more than he wanted to bother being.

But of course he didn't remember. It was such a long time ago. If she were half as smart as she claimed to be, she'd forget all about it, too.

"Come on, Heather." Looking at her from this angle, through the sports car window, required him to tilt those blue eyes up, against those thick dark lashes. He probably thought she would find him irresistible. "You can't really intend to slay this dragon alone. Millner is an ugly enemy. You need help."

"I know I need help, Griffin," she said, pressing the button that zipped open her door locks. As she lowered her umbrella, she met his warm, teasing smile with a piercingly frigid one of her own.

"I just don't need *yours.*"

CHAPTER THREE

FIREFLY GLEN, according to the brochures, had everything.

Nestled in a soft valley in the Adirondacks, it was a charming township of approximately 2,938 people.

It had quaint old houses and elegant shopping. It had hushed white winters, colored Easter-egg springs, smiling green summers, and red-gold, breathtaking autumns. It had Llewellyn's Lake, which ran thick with trout; Silver Kiss Falls, which spilled like tinsel down John's Cliff; and the Lost Logger Trail, which wound silently through dark, steepled pines.

The only thing it *didn't* have was a nanny service.

Not one single professional baby-sitting service in the whole damn town.

Disgusted, Griffin tossed the telephone book onto the end table, knocking the small metal lamp up against the wall with a clatter. He cringed at the sound, looking nervously toward the door to his office, which had become a temporary nursery.

Please God. Don't let them wake up.

They'd been in their cribs less than an hour, but Jared had warned him that Stewart, the one in red, was a light sleeper. A bird chirping, a telephone ringing, heavy rain on the roof, a shaft of sunlight touching his eyelid…that was all it took.

Oh, great. It was spring in the Adirondacks. It was nothing *but* birds and rain.

Griffin had been about ninety-nine percent joking when he suggested maybe Stewart needed a thimble of brandy in his baby formula. But Jared hadn't seemed amused. Parenthood obviously did a number on your sense of humor.

Or maybe it was the sleep deprivation that did it. Over the past seventy-two hours, Griffin had learned a lot about the exhaustion that came with having twins in the house.

Was it too much to ask them to sleep at the same time? Just this morning, he had caught himself begging an eight-month-old baby—he thought it was Stewart—to please, please, *please* go back to sleep.

The kid had just looked at him as if he was crazy. Which he was. Babies *made* you crazy. They cried for no reason, sometimes for hours. They never slept, at least not at the same time. They tried to eat everything, especially nonorganic oddities they found in strange places. If Griffin had lost a penny in 1980, these babies would find it like radar and try to swallow it whole. You were scared to take your eyes off them for a split second.

Anyhow, the lamp clatter must not have been loud enough to penetrate the closed door. The small white baby monitor remained blessedly silent.

But he couldn't go on much longer without some

real sleep. He reluctantly admitted that, though he hated asking anyone for a favor, he was going to have to get some help.

He'd already tried his friends. But they had careers, families, obligations. Emma Dunbar owed him a favor, but she was in Hawaii, enjoying a second honeymoon.

Mrs. Waller had refused to be bribed a second time, though Griffin had, in his desperation, raised his bid into four digits. She had simply folded her substantial arms again and scowled, repeating her mantra of rejection.

No. No babies. No.

That left only one hope. Though it was against his basic life philosophy to encourage any woman to think simultaneously of Griffin Cahill and babies, he had no choice. He had reached the point that he didn't trust himself to take care of the boys properly. He had caught himself dozing off this morning, while Stewart crawled toward the kitchen sink.

It was irresponsible not to get some help, wherever he could get it.

Blinking hard to force his eyes to stay open, he picked up his little black book and began to flip the pages.

TWO HOURS LATER, when Miranda rang Griffin's doorbell, he thought it was perhaps the most beautiful sound he had ever heard, better than Beethoven by moonlight, better than rippling brooks in the rain forest, better than the ching of three cherries lining up in Vegas.

It was the sound of salvation.

"Come on in. It's open."

He hoped she could hear him. He didn't dare go to the door. He was in the kitchen, parked in front of the twin high chairs, up to his elbows in smashed bananas.

In theory, he was feeding the boys. But like all theories, this one was flawed. Maybe a spoonful or two had gone into their stubborn mouths, but the rest of it was smeared across their faces and their clothes, and spattered on every surface within flinging distance.

Griffin heard the light slap of sandals across the hardwood floors. And then Miranda appeared in the doorway.

"Griffin, where is everything? Where's the Chihuly? Oh!" Her lovely mouth hung open as she took in the sight of the three banana-coated males. "Oh, my God. Griffin, what happened?"

Griffin tried to smile, but he was so tired his facial muscles weren't cooperating very well.

"I'm not sure," he said. "A couple of days ago everything was under control. And then…this."

Robert, whose blue playsuit was sticky with yellow mush, decided to greet Miranda with his favorite new joke. He spit a mouthful of bananas in her direction as forcefully as his chubby cheeks would allow, and then dissolved in a fit of giggles so strenuous it knocked him sideways in his high chair.

Miranda, who had excellent reflexes, backed out of the way just in time. She looked over at Griffin in bewildered horror.

"He thinks it's funny," Griffin explained unnecessarily. "He had a long nap, and he's in excellent spirits."

Stewart, who had dropped his spoon for the tenth time in the past ten minutes, began to cry. He rubbed his eyes, and when he took his fists away his lashes were glued into clumps with banana goo.

"Stewart, on the other hand, is now tired." Griffin sighed. "He and his brother have thoughtfully adopted a schedule of alternating naps, apparently to ensure that I'm never lonely."

Griffin watched Miranda struggle with the dilemma. Her instincts apparently were telling her to run, and run fast. She was a professional beauty, not a nanny. And certainly not a *mother.* The idea of getting smashed bananas in her hair clearly made her dizzy with revulsion.

But obviously she also knew an opportunity when she saw one. When Griffin had telephoned her, she had sounded stunned, thrilled to hear from him again so soon. His unwritten but until now unbroken rule was that women were luxuries he indulged in only on the weekends—and he never indulged in the same treat two weekends in a row.

So obviously Miranda understood that this was a rare chance. If Griffin had suddenly developed paternal instincts, she would be a fool not to adapt. She might not like babies, but she most definitely liked Griffin. A lot.

Enough to swallow down her disgust and give Robert a sickly smile.

''You are a cutie, aren't you?'' Her performance was pretty good. If Griffin hadn't seen that first instinctive recoil, he might have believed that Miranda adored sticky baby boys.

She turned to Griffin. ''Oh, Griffin, you just look exhausted.'' She came closer, a triumph of will over aversion. She ran her fingers through his hair tenderly, though Griffin noticed she did so carefully. ''Honey, how long has it been since you've slept?''

''I lost track. I may be in triple digits.''

''Well, I'm going to fix that right now.'' She took the plastic spoon out of his hand and set it on the kitchen table. ''You go get a shower and climb in bed. I'm going to finish feeding these little cuties, and then they're going to get baths, too.''

He looked at her dubiously, suddenly wondering whether calling her had been such a good idea after all.

It was a shame he didn't have Heather Delaney's number in his little black book anymore. She was probably the only woman Griffin had ever dated who had a single solitary maternal instinct written into her DNA. Even as a teenager, Heather had loved children. Everywhere they went, she had always stopped to smile at toddlers, babble to babies. It hadn't surprised anyone in Firefly Glen when Heather had become an obstetrician like her father.

But Heather's name hadn't been in Griffin's book for years. And after what had happened at the city council meeting the other day, she probably wouldn't throw him a rope if he were drowning in Llewellyn's Lake right in front of her eyes.

So instead he had names like Miranda Bradner. And what good did that do him now? Miranda had no experience—no children, no nieces or nephews. She didn't even have a younger sibling. She might not know about pennies that inexplicably appeared in forgotten corners. She might not realize how quickly a baby could crawl out of sight, slip into the bathwater, roll toward the edge of the table…

Really, it was damn terrifying all the ways infants could get hurt. For the life of him, Griffin couldn't imagine why anyone dared to have them in the first place. Except that, when they smiled, you got this strange warm feeling, as if someone had turned on a sunlamp…

His thoughts must have been written across his face like neon on a billboard. Miranda, who wasn't ordinarily the most perceptive woman in the world, understood immediately.

"Don't worry, sweetheart," she said, still using that cooing-Madonna tone. "I did about a million hours of baby-sitting when I was a teenager. I'm actually very good with children."

Somehow he doubted that. But she couldn't be any worse than he'd be if he didn't get some sleep. He'd probably drop one of the boys from sheer exhaustion.

"Griffin." Miranda bent down and put her lovely, liquid eyes on level with his. "I'm here for you, honey. Let me help you."

It was such an obvious charade. But he couldn't fight it any longer. He couldn't even keep his eyes open. And at least he could count on her eagerness to impress him. She had come here to show what a valuable partner she could be, the perfect woman to have around in a crisis. She would meet this challenge if it killed her.

"Thanks, Miranda," he said wearily, standing up. "I owe you one." He patted Stewart's gooey head as he made his way toward the door. "So long, guys. Be good for the pretty lady, okay?"

"Of course they will. They are such little darlings, Griffin. We'll be fine."

He almost laughed at that, thinking of the past seventy-two hours. But he was too exhausted to laugh, and it wasn't very funny, really. She'd find out the truth soon enough. He just hoped that, before they drove her stark, raving mad, he could manage to steal at least one blissful hour of sleep.

Actually, he got nearly two. He sat up suddenly, alerted by something...some noise he couldn't identify. Groggily he noticed that it must be well past noon. The afternoon sun lay in soft yellow stripes against his white sheets.

He glanced toward his bedroom door. Miranda stood there, looking strangely different. Her hair was a mess, and her belt was twisted sideways.

"Griffin?" Her voice had lost that gentle Madonna tone sometime during the past two hours. Now it sounded ever so slightly shrewish. "I'm afraid we have a problem."

ANNA MIZELL LAY on the examination table, listening to her baby's heartbeat with her eyes shut, an expression of concentrated rapture on her face.

Heather had already spent an extra ten minutes with Anna, and she had other patients waiting. Her nurse, Tawny, was subtly giving her the finger-across-the-throat sign that meant *cut it short.* Time's wasting.

But Heather held the microphone against Anna's stomach a little longer. The thirty-five-year-old woman had miscarried four times in the past ten years. This was the first baby she had carried long enough to have any hope of ever holding in her arms.

Now eight months pregnant, Anna had started to come in about four times a week, each time with a new imaginary crisis. Strange twinges, spotting, headaches, swollen ankles. Everything frightened Anna, and though Heather sometimes had to struggle to squeeze her into the schedule, she never really minded. She could easily imagine the dread that haunted Anna's dreams—the dread that this baby, too, would vanish in a cloud of blood and pain.

"He sounds perfect, Anna," Heather said softly, finally taking the microphone away and setting it on top of the monitor. "In fact, everything looks great. So far, so good."

Anna opened her eyes slowly, returning to the real world reluctantly. When Tawny had wiped the lotion away and pulled down her shirt, Anna put both hands over her stomach, as if she could literally hold the baby in place. Heather had rarely seen Anna in any other posture.

"Thanks, Dr. Delaney," Anna said as she wriggled to a sitting position. She looked over at Heather, her eyes misty. "You have really worked a miracle, you know. I couldn't have made it this far without you."

Heather touched Anna's shoulder. "Sure you could," she said gently. "I'm not in the miracle business. Your own body does that. I'm just here to keep notes and hold the microphone."

"But the other times—" Anna swallowed, and Heather felt her shoulder tremble slightly. "Sometimes I'm so afraid—"

Heather sat down and took the woman's hand in hers. "This baby is strong, Anna. You're already eight months along. Even if he decided to come today—which I hope he won't, because I have a waiting room full of pregnant women, who aren't exactly famous for their patience..."

Anna smiled, as Heather had hoped she would.

"Even if he comes today, he'll be fine," she assured her. "He's big enough and strong enough to make it on his own. The next four weeks are more or less icing."

Tawny cleared her throat loudly. "Speaking of that waiting room full of irritable pregnant women..."

"I'm sorry!" Anna slid off the table to a standing position, still holding her stomach. "I'll try not to bother you again this week, Dr. Delaney."

Heather smiled from the doorway. "Come any time

you're worried,'' she said, handing Anna's chart to Tawny. ''That's why I'm here.''

In the hall, she scanned the exam rooms, with their color-coded markers over the doors, designating the status of the occupants. Every one was full.

She took a deep breath. It wasn't even two o'clock, but they were already way behind schedule. She really was going to have to interview some candidates for a partner. She'd been putting it off for weeks, hoping she could wait until they had moved to Spring House. But now…

She mustn't think about Spring House. She hadn't managed to fully shake off her disappointment yet, and she couldn't afford to be distracted today.

She turned to Tawny. ''Room Four next?'' She held out her hand for a chart. ''Who is it?''

Tawny grinned. ''No chart on this one. This one is—'' She raised her eyebrows. ''Interesting.''

''Interesting?'' Heather glanced at the closed door to number four. ''I'm not in the mood for 'interesting.' I need ordinary. I need easy. I'm a half hour behind already.''

''Well, sorry, Doc.'' Tawny hadn't stopped smiling. ''Interesting is what you've got here. A double dose of interesting, you might say.''

With that mysterious comment, Tawny bustled off to deliver Anna Mizell's chart to Mary at the front desk. For one self-indulgent second, Heather stared at Room Four wearily, wishing she could maybe have just one simple, unchallenging day. Just one.

She loved her job. She had gone into medicine because she liked helping people, was stimulated by the constant kaleidoscope of challenges. Still...just one day of humdrum predictability now and then would be restful.

But a second was all she had to spare. And then she put a welcoming, professional smile on her face and briskly opened the door.

She wasn't sure exactly what she had been expecting. But she definitely hadn't been expecting this. No wonder Tawny had preferred to let her be surprised. The whole office was probably out there buzzing with the gossip.

Griffin Cahill lay on the examination table.

He was stretched out on his side, his head propped up against the knuckles of one hand. His six-foot-three body was much too long for the table, and much too male. His dark denim designer jeans covered long, powerful legs, which hung carelessly over the edge of the table. His sport shirt rippled along upper body muscles so tight and perfectly proportioned they hardly looked real.

All in all, his extreme masculinity was a serious shock in this place that specialized in estrogen. The strangest sight, though, was his utterly flat stomach. Heather hadn't realized how accustomed she was to swollen, distended moms-to-be—until she encountered the fit, sexy planes of Griffin Cahill.

For a moment she had to hold on to the edge of the door, just to keep her balance.

He obviously hadn't noticed that she'd opened the door. He was smiling, looking down, dangling one hand toward some large thing, some kind of—she squinted, disbelieving.

A *stroller.* It was undeniably a stroller, an expensive two-seater baby carriage. But what was Griffin doing with a stroller? Dimly she registered a strange clicking sound. She looked up, then realized that he was shaking a large ring of multicolored plastic keys.

Finally, after an absurd number of seconds had passed, she became aware of the other occupants of the room. The blue stroller, it seemed, was loaded with two absolutely beautiful baby boys dressed in blue rompers and tiny white socks.

Twins, she realized with a tremor of shock. Twin boys, both reaching happily for the plastic keys Griffin was dangling, burbling their pleasure at the game.

But whose twins? Griffin didn't have any children.

Did he?

She forced herself to move into the room.

"Griffin?" She wrapped her hands lightly around the two ends of her stethoscope, a classic pose of professional detachment. Besides, it kept her from having to shake hands, or reach out and touch him in any way. "What on earth are you doing here?"

He sat up quickly, swinging those long legs over the side of the table. "Heather." His smile was so bright the room seemed suddenly lighter. "Thank God you're here. I was running out of ideas. You can only keep them interested in keys for so long, you know."

It seemed that Griffin was right. One of the little boys was already whimpering, leaning over to try to extricate himself, pushing at the front bar of the stroller so hard his face began to turn red. The other boy watched quietly, but his smile had faded, so Heather suspected it wouldn't be long before he was trying to escape as well.

She bent down. "Hi," she said mildly, so that she wouldn't frighten them. "Who are you?"

"Oh, sorry." Griffin took a deep breath. "These are my nephews. You remember Jared? Well, he and Katie got married a couple of years ago, and these are their twin boys. Stewart and Robert. I'm baby-sitting for a few weeks."

She remembered Jared well. Just three years younger than Griffin, he had idolized his older brother and had stuck to him like glue, determined to go everywhere, do everything that Griffin did. Heather and Griffin had frequently resorted to some fairly elaborate tricks in order to elude him.

"Oh, how wonderful for Jared," she said, letting the quiet one take her stethoscope in his fat little fist. She smiled at the other one, so that he wouldn't feel left out. "Which one is which?"

Silence.

She twisted her head to look at Griffin. "Which one is Stewart?"

Smiling, he cocked one eyebrow sheepishly. "Funny you should ask. Actually, that's why we're here."

She stood, carefully peeling the baby's fingers from

her stethoscope. When he realized he was losing his toy, he began to whine softly and wriggle in his seat.

She looked at Griffin squarely. The expression on his face was just about as embarrassed as she'd ever seen it be. "Griffin? What do you mean?"

And he looked tired, too, she thought. Not the way other people looked tired—not wan or bloodshot or disheveled. It was just that his blue eyes were a shade less brilliant, and oddly appealing dusty shadows had formed beneath them.

"I mean I honestly don't know which one is Stewart," he said, running his hand through his blond hair roughly. "They look exactly alike. I mean *exactly.*"

"They're twins," she pointed out reasonably.

"Yeah, but I never noticed that they looked *exactly* alike, you know? They are always dressed in different colors. Stewart's red. Robert's blue. I never had to try to tell them apart. I just always went by the colors."

She glanced back down at the babies, who were rapidly going from fussy to furious now that they weren't getting any attention. They were straining at their halters, pushing at the bars. They wanted out, and pretty soon they were going to get vocal about it.

But they were definitely both dressed in identical blue rompers.

"I know, I know," Griffin said when she returned her quizzical gaze to his. "Both blue. It was a serious miscalculation."

"*Your* miscalculation?" She couldn't imagine Griffin doing anything this stupid.

"Not exactly." He sighed. "Well, yes, I suppose it was, in a way. I miscalculated by letting someone else bathe them while I took a nap."

"Who?"

Was he flushing? Surely not. But he wasn't eager to tell her, either. "A friend of mine," he said.

She started to ask who again, but she stopped herself. She knew who. His bimbo of the moment, no doubt. Rumor had it he was dating three different women, and if you added all their IQs together you'd still be on the low end of the charts.

She looked away, not wanting him to see the disapproval in her eyes. She had no right to judge him. But God, what an unbelievably dumb move!

The babies had progressed from whimpering to outright crying. Griffin reached down and tried shaking the plastic keys again, but the boys weren't buying it.

Heather spoke louder, to be heard over the din. "You still haven't explained why you're here."

Griffin hopped off the table and bent down, extricating the louder baby from the stroller and hoisting him into his arms. Heather felt a slight knock of her pulse. Playboy Cahill holding a baby was a sight she hadn't ever expected to see.

"I was hoping you might have some idea. Some trick for identifying them."

She stared at him. "You're joking, right?"

He frowned. "No. Of course I'm not joking. I have to know which one is which. I can't keep calling them 'champ' for three weeks."

The baby left behind began to howl at the injustice of it all. Griffin shut his eyes briefly, then bent again, wrestling the second boy free of his halter awkwardly, while balancing the other one on his shoulder.

Finally he rose again, this time with a baby on each shoulder. Heather felt speechless with amazement as the boys instantly sniffed back their tears and rested their fat, downy cheeks against Griffin's rigid chest muscles.

Tears still pooled around their eyes, but they began sucking their thumbs, obviously content with the safety of their new perches.

He looked at her hard, as if daring her to laugh. She didn't.

"There must be some way. Aren't there footprints on file somewhere or something? What about blood tests?"

She smiled in spite of herself. "Well, I guess we could do a DNA analysis."

"Great. " Nodding eagerly, Griffin shifted one of the boys higher. "Go ahead. Hurry."

"I was kidding, Griffin." She watched his face fall. Amazing—he was so sophisticated about some things, and yet so dumb about everything to do with babies. He'd obviously avoided the subject like the plague.

"Honestly, Griffin. I don't have any tricks for telling babies apart. There's nothing I can do for you. Maybe you should just call your brother and ask him."

Griffin shook his head emphatically, his golden hair catching the light from the overhead fixture. "No, ma'am. I'm not admitting to this, not if I can help it. Katie wouldn't ever let me hear the end of it.''

''Well, then, I guess you're stuck with the situation,'' she said. She looked at the babies, who had closed their eyes and appeared to be falling asleep, as if Griffin's hard pectoral muscles were the softest goose-feather pillows.

The sight was oddly touching. And, even more shocking, she also found that it was disturbingly sexy. It made her strangely angry to discover that she still went a little weak in the knees at the sight of him. After everything he'd done to her, that must mean she was a little weak in the head, too.

She turned around, forcing herself to stop looking. She had a room full of pregnant women waiting for her, remember? She had no time for his foolish predicament. He'd brought it on himself. Now he had to live with it.

''Good luck, Griffin. I'm sorry I couldn't help.''

''Heather, wait.''

''I'm busy,'' she said curtly. ''I have patients.''

''Please.''

But she didn't have time to wait, she really didn't. And she didn't have the strength to be in this small, intimate room with Griffin much longer. She'd come a long way in ten years. But she obviously hadn't come far enough.

She had her hand on the door when he said her name again. The sound was low and urgent. ''Heather. Please.''

''What?'' She turned reluctantly. ''I told you. I can't help you.''

He looked at her over the babies' heads. ''Yes, you can.''

''How?''

He took a deep breath, but he met her gaze squarely. ''Spend the next three weeks with me. Help me take care of the boys.''

She frowned, wondering once again if he might be joking. The idea was so utterly preposterous.

''Don't be ridiculous, Griffin. I can't do that.''

''Why can't you? You're good with kids. You're responsible and kind. You have medical training, and you're absolutely perfect.''

Though she heard the exhaustion in his voice, though she sensed real need, she steeled herself to resist it. She reminded herself of the dozens of times he had not been there when she needed him. Including last Monday, at the city council meeting.

She hardened her voice, so that he would know she was strong enough to resist him. And the babies. The whole absurd package.

''What on earth makes you think I'd say yes to such an outrageous proposition? Why should I feel the slightest obligation to help you? For old times' sake? Hardly.'' She didn't hide the bitterness she felt. ''Or perhaps as thanks for all the help you gave me over the zoning variance?''

He shook his head. ''I can still help you with that,'' he said. ''I can get Alton to call for another vote.''

"I can get him to call for another vote, too," she responded curtly. "I'm consulting a lawyer next week."

"Lawyers are expensive."

"I'll manage."

"Wait. I know," he said suddenly, looking up at her with a new light in his eyes. "I have something you want. A lot."

She shook her head. "I doubt that," she said tightly.

"But I do." He smiled, tired but more relaxed now, as if he was sure he had her. "I have your love letters."

She didn't speak, didn't even breathe for a long, empty moment. The only sound in the room was the soft snuffle of the babies' little stuffed noses.

Finally she found her voice. "All of them?"

"All of them."

She swallowed hard. "Even the one you promised to burn? The one about Silver Kiss Falls?"

He nodded slowly. "*All* of them," he said again, and his voice told her he hadn't forgotten a word that was in those letters. Those stupid, stupid letters.

She couldn't think what to say. He had promised to burn them. But then, he had promised so many things. And he had never done any of them.

She would hate it if those letters ever fell into anyone else's hands. They had been the foolish, naive ravings of a teenager newly in love, newly awake to the joys of sex. Having anyone else in the world read them would be desperately embarrassing.

She didn't really believe that Griffin would ever let

the letters go public. Not at their ugliest moments had she ever thought him capable of that level of cruelty. But even if he did, she could take it. A little embarrassment wouldn't kill her.

"I'll give them back to you, Heather. All of them."

"I don't want them." She smiled at him coldly. "They're ancient history, Griffin. I wouldn't give you a minute of my life for them, much less three weeks."

He was surprised, she could tell. Staring at her blankly, he leaned back against the examination table as if he were suddenly too tired to stand on his own. One of the babies began to wriggle and fuss, but Griffin rested his chin against the crown of his head gently, and he quickly settled down.

He looked at her over the baby's head. His face was devoid of its earlier rogue charm. He just looked tired and worried and desperate. Ironically, it made him look more attractive than ever. More real, somehow. More human.

"Oh, hell, I'm going about this all wrong. Look, I'm sorry I brought up the letters, Heather. You can have them any time you want them. No strings attached."

"I told you. I don't want them."

"Okay. But hear me out. Please. I need your help. I don't have anything to offer in return. And I don't deserve it, I admit that freely. But you have always been generous, ready to help anyone who needed it. Well, now I need it."

She hesitated. She had to set her shoulders against some stupid protective instinct that made her want to walk over and take one of the boys from his arms. Some insane impulse to lighten the burden of exhaustion she heard in his voice.

The baby began to whimper again. Absently Griffin rubbed the baby's cheek with his knuckle, and the little boy rooted sleepily toward the touch. He clamped his little rosebud mouth around Griffin's knuckle, and, sucking softly, went back to sleep.

Watching, Heather felt her stomach do something strange.

But Griffin seemed unaware of the entire episode. He had acted out of instinct, his mind entirely concentrated on her.

"I know it's an imposition, Heather. But I'm at the end of my rope. I haven't slept in three days. I'm afraid something will happen to them, something worse than two blue outfits. Please help me take care of them."

She closed her eyes, blocking out the sight of those pink, trusting lips locked around Griffin's hard, tanned finger. But when she opened them, the urge to say yes was as strong as ever.

She was a fool. No good could come of this.

She walked over and looked down at the sleeping babies. Lifting her hand slowly, she grazed the back of it across one curved, downy cheek. It was as soft and dewy as the clover that spread along the banks of Llewellyn's Lake in the spring.

"Three weeks," she said gruffly. "Not a day longer."

He nodded carefully. "Three weeks."

He paused. ‘‘Thanks, Heather,’’ he said tentatively, as if he didn’t trust his luck to hold.

She didn’t meet his eyes. ‘‘I’m not doing it for you.’’

‘‘I know.’’

‘‘I’m doing it for them.’’

‘‘I know.’’

‘‘I mean, already you’ve got the poor boys mixed up. God knows what you’d do next.’’

‘‘God knows,’’ he agreed meekly.

Finally she looked up, and she saw the gentle smile in those blue eyes that she had once loved better than life itself. And at that moment she finally realized what a dangerous decision she’d just made.

She might be able to protect the babies from Griffin and his foolish mistakes.

But who was going to protect her?

CHAPTER FOUR

OKAY, BENJAMIN BRADY, listen up. You're nineteen now—old enough to know there are no secrets in Firefly Glen. I found out when you set the boys' bathroom on fire, and I found out when you knocked out Digger Jackson's front teeth. Did you think I wouldn't find out that Sheriff Dunbar caught you doing ninety through Vanity Gap? I—

The purr of an expensive sports car pulling into the front driveway of Spring House interrupted Mary Brady's train of thought. But that was okay. She could write this particular *Listen Up* lecture, aimed at her youngest brother, in her sleep. In fact, maybe she should check her portfolio of old *Listen Up* letters. She probably still had the one she wrote when Dooley got his first speeding ticket. She could save herself some time by recycling that one.

And she was going to need all the time she could get, now that Heather had gone and made this stupid arrangement with Playboy Cahill, which was going to create tons more work for everybody.

Come to think of it, maybe the person who needed a *Listen Up* lecture right now was Heather. *Honestly!* What kind of fool agreed to let a heartbreaker ex-boyfriend and his two suspicious infants move in for the express purpose of obtaining free baby-sitting?

Couldn't Heather see what was going on here? Or was she still a little blinded by those cocky blue eyes? It just went to show you, didn't it? Even smart women made dumb decisions. Mary could already feel the beginnings of a lecture. *Okay, my dear Dr. Delaney. Listen up.*

A car door slammed. Putting down her pen, Mary cast one last look around the hastily assembled Spring House "nursery." Everything was ready. She sighed. Like it or not, Griffin Cahill had arrived. Time to play welcoming committee.

As she trotted down the curving staircase, she could see Griffin through the beveled glass that framed the front door. He had his backside to her, bending over to retrieve the babies from their car seat.

It stopped her in her tracks. Normally, Mary didn't go all breathless and poetic about the male body. Growing up with four brothers had cured her of that. But, even so, she had to admit that, from this angle, Griffin Cahill had a rather nifty little backside.

Too bad he was such an ass.

She grinned, enjoying the play on words. She stood there watching, chuckling, until Griffin began to climb the steps toward the porch, a sleeping baby in each arm. Then she finally took the rest of the stairs and opened the door.

"Need any help?" She made no move toward him,

and the tone of her voice made it clear that only one answer would be acceptable.

"No, thanks," he said politely, obviously getting the message. Nobody had ever accused Griffin of being stupid. Not even Mary.

Shifting the baby in his left arm slightly, he flicked a glance into the foyer behind her. "Where's Heather?"

"She's working."

"Working?" He looked genuinely surprised. He probably had expected Heather to be waiting by the door with bells on.

Mary smiled. "Yes, working. It's a darling little idea they've invented. You go to an office, and you spend a few hours being useful. Afterward, they pay you."

"How clever," Griffin said, all admiration. "I should try it sometime." He raised one eyebrow. "Oops. That was probably supposed to be your line, wasn't it?"

Maddeningly, Mary couldn't think of a witty reply. So she didn't try. She just stepped aside grimly, letting Griffin stride into the house, which he did as if he owned it, the cheeky bastard. He'd probably walk into heaven itself with that same cocky stride.

But a few feet inside the door, he stopped cold. Whistling just under his breath, he scanned the large hall slowly, obviously stunned by the restored beauty around him.

Mary waited. She had wanted him to be impressed, and yet now she was strangely annoyed by his surprise.

Of course Spring House was beautiful. Why wouldn't it be? From the moment Heather Delaney had bought it, she had pampered this sad old relic like a baby. She had spent her entire inheritance renovating it.

Thanks to Heather, sunlight poured in through the beveled glass side lights, tossing quivering rainbows onto the polished honey-wood floors. An elegant gold-and-green patterned carpet rose up the graceful curve of stairs toward the upper stories. Sparkling mirrors bracketed by gleaming brass sconces offered glimpses into other rooms of equal beauty.

You never would have guessed that only two years ago Spring House had been a dark, creaky, moldering old mess, good only for haunting or tearing down.

Griffin turned back to Mary, a ridge forming between his brows. ''I thought Heather was turning it into her offices. Into a clinic.''

''Not this part,'' Mary explained impatiently. ''Just the back, where the old kitchen and pantries and servants rooms used to be. She was very careful to keep the clinic from spoiling the rest of the house. She even put the parking at the back, so the cars wouldn't annoy the neighbors.''

Griffin nodded thoughtfully. ''Still. It's incredible.''

''I don't see why you're so shocked, Griffin. Heather presented the plans to the city council when she applied for the zoning variance. Didn't you even bother to look at the blueprints?''

Griffin glanced over at her, his chin brushing the

forehead of a sleeping baby. ''I didn't see any need to. I knew I was going to vote yes.''

''Really.'' Mary narrowed her eyes. ''Then it's too bad you didn't.''

''Oh, I see.'' He tilted his head quizzically. ''Is that what's eating you, Mary? The vote? Is that why you were standing at the door doing that over-my-dead-body routine?''

''You bet it is.'' Mary saw no reason to beat around the bush. ''Well, that's part of it, anyway.''

As if sensing the animosity around him, one of the babies began to stir and whimper. Griffin bent his lips to the little half-bald head and whispered something. The baby nuzzled his chest drowsily for a minute, then subsided with a powdery sigh and fell back asleep.

Griffin was still looking at Mary. ''Okay. The vote is part of it. What's the rest of it?''

''The rest of it could fill a book,'' she said irritably, annoyed with the baby now, too. Even a baby should know better than to fall for this jerk's whispered promises. ''But in a nutshell, the rest of it is that I like Heather Delaney. I think she's a damn fine person. I think she deserves to be happy.''

''Me, too.'' Griffin shrugged. ''I'm only going to be here for a couple of weeks, you know. I don't intend to interfere with anybody's long-term happiness.''

Mary kicked her heel against the wood floor, though she knew someone would have to polish out the scuff mark. ''Yeah, well, you may not intend to, but you always seem to have a way of doing it anyhow.''

"Really? How?"

"Just by being around, damn it. Just by being you."

He grinned. "Gosh. You make me sound pretty powerful."

"Don't kid yourself, blondie. You're not powerful—you're just Trouble. Like the time you stole Eddie's prom date and had sex with her out behind the gym."

Griffin laughed softly. "Come on, Mary. That was more than fifteen years ago. And we didn't actually have sex."

"They found her corsage in your underwear."

He laughed out loud, startling the babies, who jerked in their sleep. Silencing himself quickly, he winked at her. "That's nothing but an urban legend, and you know it."

"Okay, how about the time you and Dooley went joyriding in Hickory Baxter's Cadillac?"

"Twenty years ago," he said. "Even Hickory has forgiven us by now. Come on, Mary. You can't still be this ticked off about a bunch of teenage nonsense. Other than missing the city council meeting, which, by the way, was not my fault, what sins have I committed lately?"

She looked him straight in the eye. "Well, there was that charming episode with Emma Dunbar. That was just a couple of months ago. Recent enough for you?"

Mary was pleased to see that Griffin finally looked uncomfortable. As well he should. Emma and her husband, Firefly Glen's Sheriff Harry Dunbar, were getting along fine now, but a couple of months ago their marriage had been in real trouble.

And the trouble was spelled "Griffin Cahill."

"Been listening to gossip, Mary?"

"It isn't just gossip," she retorted. And it wasn't. Harry himself had caught Griffin with Emma, kissing her, and God only knows what else. The two men had squared off in Emma's pretty little Paper Shop on Main Street, with half the town watching through the plate glass window.

"Are you so sure?"

"Darn right I am." She lifted her chin, daring him to downplay the situation. "I knew you were a tomcat, Cahill. But I honestly thought you drew the line at married women."

For a long minute he didn't answer her. He just idly stroked the pink cheek of one of the sleeping babies with the tips of his fingers.

It made Mary madder than ever. "Well? Haven't you got any explanation at all?"

He smiled. "As a matter of fact, I do."

Mary snorted. "And?"

"And, in spite of your obvious curiosity, I don't feel any particular need to share it."

God, he would never change, would he? He'd always been too handsome, too rich, too bloody full of himself. Too...she felt her vocabulary stuttering with annoyance. Too blond.

Maybe he was the one who ought to get her next *Listen Up* lecture. But what a waste of good ink and paper that would be. He wasn't the type to listen up to anyone.

"Besides," he added, eyeing her with a glimmer of real curiosity, "I'm not sure you have a dog in this race, do you, Mary? You're not Emma's guardian. Or mine."

"No, I'm not," she admitted. "But here's fair warning, blondie. Starting right now, I'm Heather's."

OH, YOU FOOL. You idiot. You complete and utter moron.

No, worse than moron. Much worse. Heather wished she had a thesaurus. There must be a bigger word, a word with five-inch fangs. An absolute ogre of a word for people like her, people who were dumber than dumb.

But she couldn't think of one. She could hardly think at all. For five solid minutes, she had been standing in the front hall, her briefcase in one hand and her keys in the other, frozen in place by the sounds that floated down to her from the upstairs bathroom.

Thumping. Splashing. Giggling. Laughter. A baby's exuberant soprano. A man's calm baritone.

Fairly normal sounds, really. Just the noises any mother might hear when she got home from work. The noises of a happy young family at bath time.

The only difference was that she wasn't a mother.

And this wasn't her family.

Oh, how could she have been so stupid? She let her briefcase slide out of her fingers with a soft leather plop and stared at herself in the hall mirror. Why hadn't she just offered to take the babies and let Griffin go his merry way? She could have handled them alone somehow. Even if it had meant doing completely without sleep for three weeks. It would have been worth it.

Anything would have been preferable to this—to Griffin Cahill living in Spring House. With her.

It had seemed so sensible yesterday. Obviously, if they were going to be a team, they'd have to sleep under the same roof—but setting up camp at Griffin's bachelor den was out of the question. She'd been there once, at a party she couldn't avoid. He collected ridiculously expensive art glass, for heaven's sake. And all those metallic angles, all those highly polished hardwood floors, that modern, free-floating staircase…

Ultra-elegant, no doubt. But a nightmare for infants.

Besides, to be brutally honest, she had simply wanted the home field advantage. She'd wanted him to be the "guest," the one who had to make all the adjustments, the one who had to politely request every glass of water he drank.

But, in all her strategizing, she hadn't realized one simple thing. She hadn't realized how…how difficult it would be to come home and find him here.

Suddenly a prickle of unease broke into her thoughts. Tuning into the bath time sounds, she realized that the squealing laughter had changed. As in a complicated piece of music, a new note had been introduced. Under the laughter, a wail of frustration. Maybe even distress.

Finally, thankfully, Heather's paralysis lifted. Dropping the keys in the cut-glass rose bowl, and shedding her ridiculous case of nerves at the same time, she hurried up the stairs, ready for anything. She didn't dash, but she covered the steps with quick efficiency, her lab coat ruffling out behind her. Yes, this was more like it. She was a doctor, after all. Not a silly, dithering, hand-wringing ninny.

She didn't slow down until she reached the threshold to the bathroom—but then she stopped dead, stunned by the chaos in front of her.

Water was everywhere. A hurricane of droplets dappled the mirror over the sink and pooled in the cracks between the floor tiles. Griffin had obviously caught the worst of it. His T-shirt stuck to his chest, and the soaked front of his jeans lay dark and heavy against his thighs. His blond hair tumbled over his forehead, wetly tickling his eyebrows.

One of the babies was trying to crawl out of a large white plastic tub that had been placed on the counter next to the sink. Drenched and shining, wriggling and giggling, he looked for all the world like a baby pig.

The other boy was in a small playpen, naked and red faced, holding on to the rails of his prison and screaming his indignation at being left out of the fun.

Griffin stood between the two, contorted into an almost impossible position. He was leaning sharply forward, holding on to the baby in the tub, but he had one hand desperately extended behind his back, shaking the multicolored ring of plastic keys at the baby in the playpen, who couldn't have been less interested.

"I kid you not, Stewbert. You've gotta give me a break here, pal." Griffin's baritone was raspy with frustration. He jiggled the plastic keys behind his back feverishly. "Your dad said this damn thing was your favorite toy, remember?"

Heather didn't wait for Griffin to notice her. She just kicked off her work shoes and waded, stocking-footed, into the fray. She leaned over the playpen and gathered the naked, wailing little boy into her arms. He stopped crying instantly, and smiled up at her through his tears, as if to say it had all been a grand joke.

"Yes! Attaboy, Stewbert," Griffin said without turning around, still jiggling the noisy ring of plastic keys frenetically. "That's it, pal. Just give your Uncle Griffin sixty seconds of peace and quiet, and maybe he won't go stark, raving crazy after all."

Heather reached out and covered the clacking keys with her free hand. "I don't know," she said mildly. "It may be too late."

"Heather?" Griffin swiveled his head without letting go of the baby in the tub. The expression on his face was ten percent embarrassment and ninety percent pure, unabashed relief.

"Thank God," he said simply. He dropped the keys on the floor and, using both hands, gave the baby in the tub one good rinse, then plucked him out. Ignoring the boy's immediate squeals of protest, Griffin flicked a towel from the rack and draped it across the wet, wriggling little body.

Then he turned around and gave Heather a smile that

caught a glistening drop of water in one dimpled corner.

"Hi," he said sheepishly. "It may be hard to believe, but the Stewberts and I actually had decided that being all cleaned up would make a great first impression when you got home." He blinked away a damp strand of hair that had caught on his lashes. "I'm willing to admit I may have miscalculated just a little."

She looked around the soggy room. "Just a *little?*"

He grinned and began rubbing the baby dry with the soft blue terry towel. "I know. But remember...you didn't see what the Stewberts looked like *before* their baths. Maybe I shouldn't brag on my own nephews, but I have to say they do things with pureed peas that are really quite creative."

She chuckled. She couldn't help it. For no apparent reason, the baby she was holding had decided it might be fun to look at the world upside down. He had dropped his head and was now leaning so far back his little belly button was pointing at the ceiling.

She righted him with effort, but he flopped back immediately, determined to slither headfirst out of her arms. It was like trying to hold on to a wet eel.

"The Stewberts?" She looked at Griffin over the writhing little boy. "That's what you're calling them?"

"Well, I had to split the difference," he explained reasonably. "'Stew' for Stewart and 'Bert' for Robert. I tried other combinations, but 'Bert-wart' sounded almost vulgar."

She laughed, which caught her baby's attention. He

stopped twisting abruptly, pulled himself erect, and stared at her. Frowning, he reached out and pressed his tiny forefinger against her teeth curiously.

She planted a small kiss on the exploring hand. "Still," she said, "you're going to have to fess up sooner or later." She glanced at Griffin, who was sharing the towel with his nephew, alternately rubbing the baby's wet face, then his own. He had spoken to Jared several times, assuring him that the boys were all right and letting him know about the temporary move to Heather's house. But he'd never mentioned the mix-up in names. "Why don't you just call Jared and ask him what the secret is to telling them apart?"

"I can't. I still have my pride, you know." Griffin took one step and landed with a piercing, falsetto squeak on a yellow rubber duckie. "Well, some of it, anyway."

Heather didn't know an awful lot about babies—at least not once they were born and turned over to the local pediatrician. But she did know that it was probably courting disaster to postpone the diaper process much longer. "How about if I help you get these guys dressed?"

Griffin smiled. "That would be great. Thanks."

She turned toward the large dressing room, which she had hastily converted into a makeshift nursery late last night. It was conveniently located between the spacious his-and-her bedrooms so common in Victorian floor plans. Griffin would sleep on one side, Heather on the other. Both of them would be within earshot of the boys.

"Heather." Griffin's voice came from behind her.

She turned around. "What?"

"I really mean it," he said softly. "Thanks. For everything."

He sounded sincere. She felt herself start to melt a little around the edges, just looking at the sweet picture of man and baby, both damp and tousled, both staring solemnly at her with blue eyes so clear and open their souls seemed to shine through.

It was so strange. It made her feel a little lightheaded. She'd seen him just like this in dreams, a thousand times. Her husband. Her baby. She remembered waking up and hugging her pillow, not wanting to let the dream go. Of course, that had been a long time ago. At seventeen, she had still had complete faith that the dream would one day come true.

"Heather, I—" He let out a slow breath, as if he weren't sure where to begin. He stroked the baby's back idly. "Listen, I've always wanted a chance to tell you that I—"

Suddenly his expression changed. He looked down.

"What the—?" Holding the smiling baby at arm's length, he cursed, sharp and hard. "God damn it, Stewbert, couldn't you have waited one more lousy minute?"

Heather looked at Griffin's shirt. It had always been wet, so she couldn't discern anything new, but obviously he could. He was glaring at his nephew, and the horrified shock on his face couldn't have been any greater if the baby had just shot him with a popgun.

She began to laugh, sorry for Griffin, but relieved that the weirdly intimate moment had passed safely. She wasn't up to exchanging confidences with him now. It was too late for that. Years and years too late.

"It's not funny," he said, transferring his glare to her.

"Yes, it is. You should see yourself."

"It could be you next," he growled. "I hope it is, you heartless—"

She grinned. This was a whole new side of the ordinarily suave and glossy Playboy Cahill. This man was disheveled. Clearly perplexed. Practically inept.

He came shockingly close, in fact, to being human.

Still smiling, Heather turned toward the nursery. Griffin followed quickly, still holding the baby out with stiff arms, as if he were an unstable time bomb.

"Well," he observed wryly as they paraded down the hall, "it's nice to know that you find my predicament so amusing."

Heather crossed the room, picked up two diapers from the changing table and handed him one politely.

"Yes," she agreed, her smile broadening as she watched him try to open the diaper and lay it on the table without letting the baby within striking range. "In fact, I'm starting to think these next couple of weeks might just be extremely entertaining."

CHAPTER FIVE

TEN O'CLOCK AT LUCKY'S LOUNGE. Typical Friday night full house, lots of noise and smoke. A hot, greasy pizza waiting back at the booth. A well-chalked cue in his hand and a Knicks game on the overhead television. The twelve ball sinking into the corner pocket just as the go-ahead shot sinks into the TV basket, nothing but net either place.

And best of all, not a baby in sight.

It was, Griffin decided as he racked his cue and joined Parker Tremaine at their corner booth, about as close to heaven as the average guy ever gets.

Well, a beer might have nudged him an inch or two closer, but for the time being alcohol was off-limits. Still a field general in disguise, Heather had posted a complicated rotation of responsibilities. According to her typewritten schedule, Griffin had Daddy Duty in just over two hours.

Setting his jaw, he picked up his diet soda and tried not to smell Parker's Michelob from across the table.

"So. Tell me the God's truth, Griff." Parker leaned back and wiped the foam from his upper lip. "How tough is it?"

Griffin shrugged and stalled by taking a swallow of

his cola. He couldn't exactly tell Parker the truth. Parker's wife, Sarah, was going to have a baby this summer, and Parker was clearly scared to death.

So he couldn't say, *It's hell, pal. Run for your life.* But he wasn't going to lie, either.

"It's weird," he said, grimacing as the cola went down. *God.* This stuff could ruin a good pizza. "I mean, they're cute. Sometimes they're so damn adorable you just can't believe it. But they're after you all the time, you know what I mean? They need something every fifteen seconds. I've never been so tired in my life."

Parker blinked, then took a fortifying swig of beer. Griffin looked away. It was strange. He used to scoff at his friends who seemed so emasculated by the arrival of a new baby. Weaklings, he had thought them, with their shadowed, tired eyes, their fretful double-checking of their watches, their frequent calls home to check out mystery fevers and erupting teeth.

And what happened to their conversation was a crime. Brilliant men could deliver twenty-minute monologues about burping, and CEOs would discuss projectile vomiting until you practically lost your lunch.

Yeah, he had thought they were pretty pathetic. And now here he was, in the same boat. For the past hour, all through the first half of a damn good Knicks game, he'd been fighting an urge to call Heather to find out if Stewbert was still refusing to eat.

"You in?" Micky Milligan, the seven-foot bartender who had been collecting the "TV tax" at Lucky's ever since Griffin was a teenager, came by with his hand out. Everyone at Lucky's knew that the TV tax was just a clever ruse to get around the prohibition against gambling.

Tonight they were betting on the point spread in the basketball game. When he handed over his five-dollar bill, Parker called for the Knicks by two. Griffin felt wilder. He guessed the Knicks would blow it out by twenty.

Parker laughed. "Haven't you even been watching the game? The Knicks are down by six, with only five minutes left." When Griffin just shrugged, Parker narrowed his eyes curiously. "You didn't have a clue what the score was, did you? What's with you tonight? Is anything wrong?"

Griffin shook his head. Was anything wrong? Besides the fact that his brother had just saddled him with two babies who never slept, which meant he didn't sleep, either? Besides the fact that he had to drink swill with his pizza?

He downed the last watery dregs of his cola. "Nothing's wrong. I just believe in the Knicks." He smiled at Parker. "I notice you handed over your hard-earned cash without a second thought. Sarah doesn't mind your gambling away the baby's college tuition?"

Parker smiled that goofy smile he always got when he talked about Sarah. The man was so in love it was funny. "She'd mind if I didn't. The first time she came here, she won the whole pot, so she thinks it's good luck."

Parker drained his beer. "Besides, you know Sarah. She's not the judgmental type."

That was true. Parker was a lucky son of a gun. He had a wife who was beautiful and smart and gentle—and one of the most easygoing women Griffin had ever met. She was that rare female who loved her man just as he was. She had no interest in changing him, holding out hoops for him to jump through, setting up hurdles for him to clear before he could be considered worthy of her.

Not, to put it bluntly, at all like General Heather Delaney.

Griffin tried to imagine himself married to Heather, with a baby on the way. The sex would be fine. In fact, it would be fantastic. He remembered that, all right. But hell. What was he thinking? They probably would have stopped making love within two weeks of the wedding. The first time Griffin came home late, or looked at another woman walking by...

God, he hadn't thought about all this in years—and he'd be better off if he didn't think about it now. He had no idea what marriage to Heather would be like, but he was fairly sure it wouldn't involve beer at Lucky's and betting on the Knicks game.

"Stop daydreaming, Cahill. Shove over and make a little room. And while you're at it, pour your long-lost friend a beer."

Griffin looked up, shocked by the sound of the familiar voice.

"Troy?" He shook his head, disbelieving. But it was

definitely Troy, his friend and sometimes partner, the writer who provided the copy to go with his pictures. Troy, complete with his movie-star tan, his shaggy Beatles haircut, and his compulsively buffed body, all of which worked hard at disguising the fact that Troy Madison was standing on the other side of what he called "the great divide"—his fortieth birthday.

"What the hell are you doing in Firefly Glen, Madison? I thought you were in Acapulco, interviewing that actress."

"Naw. I cut that short. She turned out to be completely plastic." He grinned at Griffin's raised eyebrow. "Her personality, you filthy-minded animal. I wouldn't know about the rest of her. I'm a married man, remember?" He slid into the spot Griffin had created. "For the moment, anyhow."

Griffin didn't take the bait. Troy was a gifted writer, but a lousy family man. He had been complaining about his rotten marriage for the past ten years. Every time Griffin worked with him on an assignment, Troy would swear that a divorce was imminent. But after a decade of grousing, the man was still wearing that little gold ring.

"You remember Parker Tremaine, don't you, Troy?"

Troy brushed his brown hair out of his eyes and extended a hand across the table. "Of course. Good to see you, Sheriff."

"Not the sheriff anymore," Parker explained. "I

traded in my badge for a shingle. I set up my own law practice in town a few months ago.''

Troy grinned. ''Maybe I could use you. Do you do divorces, Counselor?''

''I haven't done any yet. Haven't done much of anything yet, actually. A couple of wills, a couple of trust funds, nothing too exciting.''

''That's what you get for living in Firefly Glen, where when they want a real thrill millionaires dress up like loggers so they can spend Friday nights in dumps like this.'' Troy looked around, exhaling a sigh full of pity. ''God, what a yawner. You probably couldn't even get a good fight going in this town unless you insulted somebody's mutual fund.''

Parker smiled. ''Or dinged their BMW.''

''Hey.'' Griffin tilted his empty glass toward Parker threateningly. ''You leave my BMW out of this.''

Troy groaned. ''Rich people have got to be the most boring people on earth.'' Reaching over, he shamelessly poached a slice of pizza from Griffin's plate. ''But don't worry, my small-town friend. I've come to take you away from all this.''

Griffin watched him eat half the pizza in one bite. ''You don't say.''

''I do say. I've got a proposition you'd be a fool to refuse. And you're no fool.'' Troy scowled at the table. ''Hey, where's the beer?''

''Griffin isn't drinking tonight, Troy,'' Parker put in, a mischievous glint in his eye. ''He's got to go home soon. He's got a curfew. He's got to take care of the babies.''

Troy froze, his mouth half-open, which wasn't a pretty sight. ''The what?''

Parker's grin was splitting his face. ''The babies.''

''Shut up, Parker.'' Griffin gritted his teeth. ''It's not like that. I don't have any babies. I mean, I have babies, but—''

''Later. You can tell me the baby story later.'' Troy held up both hands. ''Right now just listen. Forget the babies, whoever they are. Forget everything. I've got an assignment for us.''

''But I can't—''

''Just listen, I said. This is special, Griffin. This is the one we've been talking about, the one we've been waiting for. It's Nepal.''

''Nepal?'' In spite of himself, Griffin's heartbeat revved a little. This really was special.

''Nepal. And that's not all. Get this. It's *National Geographic,* man.'' Troy nodded his head, his tan glowing almost copper with rising excitement. ''It's the one and only *National Geo*-Chance-Of-A-Lifetime-*graphic.*''

Griffin's mouth wasn't working right. He couldn't seem to get it to form the word ''no.'' He just looked at Troy, whose eyes were shining. Then he looked at Parker, whose eyes were not. Parker's kind blue eyes were dark, and somber.

Parker understood.

''Well?'' Troy sounded indignant. ''What are we

waiting for? Go home and get packing. If we leave tonight we'll have a couple of weeks to play around before the shoot officially begins."

"Troy," Griffin began slowly. "I think maybe I'd better tell you the baby story now."

"Oh, come on, Griff—" Troy paused. As he looked around, he finally seemed to register the grim expressions on the faces of the other men. "Damn, Griffin. You haven't done something really stupid, have you? They aren't yours?"

"No. They're not mine." Griffin took a deep breath. "But for the next three weeks they might as well be."

"Well, if they're not yours, then what difference does—"

"If you'll listen, God damn it, I'll tell you."

Troy tugged on his shaggy hair irritably, grabbed another piece of pizza and settled back with a grunt.

"Okay," he said flatly. "But I'm warning you. I'm not taking no for an answer."

MARY HAD STRAIGHTENED up only about half the magazines in the waiting room when somebody began knocking at the front door.

"We're closed," she muttered under her breath, bending over to retrieve an issue of *Fortune* somebody had kicked under a chair. It was Saturday, for Pete's sake. Even Heather Delaney, guardian angel of the entire hopelessly dependent female population of Firefly Glen, deserved to close up shop on Saturday.

But apparently whoever was out there didn't agree. The knocking continued.

Mary growled and walked over to the glass doors, prepared to shoo the pest away. To her surprise, though, it wasn't a pregnant female. It was a male. A very male male.

He looked to be in his late thirties or early forties, and he was aiming a fairly charming smile at her through the glass. Not charming enough to get her to open that door, though. Saturday afternoon was her only time for writing, and her writing was much more important than any pair of nicely tanned, rather broad shoulders.

She pointed at her watch, then pointed at the door, where the office hours were clearly stenciled. ''We're *closed,*'' she mouthed broadly, so he couldn't mistake her meaning. But she smiled. He might come back on Monday, and she'd like him to remember her warmly.

''Am rucknggh pr Gffarn Chll,'' he mouthed back, returning the smile. He tilted his head, laced his fingers together in supplication and managed to make one word come through clearly. ''Please?''

Oh, heck. Mary reached up and twisted the dead bolt.

''The doctor isn't here,'' she said firmly. ''We're closed.''

''Actually, I'm not looking for the doctor,'' he explained politely. ''I'm Troy Madison. I work with Griffin Cahill. I was wondering if he might be here.''

He *worked* with Griffin Cahill? That was a joke.

Cahill hadn't worked in his whole spoiled life. But she felt a small drag of disappointment. She should have known that this man, with his major-league good looks and his cheerful assumption that any door he knocked on should miraculously fall open, would be buddies with Playboy Cahill.

"Well, he's not." She let the door narrow an inch. "Listen, I hate to be rude, but I'm pretty busy here."

Troy, or whatever his name was, quickly adopted an apologetic expression. "I know. I am sorry. It's just that Mrs. Burke at the café said she thought Griff was coming here, to see Dr. Delaney. And I really need to talk to him. It's important."

She tried not to fall for it, but he was awfully good. She liked it that he had bothered to find out Theo's name at the Candlelight Café. And she liked it that he called Heather "Dr. Delaney." That showed respect.

"You see," he went on, as if he sensed a chink in the fortress, "it's about a job. It's rather exciting, really, and a decision has to be made quickly. Otherwise, I wouldn't have dreamed of bothering you when you're closed."

He even sounded sincere. And he had an open face. He really did look excited about something.

"A job? You're a photographer, too?"

He laughed, as if that were very funny. "Gosh, no. Even at Christmas I mostly end up taking pictures of my thumb." He pantomimed fumbling absurdly with an imaginary camera. "Actually, I'm a writer. That's why Griff and I make a good team. I come up with the words, and he provides the pictures.''

''Really? You're a writer?'' Mary hoped she didn't sound like an ingénue. But she didn't meet many writers, buried here in Firefly Glen. Most of the men she met were either loggers, like her brothers, or millionaires, like Griffin, who didn't do anything but play with their stock tickers. ''For a living?''

''Yes, I am. I mostly do travel pieces. But of course I'm working on a novel that I may even finish someday, if I live long enough.''

She looked at him, fascinated by the blasé way he made that announcement, as if everyone understood about writing novels, as if everyone probably had one half-completed in a drawer at home.

She had to bite the inside of her cheek to keep from telling him about the box full of stories she kept under her bed, stories she had written to amuse her little brothers after their mother died. The stories weren't much good—strictly amateur, family stuff. But sometimes she dreamed she'd polish them up a bit, send them to an editor and see what happened.

It wasn't a fact she usually felt like broadcasting. Not anymore. She'd made the mistake of telling Dooley about it one day, and he'd laughed so hard lemonade had come running out his nose. He'd been showing off that trick at parties ever since.

That was her world. The world everyone thought she ''belonged'' to. But someday, she'd vowed that afternoon, as she tossed her paper napkin to Dooley, someday she'd show them all how wrong they were.

She wondered if this man, this Troy Madison, had ever felt the need to show anyone anything. Probably not. He looked as if his parents had been called Scott and Zelda, and read each other poetry after dinner. He looked as if he'd been born in a thirty-room country house that had a library lined with a hundred thousand books.

She, on the other hand, had been born with only a dog-eared library card. In spite of that discrepancy, she felt a strangely powerful kinship with him now.

"So what is this exciting assignment you mentioned? Is it a travel story?"

He beamed. "Yes. It's in Nepal. I've been sending the idea around for years, and somebody finally bit on it. And not just 'somebody.' *National Geographic.*"

He looked absolutely adorable, with that proud, happy grin. And why shouldn't he be proud? *Nepal.* She liked the exotic sound of it. And she definitely liked the idea of Griffin Cahill in Nepal.

"Actually, Griffin was here about twenty minutes ago," she said, suddenly deciding it would be a good idea to cooperate. She could tell Troy was surprised by her abrupt change of topic, but he nodded attentively. "He did come to see Heather. He was planning to take the babies to the park."

"And what? He wanted her to go, too?"

"I guess so. He didn't exactly ask her, but why else

would he have come here? He doesn't have to clear all his movements with her.''

''And did she go?''

''Followed him within five minutes. Like he had her on a string.''

Probably, Mary figured, she shouldn't be so obvious about her displeasure. But Heather had shocked the heck out of her this afternoon. Heather didn't believe in wasting time. She always spent Saturday afternoons, when she had no patients, going over medical records. She never just went to the park, for no good reason. Never.

Not until Griffin Cahill and his two pudgy bundles of joy—drooling all over their identical blue rompers—had strolled in here today.

''I think she was concerned that he couldn't handle them alone.'' At least that was the explanation Mary preferred.

Troy looked thoughtful. ''Oh, man, if there's a female involved...'' He shook his head, as if to himself. ''No. A doctor would be too serious. Not his type. And we're talking *Nepal* here.'' He scratched his ear and frowned at Mary. ''You don't think that he...that she...''

She recognized the concern in his face quite easily. It was a mirror image of her own.

He started again. ''I mean, you don't think that they—''

''Not if you get there fast enough,'' she said. Smiling, she strode over to the front counter and tore a blank sheet from the sign-in clipboard. "Here. I'll draw you a map."

WHEN HEATHER REACHED THE PARK, she wished for the first time in her life that she could take photographs the way Griffin could. She would have liked to have a picture of this day, to look at when she was cold, when the sky was low and gray, when it was winter again.

It was one of those magical early May days, when everything was washed in gold. It wouldn't last. Soon spring would gather a vigorous green strength. But today—maybe only today—the blue-gold sky rose clear for miles; the emerald-gold grass was tender underfoot. The sable-gold trunks of budding oaks grew alongside white-gold birches, and daffodils shone like cups of honeyed champagne.

Add to that the peachy-gold cheeks of the laughing Stewberts, and Griffin's golden hair—and you had a scene that begged to be captured, and kept forever.

But Heather had no camera. So she just stepped into the picture and became a part of it.

The boys already sat in a pair of baby swings, fully harnessed, and Griffin stood centered behind them, gently pushing one with each hand. The Stewberts clearly loved it. With each rhythmic arc, they crowed delightedly and kicked their tiny legs like baby frogs trying to swim through the air.

Griffin must have been very sure she would follow him, Heather thought wryly. He couldn't have heard her coming up behind him, but he turned his head and smiled at her over his shoulder, unsurprised.

"Hi," he said. "You must have ESP. I was just wishing I had another pair of hands."

She stepped into place in time to catch one of the Stewberts on the downswing and give his padded bottom a push. "Really? I thought you seemed to have things remarkably well under control."

"An illusion," he assured her. "They're trying to lull me into a false sense of security, and then they'll hit me with it."

"With what?"

"Whatever. Crying. Screaming. A tumble. A pinched finger. A runny nose. A leaky diaper." He grimaced. "Projectile vomiting."

She laughed, which was a mistake, because it caused Stewbert to writhe in his harness, trying to get a look at her. She caught the swing. "It's just me, sweetie," she said, kissing him on the top of his head.

He smiled at her broadly, his two white front teeth gleaming in the spring sunlight, and he let go of the chain, reaching out for her with a low gurgle of recognition.

She felt a small, sweet pinch somewhere in her chest. But she fought the urge to pick him up. Taking his little fist and planting it back on the chain, she twisted him face-forward and gave him a new push. His feet began to kick contentedly again.

She glanced over at Griffin, who had been watching her with a strangely admiring half smile on his face.

She felt herself flushing, but she squelched it somehow, concentrating on pushing the swing. *You've seen this before,* she reminded herself. *It's just that old, cheap Cahill charm.*

"You know what, Dr. Delaney?" Griffin spoke softly. "I think maybe you're a natural."

She eyed him coolly. "And I think maybe *you're* full of—"

"Cahill? Cahill! Can I borrow you for a moment?"

They both looked toward the edge of the square, where the sidewalk traced the perimeter of the park. Alton Millner stood there among the daffodils, waving awkwardly, looking stiff and overdressed for a mild Saturday afternoon in a dark suit and tie. But then he always overdressed. He probably thought it made him look mayoral.

Griffin waved back politely, but without enthusiasm. He sighed and turned to Heather. "Sorry. Are you okay alone here for a minute?"

She nodded and watched as Griffin loped off toward the other man, his corduroy pants and light brown bomber jacket gilded by the April sun. His movements were light and graceful, she thought.

After Griffin reached the mayor, Heather looked away. She wasn't going to try to guess what they were talking about. She kept her attention on the Stewberts, pushing them back and forth, back and forth, like clockwork.

Griffin was gone a good bit more than a minute, which could have been predicted, considering what a talker Mayor Millner was. The babies began to tire of their game. One of them started to whimper.

Heather had already discovered that whenever one of the twins switched moods, the other wasn't far behind. She circled round to the front and began unhitching the first baby. The harness was a diabolical contraption, though. It would take a civil engineer to extricate Stewbert from its clutches, especially while the little boy was wriggling and twisting like this.

Her fingers flew, but the latch wouldn't give. The baby seemed to sense that he was trapped. She heard the first ominous sputters, the short grunts that signaled the onset of a full-blown tantrum.

"Oh, Stewbert, please," she begged in a whisper, tugging at the straps. "Not yet. Not now."

But it was too late. Stewbert sucked in a deep breath, tilted back his head and let loose the most bloodcurdling scream Heather had ever heard. The other baby frowned, openmouthed with shock, and then decided to join in vigorously, for no apparent reason except that he refused to be outdone by his brother.

It was like being the star of a nightmare. Parents all around the park turned and watched in horror. A pair of terrified starlings shot out of the treetops. Even the squirrels seemed to freeze, mid-acorn, and stare.

Of course Griffin chose that moment to return. He squinted at the god-awful noise, then squatted down beside Heather and put his hands over hers.

"Here. Let me," he said. "I already figured it out once."

Gladly. She pulled her shaking fingers away and let him work. Within seconds he had the baby loose. He handed the screaming boy to Heather, then went to work on the other swing.

In less than a minute, both babies were free, and, miraculously, silence had returned to the golden spring day, except for their small, watery hiccuping and the terrified pounding of Heather's heart.

Griffin smiled. "I take it back," he said, patting his baby's damp head. "I guess you're not a natural after all."

She shuddered. "There was *nothing* natural about that sound," she said. With one last hiccup, Stewbert lifted his head and smiled at her, all dewy innocence. She shook her head. "You can't fool me," she told the baby soberly. "There's a demon inside you, and that's a fact."

Griffin chuckled. "At least now you see that it really does take two people to handle this."

"Three or four might be even better." But the little demon had placed his cheek against her collarbone, put his thumb in his mouth and closed his eyes, soggy lashes brushing pink satin cheeks. It was amazingly difficult, she realized, to stay out of sorts with any creature this soft and warm and trusting.

Which must be the way Nature planned it. Otherwise, who would dare to have children at all?

The other baby had shut his eyes, too, so by mutual, unspoken agreement Griffin and Heather began walking slowly back toward her office. It wasn't far—nothing was far from anything else on the quaint little streets of downtown Firefly Glen. Besides, Heather's shift was next, and they'd make the transfer there.

"I'm sorry to have left you alone so long," Griffin said, speaking quietly so that he didn't get the twins stirred up again. "But Alton is such a windbag."

"What did he want?"

Griffin hesitated. "He wanted to offer one of his daughters as a nanny—just in case the arrangement I made with you wasn't working out."

She felt a surge of irritation, but she kept her voice low somehow. "One of his daughters? Who? Mina? She's only fifteen, for heaven's sake! And she's the most ditzy teenager in town."

Griffin nodded. "I know."

"I mean, *really* ditzy. She had to quit the cheerleading squad because she couldn't remember the cheers." Heather stroked Stewbert's back protectively, hoping he wouldn't sense the quietly furious pumping of her heart. "Honestly, how absurd! He can't really believe that Mina could possibly handle it. Her judgment is terrible and—"

"Hey." Griffin put his hand on her arm. "Relax. It's okay. I told him no."

Heather looked at him blankly. His smile was slightly quizzical, and he looked both amused and curious. She took a breath, suddenly aware that she must have been overreacting.

She resumed walking. "I mean, it's not that I wouldn't be delighted if you could find someone else to help you out. I've got my practice to think about, and I hardly have the time to moonlight as a nanny. I just think it ought to be someone mature. Someone responsible."

"I agree completely," he said politely. "Much better for it to be an older woman, like you."

She looked at him hard, but his smile was so open and infectious that she couldn't help smiling back.

"Besides," he added thoughtfully, "I think Alton knew I wouldn't go for it. He was just clutching at straws. I think it shocked him to see us working together on this. Or anything."

"It has probably shocked a lot of people." She sidestepped around Theo Burke's cat, who had found a sunny spot in the middle of the sidewalk outside the Candlelight Café and claimed it. "Frankly, it even shocked me a little."

Griffin smiled. "Me, too, for that matter. But I think it particularly confuses Alton because he was counting on our somewhat—" he seemed to choose his next word carefully "—*complicated* history to keep us at odds. He apparently assumed that just because we used to be engaged we must be enemies."

"Imagine that," she said, allowing herself the slightest hint of sarcasm. "Of course, the fact that we live in the same small town but hardly ever even speak to each other might have contributed to that notion."

"Might have," Griffin agreed easily. "Anyhow, I think he had been assuming I was on his side of this zoning battle. Apparently he was taking it for granted that I would be only too happy to vote against you the other day.''

Heather didn't say anything. She concentrated on walking softly, rhythmically, lulling Stewbert to sleep. The sunshine blinked in and out of newly leafed maples and pale green oaks like a golden strobe.

But she knew Griffin was looking at her, waiting for her response.

''Heather,'' he said finally. ''You do know that, if I had been able to get there on time, I would have voted for your variance.''

She still didn't answer. What was there to say?

''Heather. Tell me you know that. Tell me you know I would have voted yes.''

She turned, then, and leveled her gaze at him. ''Actually, I don't ever spend much time thinking about what 'would have' happened in life,'' she said. ''It doesn't really get you anywhere, does it? He managed to kill the zoning variance. That's the reality I have to deal with. And I am dealing with it.''

They had finally reached his car, which was parked in front of her office. That elegant little whip of a vehicle, always so streamlined and racy, looked strangely alien today, she thought. And then she saw why. The top was down, and the soft leather seats were filled with large plastic baby restraints.

She had hardly absorbed the incongruous sight when Griffin turned to her abruptly.

''Damn it,'' he said roughly. ''The son of a bitch isn't going to get away with it.''

"With what?" She put her hand over Stewbert's head instinctively, as if to protect him from Griffin's sudden vehemence.

"With vetoing the variance. I told you I'd get him to change his mind, and I meant it. You'll get your variance, Heather. I promise."

She tensed. She wasn't quite sure how to react to this Griffin, who was so uncharacteristically earnest. And besides, he had promised her things before. So many broken promises littered the past that no one could safely stroll down Memory Lane anymore.

"I didn't ask for your help," she said carefully. "I never asked for anyth—"

"God, Heather, do you have to be so stiff-necked? I asked you for a favor, didn't I? Can't you ask me for one in return?"

"No," she said, civilly but firmly. "I can't."

His face darkened. He looked angry for a moment, but almost as soon as the expression appeared it vanished. He stared at her blankly for the second it took him to adjust, and then his old, sardonic smile slowly returned.

He tilted his head, catching the afternoon sunlight in his hair.

"All right, then, I won't do it for you. I'll do it for Lady Justice. Like any good superhero, I'll stop the bad guy in the name of fair play."

She raised her brows. "So you're a superhero now?"

He grinned. "Superuncle, they call me." He looked

down at the baby, who still slept in his arms. ''That's right, Stewbert. I'd love to stay and change your diapers, but I have to be going. Your Uncle Griffin is off to fight for truth, justice, and the Firefly Glen way.''

CHAPTER SIX

WHEN THE PHONE RANG that rainy Sunday afternoon, Heather was working in her office at Spring House, going over the results of Mrs. Mizell's most recent blood tests.

She didn't bother to answer it. Griffin was officially on duty until six o'clock, and they had agreed that whoever was in charge of the babies was also in charge of the house. That way, whoever was *off* duty could get some real relief—could actually sleep or work or just relax.

Surprisingly, the schedule she'd designed was working fairly well. Even so, she had to admit she hadn't been this exhausted since medical school. She knew Griffin was tired, too, though he dismissed the notion with his usual insouciance. But once, when she reported for her shift, she'd found him sprawled out on the floor of the nursery, sound asleep next to the cribs.

It was an oddly appealing sight, his golden head pillowed by a stuffed caterpillar, his feet bare, a cloth ABC book lying forgotten on his chest. She had hardly been able to bring herself to wake him.

Who would have thought he'd be so good at this daddy thing? She had been listening to the three of them upstairs while she worked. She caught muffled notes of music—the Stewberts loved music—and once or twice some laughter, then the mysterious sound of something scraping across the floor.

Maybe Griffin was down on all fours, playing roaring tiger games, the way he had been last night. Or maybe he was moving the crib closer to the window, so that Stewbert could watch the rain.

It was strange, she thought, laying aside Mrs. Mizell's Rh readings for the moment. Griffin and his nephews had been at Spring House not quite a week. And yet, somehow, it seemed as if they had always been here.

In fact, when she tried to remember life before the Stewberts, she sometimes had difficulty remembering exactly what she had done with all her free time.

"Sorry to interrupt, but I think I may have bad news."

Griffin was standing in the doorway, looking so crisp and fresh it was hard to believe he'd just been wrestling with a pair of twin infants.

"What is it?" She put her pen down carefully. "Are the boys all right?"

"They're fine. They're asleep. But Missy Stoppard just called. She's still twenty miles outside of town. Her car broke down, and she doesn't know when she'll be able to get home."

"Oh, no. Missy's childbirth class meets here this afternoon. It starts in—" She looked at her watch and groaned. "Two minutes."

He smiled ruefully. "I guess that explains why three minivans have just pulled up in your back driveway."

"Oh, heck." She began closing files and stacking them in the desk drawer. "They're here already?"

But the soft chime of the office door opening answered her question before Griffin could. A babble of happy voices filled the waiting room, which was, thank heaven, pristine and ready. Here at the Spring House office, every room was always pristine, always ready and waiting. The rooms had never been used and—if Alton Millner had his way—never would be.

Except for Missy Stoppard's childbirth classes, which were sponsored by the local hospital and thus somehow got around the zoning problems.

"Do you want me to tell them Missy's not coming?" Griffin had automatically begun helping her with the files. "Want me to send them home?"

"No. I always fill in for her when she can't make it. Before she came to the Glen last year, I used to teach these classes."

"Really?" Griffin paused, obviously surprised. "I didn't know that."

Heather looked at him. If the parents-to-be weren't already out there waiting, she might have succumbed to the temptation to tell him just how many, many things he didn't know about her.

He'd been gone a long time—he'd peeled out of Firefly Glen the day she handed him back his diamond ring, and he'd spent the next eight years traveling. He had returned only about a year ago, surprising everyone, especially Heather.

And during that year, they had hardly spoken beyond a civilized "hello" if they passed on Main Street. So, actually, Griffin Cahill knew as little about Heather's present life as, say, newcomer Missy Stoppard did.

But the parents-to-be *were* waiting. And what was the point in bringing all that up anyhow?

So she settled for saying, "You weren't here then."

She walked to the door and headed briskly toward the reception area. She didn't even know whether he followed her or took the other way out, back to the residential part of the house.

The waiting room was full. Five couples had enrolled in Missy's class this time, and the women were sitting on the floor, chatting companionably with each other. The men had begun to shove chairs out of the way, making room for everyone to practice.

This was the fourth of six sessions. Clearly they were already pros.

Heather smiled. "Hi, everybody. No, no," she said, waving her hand playfully, "you needn't get up!"

A chorus of chuckles swept the room. Most of the women were round and bulky, somewhere near their eighth month of pregnancy, and needed help climbing to their feet anyhow.

"Sorry, ladies and gentlemen, but Missy's not able to make it tonight," Heather announced. "So you're stuck with me."

She didn't expect anyone to be particularly upset.

All the women were Heather's patients anyhow, so it wasn't exactly like asking them to work with a stranger.

But Sarah Tremaine let out a low, disappointed groan. "Oh, darn, Heather, I was hoping you'd be my partner tonight."

Heather looked toward Sarah, noticing with surprise that her friend was alone. Parker Tremaine and his petite, honey-blond bride had been almost inseparable since their wedding last winter. Parker caught a lot of ribbing about it, but actually the newlyweds were one of the Glen's favorite love stories.

"Why? Where's Parker?" Heather couldn't believe the doting bridegroom had picked such an important time to go missing.

"He's sick, poor guy," Sarah said, and so much worried tenderness crept into her voice that it made the other couples grin. "He wanted to come anyhow, but I told him he couldn't risk giving germs to everyone else."

"Yeah, I'd heard he was sick," Joey Stillerman put in mischievously. "Lovesick, that is. I didn't know it was contagious."

Aleen Stillerman hit her husband over the head with the pillow they'd brought along. "Too bad it isn't," she said. "I wouldn't mind if you caught a little of what Parker's got."

"Oh, yeah?" Joey reached over and tickled his wife, and the two of them ended up in a rolling heap on the floor.

Sarah folded her hands over her stomach and sighed. "If you've got to teach tonight, Heather, who am I going to work with?"

Heather thought it through. Maybe, if she worked it right, she could do the teaching, and spend at least a little time coaching Sarah, too. But it would mean juggling the—

"How about me?"

It was Griffin. Heather turned, surprised. Apparently he had followed her after all.

He certainly knew how to command the attention of an entire room. Everyone stared at him in silence. Even Joey and Aleen stopped wrestling and sat up straight.

One of the dads—it might have been Boomer Bigwell—made a low, whistling sound. "Pinch, me, Betty. I'm dreaming. I thought I saw Playboy Cahill standing in a room full of pregnant women."

Heather spoke under her breath. "Don't be silly, Griffin. What about the babies?"

He shrugged. "For once, they're both sleeping. I have the portable monitor in my pocket."

She felt herself fumbling, but she needed a polite way to send Griffin away. Surely, given the stories she'd been hearing about Griffin and Emma Dunbar, who was Parker Tremaine's adored little sister, this wasn't a good idea. Sarah herself was probably horrified, but too kind to hurt Griffin's feelings.

"I'm serious, Sarah," Griffin said. "If you tell me what to do, I'll be glad to pitch in."

Joey Stillerton grinned. "I don't know, Cahill. If you

spend the next two hours with your hands on Sarah's belly, Parker just might rise up off his sickbed and kick your—''

''I'd love it,'' Sarah broke in. Her voice was firm. The smile she aimed toward Griffin was both grateful and welcoming. ''Thanks, Griffin. You're a lifesaver.''

Heather cast Sarah a quick, questioning glance. But Sarah nodded subtly, assuring her that everything was fine. Heather caught the determined look in Sarah's eyes and decided not to interfere.

She settled for aiming a cautionary glare at Griffin as he passed. She caught his arm. ''This class is serious, Griffin,'' she whispered. ''It's not an excuse for a flirtation. And Sarah is a friend of mine, so—''

''Hey, lighten up, Doc.'' Griffin's smile was wry, but it didn't quite make it to his eyes. He put his hand over hers, hard. ''I'm pretty sure I can control my animal instincts for an hour or two.''

Warned by the taut quality of his voice, she pulled her hand away and turned to the others. ''Okay, then. Partners, get into position. Let's review the first breathing technique.''

She watched as Griffin took his place on the floor beside Sarah. Heather didn't like this arrangement—maybe just because she suspected Parker wouldn't like it—but she couldn't prevent it. Though Sarah might look fragile, she was actually a very strong woman. If she'd decided to work with Griffin, that was exactly what she'd do.

"Okay, ladies, take a deep, cleansing breath. And...*contraction begins.*"

Heather roamed the room, checking on each of the couples, making sure they were using proper technique, occasionally cheering excellent teamwork. But all the while, out of the corner of her eye, she was watching Griffin and Sarah.

He clearly hadn't ever done anything like this before. Sarah had to fill him in on each step. But by the end of the class, Heather had to admit that, to her complete surprise, Griffin made a terrific partner.

He had good instincts, a soothing voice and gentle, deft hands. He read Sarah's body like a pro. He saw where she was still tense, where she needed to relax more. During the simulated "contractions" they communicated as easily as any couple in the room.

And unfailingly, when he massaged Sarah's stomach, or her back, he touched her like a brother. He was warm, confident, comforting, focused—without any inappropriate sensuality. His professional calm eliminated any hint of the wolfish liberties Heather had feared.

In fact, she felt a little foolish for having let herself think such things. She knew that Griffin had been angry. Perhaps he had been justified. He wasn't an animal, was he? She stared as he bent over Sarah, their gazes locked for focus, his gentle hands tracing light circles across her swollen stomach.

No, not an animal. Far from it.

Miraculously, the Stewberts continued to sleep

through the entire class. Their first wriggling, snuffling noises had just begun to sneak through the baby monitor while Heather was congratulating and officially dismissing the class.

Griffin helped Sarah to her feet with a smile. "Terrific job, Mrs. Tremaine," he said, smiling down at her. "You were pretty darn impressive."

"I couldn't have done it without you," Sarah answered. And then she raised herself on her tiptoes, took his lean, tanned, handsome face in her hands and kissed him on the cheek. "Thank you, Griffin."

Heather looked away. She hated to discover that the only inappropriate sensuality in this room was in her own mind. She hated it, but it was true. The sight of Griffin's hands on a woman's body, however brotherly the touch, made her heart skip a little too fast.

She knew how those hands felt. She thought she had forgotten. Her brain probably had forgotten. But her skin remembered, and it tingled now with a primitive awareness. As meaningless as a sneeze, or a shiver—but just as uncontrollable.

"Mmmm...bamagadada," the monitor sang suddenly.

The Stewberts were awake. Almost instantly a second voice joined in fretfully. "Bagagada. Damamadada. Geep."

The babbling was so ridiculous—and yet so adorable—that everyone had to laugh.

"Uh-oh, stud," Joey Stillerman said, slapping Griffin on the shoulder. "Looks like somebody is paging his papa."

"Playboy Cahill," Boomer Bigwell called out with an irreverent grin. "That's what that 'goo-goo' stuff really means. It means, 'Playboy Cahill, please report for stinky-diaper duty.'"

"For heaven's sake, guys," Sarah said, frowning. "Stop teasing him."

"It's okay," Griffin assured her with a smile. "They'll be standing in my shoes one day soon."

He turned, raising the monitor in a playful goodbye salute to the other men. "But by then, gentlemen, I'll be in Tahiti, sipping drinks from coconut shells. You see, I've only got two weeks left in my sentence. You, my friends, are in it for life."

I'VE ONLY GOT two weeks left in my sentence.

You're in it for life.

The sardonic phrases played in Heather's head, over and over, as she and Griffin bathed and fed the babies. His shift had ended at six o'clock, but during the six-to-seven hour each night, they worked together. Then Heather took over for her shift, which would run till midnight.

The routine was complicated. But she had thought it was all working fairly smoothly. She had even, occasionally, thought perhaps Griffin was enjoying himself, just a little. She hadn't been dumb enough to think he would suddenly fall in love with the idea of home and hearth and dirty diapers, but sometimes when he smiled at Stewbert, or made those silly lion roars…

She'd been a fool, that was all. He couldn't have made his position any more clear, could he? *Two weeks left in my sentence.* This enforced domesticity was like a prison term to him, and he was counting the days until his parole.

Well, so was she. She also had a life to get back to.

In the long, bronze shadows of sunset, she sat on the nursery chair, rocking Stewbert, who, after a big meal of mashed lamb and rice, and a sudsy, warm bath, was fighting the need for sleep. He lay in her arms, sucking on his bottle and gazing up at her with softly unfocused blue eyes.

He had wrapped his fat fingers in the long ponytail that draped over her shoulder. Now and then he would tug lightly on it, as if to reassure himself that she was still there. But he was losing his battle with sleep. His eyes were almost completely shut.

Griffin was slowly pacing the room, with the other baby cuddled up against his chest. That Stewbert wasn't ever as easy to get to sleep.

Though at first Heather had thought the babies were identical, she knew them apart quite easily now. There were a hundred tiny signs. One had a dimple in his left cheek. The other had a cowlick forming in his pale, feathery bangs. One talked much more than the other. One kicked his leg like a metronome when he was drinking from his bottle. One ate pureed peas like candy—the other would scream at the sight of them.

If only she knew which was Robert, and which was Stewart. If she could put names to them now, she thought, she'd never get them mixed up again.

She placed the sleeping baby in his crib, glancing over at Griffin, who was still working on the other Stewbert. She held out her arms, asking silently if he'd like to turn over the job. He shook his head almost imperceptibly, so that he wouldn't disrupt Stewbert's descent into dreamland, and kept walking.

Heather could only wait.

The twilight was turning from bronze to the deep red of ripe grapes. The doors to the sleeping porch were open, so Heather strolled out there, drawn by the trill of a nightingale in the nearby quaking aspen, which was white with spring bloom. The air smelled of the violets she had planted last year.

God, she loved spring in Firefly Glen. She breathed deeply, taking its mild sweetness into the bottom of her lungs. It was hard to believe that, up on Lost Logger Trail, patches of snow still lingered.

She always rushed the season. One year, she'd lost every single flower to a mid-March frost, because she had planted far too soon. But sometimes, she thought, sometimes you couldn't stop yourself. Sometimes you wanted the new, fresh birth of spring so much that you simply closed your eyes and pretended there was no such thing as winter.

She felt oddly like crying, which was absurd, especially on such a beautiful evening. She hoped that Griffin would be gone when she returned to the nursery.

She didn't feel up to trying to hide her fragile edginess from him any longer.

Oh, what was wrong with her tonight?

It had all started during the childbirth class. But why? She had taught that class a hundred times, and never let it bother her. She had never let herself yearn to trade places with her patients, to be heavy with pregnancy, to be cherished and protected by a husband, to be initiated into the deepest mysteries of love and life.

She had never, ever, let it become personal. So why today? Why had it been so different today?

She recoiled from the answer her heart offered up. *No,* she said. Not Griffin. *No, no, no.*

She heard movement behind her. Griffin had come out onto the porch, too. He didn't speak, but she knew. She could tell by the small, cool current of air that opened and eddied, accepting his presence, and by the faint scent of baby powder that joined the smell of violets.

''Heather?'' He was only inches away. His warmth touched her shoulder blades and trickled down to the small of her back. ''Is anything wrong?''

''No,'' she lied. ''I'm fine.''

''Are you sure? You seem tense.''

''I'm fine.'' But she didn't turn around. She *was* tense. She had been tense since the day he moved into her house. She would be tense until the day he moved out.

''I don't believe it.'' He touched her shoulder. ''God, you're positively humming with tension.''

''I'm not,'' she said tightly. ''Honestly, Griffin. I'm just tired.''

''All right, then, prove it. Let me check.''

Still standing behind her, he reached his right arm across her body and took hold of her left arm. He gripped her by the elbow, shaking her very gently, to see if her wrist would flop.

It was one of the moves she taught in the childbirth classes. He learned fast, she thought. He learned well.

And of course her body betrayed her. Her arm was stiff, though she fought to relax it, the way she had always told her students to relax. But how could she? How could she be calm with him standing so close?

''Relax, Heather,'' he said softly. ''Just let go.''

She tried, but this was harder than it looked, this isolation of certain muscle groups, this total focus and control. Her arm remained awkward, inflexible. God, what had she been thinking—all this time, teaching things she knew nothing about?

She inhaled shakily.

''That's right,'' he whispered. ''Breathe. Take a deep, cleansing breath, all the way in.''

But she could hardly breathe at all. His cheek was against her cheek, warmth to warmth. She hadn't been in Griffin's arms in so long. How could it be so strange, so erotic—and yet so terrifyingly familiar?

Her heart was like something caught in her chest, bumping into things in its panic.

''Breathe in through your nose. Come on, deeper.''

She couldn't. It was hopeless. Her lungs just

wouldn't cooperate. She made a small move to get away. But his fingers on her elbow and the light band of his arm across her chest were enough to stop her.

She realized that she was strangely powerless, desperately frightened. And shamefully excited.

"Shh," he whispered, the way he might have done to the baby, or to a lover about to climax. "Don't fight. Just breathe."

And then, pressing himself against her from behind, he put both hands on her stomach. She gasped, but he ignored her. He began to move his fingers in slow, sure circles.

"Remember what you said—it's like a wave. Just ride it." He put his lips against her neck. "Come on, breathe deeper. That's right. Just like a wave."

Like a wave. Damn him. Those were her words, the words of her class. The words of the delivery room. In her years as a doctor, she'd heard a hundred ashen-faced men whisper them to their brave, terrified wives.

They were words of struggle, of pain, of survival, miracles, birth.

Not words of shallow seduction and sex.

But because shallow emotions were all he knew, he couldn't possibly understand. He knew nothing. *Nothing.* He was taking her words and twisting them, distorting them. Cheapening them.

And even worse—she was falling for it, melting under the spring sun like the last lacy edges of ice.

In her disgust—with him, with herself—she found enough breath to speak. She pulled away.

She stared at him.

"I knew you'd do it," she said between clenched teeth. "I knew you'd abuse what you learned there today. I knew you'd turn it into a joke."

His face was hard to read in the deepening shadows. "I'm not laughing, Heather," he said softly. "And neither are you."

"No," she agreed. "Because it isn't funny. It's pathetic. Pathetic that you would take something as profound as that and turn it into a cheap pickup line."

He hesitated, standing very still. "Is that what you thought I was doing?"

"You bet it is," she said tautly. "But you can save the performance for some other woman, Griffin. I'm not interested."

"Heather," he began gruffly. "Damn it, Heather, I—"

"I said I'm not interested." She lifted her chin. "But don't be too disappointed, Griffin. You'll get out of jail soon. You only have two weeks left in your sentence, remember?"

CHAPTER SEVEN

ALL RIGHT, TUCKER BRADY, listen up. You may think tattooing a fire-breathing dragon on your bicep will make you look like Killer RockHard ThugMan, but it won't. It will just make you look like a puny little goofus who dreams about being tough. Face it, Tuckie. You weigh about one-twenty dripping wet. If you've got fifty bucks to burn, burn 'em at the gym.

Mary was composing her latest *Listen Up* letter as she climbed into her car. *That idiot Tucker.* She growled as she searched for her key, which had fallen to the bottom of her purse. *Fire-breathing dragon, my foot.*

Actually, she might need to soften this letter up a little before she sent it to Tucker, who was only eighteen, pimply and painfully insecure. But right now she didn't feel like sugarcoating anything.

It had been a long, frustrating Monday. Nothing had gone right. Every patient had been late, or early, or grumpy, or too chatty, or ready to argue about the bill. Test results had been late or wrong or misfiled. The new girl in the office had lost the prescription pads and dropped a delivery of test tubes.

Worst of all, Mrs. Mizell had shown up again, convinced that her backache meant she was about to miscarry. Calming her down had taken Heather nearly an hour and had blown the afternoon schedule to bits. Then, leaving the office in turmoil behind her, Heather had gone racing home right at six, eager to play nanny to Griffin Cahill's drooling twin blobs.

But, thank God, the workday was finally over. Mary was going to go home and sleep for a month.

She put the key into the ignition and turned. Nothing. She glared at the car, a 1957 Thunderbird that Dooley had bought and restored for her last year. She hadn't wanted the darn thing. Dooley had just used her as an excuse to buy it, because he thought it was cool.

Well, you couldn't prove it by her. She hadn't ever thought a car was cool. As far as she was concerned, they were just transporting machines. And this one was a damn sorry transporter. It rarely went more than fifty miles without breaking down.

She turned the key again. "Listen up, you rusty bucket of bolts," she said fiercely. "Start, or you're headed straight for the junkyard."

But no matter how hard she whipped it, the motor just whined and struggled, coughed, shuddered, and finally passed out with a rather ominous *thunk.*

"I'm going to kill you, Dooley," she muttered, her knuckles white on the steering wheel. "And then Tucker. And then the rest of you, one by one, until I feel better."

"Hi." Troy Madison's ridiculously cheerful voice floated in through the window. He bent down and smiled at her. "Wow. What a car—'57, right? Look at those fabulous fins!"

She narrowed her eyes. "I'm going to pretend you didn't say that."

"Why?"

"Because otherwise I'd have to kill you."

She tossed the key back into her purse, where it would undoubtedly get lost again, and reached over to shove open her door. Troy, who thankfully was a pretty smart guy, backed out of the way quickly. She climbed out, slammed the door shut behind her, then kicked the fabulous fins for good measure.

"Oh." Troy glanced at the Thunderbird, then at her face, which undoubtedly looked a little scary. "Car trouble?"

"You might say that. For the price of a bus token, I'm selling it to the first person who walks by. Well, gosh. That would be you, wouldn't it?" She held out her hand. "A buck fifty."

He chuckled. "How about if I just give you a ride home? I've got a rental car down the street." He tilted his head charmingly. "Of course you'll have to promise not to kill me."

She felt her irritation subsiding. He really was kind of a cutie, even if he was Griffin Cahill's friend.

"You're probably pretty safe," she said, almost smiling. "You're at the end of a very long list."

She locked up the Thunderbird—though frankly if anyone could steal the useless thing, that was fine with her—and then they walked to his car, which was at the other end of Main, down by the City Hall.

It was a little chilly, one of those May days that were really more kin to April. Now, with sunset coming on, the sky was a frosty purple over the rolling black humps of the mountaintops.

She shivered—in her fury, she had left her sweater in the back seat.

Troy took off his camel-hair jacket and held it out. "Here. This might help."

She thought about refusing it, but a gust of icy wind puffed around the corner of the Candlelight Café and changed her mind.

"Thanks," she said, pulling it together in the front, enjoying the way it was still warm from his body. She slanted a sideways glance at his face, hoping he knew this wasn't flirting. She really was cold.

But he didn't have that smug blowfish look guys usually got when they thought they were going to get lucky, so she relaxed. They walked the rest of the way without saying much, just an occasional pleasantry to shopkeepers closing up for the night.

His car, when they reached it, was a no-nonsense, generic sedan, the kind she would have bought if Dooley had let her pick out her own. Newish, boring, reliable. She loved it on sight.

Of course, it started perfectly. She gave him general directions to her house, then leaned back and let herself go limp for the first time all day.

He was amazingly good company. He was one of

the few men she'd ever met who knew when to shut up. They were almost at her house before he spoke.

"So," he said playfully, "who is ahead of me on this hit list of yours?"

She opened her eyes and tilted her face to look at him without lifting her head. "Let's see. All four of my fool brothers. That useless mechanic. The shyster who sold us the car in the first place."

She pointed to the half-hidden turnoff that would lead them to her road. "That way. Oh, yeah, and if I have time, Griffin Cahill, too."

Troy glanced over at her briefly, though he needed to concentrate to maneuver his way safely down the pocked road. "Why? What has Griffin done?"

"Nothing," she said, making a small scoffing noise. "That's Griffin's specialty. He does a whole lot of nothing, while Heather works herself half to death trying to keep up with his bratty nephews."

Troy smiled. "You sure don't think much of Griff, do you?"

"Sorry. I know he's your friend, but—"

"No, it's okay. It's actually kind of refreshing. You may be the first woman I've ever met who wasn't drooling over him."

"Yeah, well, I hate useless people." She pointed to a small dirt track between the pines. "Go through there. The house is at the end of that path."

"Useless?" Troy sounded perplexed. "Sorry, I've got to disagree. Griff's a lot of things, but he's not useless."

"Are you kidding? The man wouldn't dream of really working at anything. It might muss his hair. I based every single detail of Prince Dudley Do-nothing on Griffin Cahill, right down to his curly eyelashes and his nifty velvet pants."

"What?" In spite of himself, Troy was laughing. "Prince who?"

"Prince Dudley Do-nothing. He's—" She shook her head, suddenly embarrassed to have mentioned those silly stories to a real writer. "Oh, he's nothing. Just a character in some stories I wrote to keep my younger brothers out of trouble. They thought Griffin was the ultimate, and I had to find some way to keep them from imitating everything he did." She grinned. "Or didn't do, as the case might be."

They had arrived at her big, rambling country farmhouse, home to the whole Brady clan, including all four brothers, two wives, two babies and Mary.

She had expected to feel self-conscious. She appreciated its history and its unpretentious charm, but she could imagine how weird and ramshackle it must look to a world traveler like Troy.

Strangely, he didn't even seem to notice it. He had parked the car and turned toward her, his eyes lit with curiosity.

"I didn't know you wrote," he said eagerly. "That's terrific."

"I don't. Not like you do, I mean. Not real writing. It's just dumb stuff. Kid stuff." She bit her lip to stop her inane babbling. Why was she being so stupid about this? She was a rather astringent woman of almost thirty, not a stammering ninny. And her stories weren't anything to be ashamed of. The boys had loved them.

"All writing is 'real' writing," Troy said firmly. He moved his arm, which had been resting across the back of the bench seat, and touched her shoulder. "I'd love to see some of your work, if you'd feel comfortable showing it to me."

It was almost dark, which frustrated her. She wanted to see his face, wanted to see whether he looked sincere. Probably he was just trying to flatter her, hoping he could butter her up until she just slid right into bed with him.

"That's nice of you," she said, carefully noncommittal. "But not tonight. I'm tired and hungry. It's been a rough day."

He made a disappointed sound. "Wait. I know. I could take you out for dinner, so you wouldn't have to cook. You could bring a few of your stories along, and we could talk about them."

Well, at least he hadn't offered to fix her a quiet dinner at his place. Or, even worse, to come in and fix dinner for her here. But he could probably tell from all the other cars in the driveway—many of them "collectibles" like the Thunderbird—that no one could expect any privacy in this house.

As she sat there trying to gauge his motives, the screen door of the farmhouse slammed, and a young, gawky bundle of bones came loping out toward one of the cars. Oh, heck. Tucker was probably on his way to the tattoo parlor, and she hadn't had time to finish his *Listen Up* letter.

She rolled down the window. ''Hold it right there, Tucker Brady. You're not going anywhere tonight.''

The poor boy froze like a cartoon character and squinted guiltily through the dusk, trying to identify the unfamiliar car.

Mary turned back to Troy with a smile.

''Thanks, anyway,'' she said. ''I hope you'll give me a rain check, but I really am tired. And I have to see a man about a tattoo.''

GRIFFIN STARED at the mishmash of cards in his hand and sighed. A three, a five, two deuces and a king. And the way his luck was going tonight, there was no point drawing for an inside straight.

''I'm out.'' He folded his cards and set them down. ''Damn it, Troy, if you're not going to deal me anything better than this, I might as well go read a book.''

Troy rubbed his hands together gleefully, then made a conspicuous display of raking in the pot. ''Maybe you should just go to bed, like Mommy told you to,'' he suggested helpfully, cocking his head toward the baby duty schedule Heather had printed out and taped to the kitchen wall. ''See? Eight to midnight, Heather on duty. Little Griffie takes a nap.''

Griffin ignored him, concentrating on shuffling the cards. Troy had been teasing him about that stupid schedule ever since he'd arrived an hour ago. It was annoying as hell. But Griffin's theory was that if Troy didn't get a rise out of him, he'd eventually get tired of the game and move on to another topic.

But apparently he wasn't bored yet.

"Does anybody really do that?" Troy grinned. "Sleep from eight to midnight?"

God, he was like a dog gnawing a bone. Griffin dealt new hands without answering.

"Playboy Cahill doesn't, that's for sure," Troy said. "I mean, does this lady *know* you, Griff?"

"She knows me. Pick up your cards."

"Okay, okay. Listen, Griff. I gotta be honest with you, buddy." Troy popped a potato chip into his mouth and arranged his cards while he chewed. "At first I was afraid you might have a thing for this doctor lady. I mean, you guys are living together, and she is gorgeous, right? The package might be wrapped a little too tight, if you know what I mean, but she's still a knockout."

Griffin didn't look up from his cards. "So what if I did? Since when do you worry about which women I 'have a thing' for?"

"Since I need you to come to Nepal with me, that's since when. What do you think I'm hanging around for? If you're really just baby-sitting your nephews, I'll talk you into the trip sooner or later. But if you're actually in the middle of a hot thing with this doctor lady..."

Griffin tightened his grip on his cards, which were rotten, of course. "Troy, you're missing the mark in so many ways I hardly know where to begin. First off, I'm not in the middle of any hot thing.''

''I know,'' Troy assured him, grabbing another fistful of chips. ''Believe me, the minute I saw that schedule on the wall, I knew I was wrong about you two. I mean, it's like being in prison, isn't it? With her as the warden.''

Griffin was strangely torn. He had this instinctive urge to jump to Heather's defense. How dare Troy criticize her? What did Troy really know about her, anyhow? He'd only met her yesterday, for about fifteen minutes.

On the other hand, deep inside, Griffin agreed with him. Heather was bossy, rigid and judgmental—she always had been. It had come between them ten years ago. And it would come between them now, if he were fool enough to try to start anything.

Which he wasn't. She hadn't changed a bit. She still went through life wearing a straitjacket.

Take last night, for instance. She'd gone off the deep end just because he'd tried to give her a back massage.

Hell, he should have known better. But he'd acted on impulse. Just an impulse, damn it, not an agenda. Certainly not a seduction. Frankly, when he set out to seduce a woman, he was a hell of a lot more systematic and, at the same time, more subtle.

And definitely more successful.

Last night had been different. His intentions, for once, had been ridiculously honorable. He had felt close to her. Cozy. Intimate. Like a brother. Like a friend.

Like an idiot.

Maybe it had been how young and gentle Heather had looked there in the nursery, her head bent over the drowsing Stewbert. For a minute he had seen, not the General Delaney she was today, but the teenaged Heather, the innocent Heather, the laughing girl he remembered mostly from dreams.

But actually his strange mood had begun even earlier—during the rather surreal experience of Heather's childbirth class.

If he'd made a list of the top ten places he never wanted to end up, a childbirth class would be on it. He'd only offered because he liked Sarah Tremaine. And, frankly, for the fun of shocking Heather, who obviously expected him to bolt like a scalded cat in the other direction.

And yet, gradually, as he had knelt there, working with Sarah, he had begun to feel something very strange, something that felt a lot like...envy.

Not envy of Sarah herself. No, nothing that simple. He'd felt envious of something he couldn't even name. An elusive truth he had glimpsed in the face of every woman in that room.

The women glowed, there was no other word for it—as if they were lit by some source Griffin had never seen. And the smiles they turned upon their husbands held such courage and faith and joy and promise that when the men smiled back their eyes were full of tears.

Those smiles had made Griffin feel strangely hollow. As if all these people—even dense, affable Boomer Bigwell—knew something he didn't know. Something exciting. Something about happiness.

Something about love.

Oh, hell, he'd been back in Firefly Glen too long. Tucked away in this sheltered little valley, you could forget that the world was chaotic and cruel, that love mostly went sour in less time than it took to make a baby, and that, out there, nobody really lived happily ever after. Nobody.

Maybe he ought to go to Nepal with Troy after all. Coping with foreign languages, strange currency, mysterious foods and unpaved roads would be much simpler than coping with General Heather Delaney.

"Hello? You going to bet or what? This isn't a game of chess, you know."

Griffin threw in a couple of blue chips, though he knew he would lose them. "Too bad," he said. "I could beat you at chess."

That was when the tapping started. Light, but insistent, like pebbles at the window.

Griffin frowned. "What the hell—?"

But Troy was already on his feet, smiling and heading for the kitchen door. "Hot damn," he said happily. "I bet it's the girls."

Griffin felt frozen in his seat. This did not sound good. "The girls?"

"Yeah. The girls from Lucky's. Margie and Barb. Or Barbie and Marge. I forget which." He scratched his cheek. "Whoops. Did I forget to tell you I invited them to stop by here after they ate?"

"It must have slipped your mind," Griffin commented dryly. "Not that your mind was involved in the decision, I suspect."

"Damn. You're starting to worry me, Griff. Look, just repeat after me—I am a consenting adult. Those babies upstairs are not really mine. I am allowed to have fun." He scowled at Griffin's pointed silence. "Okay, don't repeat after me. But you'd better put a smile on your sour puss, buddy, because I promised these ladies some laughs."

BP 155/90. THAT WAS TOO HIGH for Anna Mizell, even during a panic attack. How high had it been last time?

Distracted and slightly anxious, Heather walked down the back staircase carefully. She held on to the banister with one hand and tried to flip Anna's chart with the other, while, with any kind of luck, she'd avoid dropping the pair of empty baby bottles she had tucked under one arm.

The Stewberts were going to wake up soon. She could tell by the restless shifting in their sleep. She wanted to be ready, with fresh, warm bottles in hand.

Let's see...Only 130/85 last time. Nearly normal. But still...Can't risk preeclampsia at this point. What about weight gain?

Still squinting at the chart, searching for clues, she moved though the darkened dining room, the quickest route to the kitchen. The baby monitor swayed heavily in the pocket of her robe. No noise from the babies yet—if she hurried, she'd make it back before they began to cry.

As she shouldered open the swinging door to the kitchen, the unexpected sound of laughter stopped her in her tracks. Who on earth was in the breakfast nook at this hour? It was nearly eleven. She had thought she was alone in the house.

There it was again. It wasn't really laughter, not exactly. It was giggling. Girlish giggling. And from more than one girl.

She had a mindless impulse to back out again before she was seen. But her foot caught in her robe, and she stumbled, dropping the baby bottles on the bare tile floor with a loud plastic clatter.

Glasses clinked, chairs scraped back, voices whispered…and then four faces emerged from the breakfast nook. Troy Madison held a handful of cards, and was red faced, transparently guilty, like a little boy caught licking the icing off the cake.

He stood awkwardly between two young—very young—women. Improbable blondes, they were smacking gum like a synchronized act and staring anxiously at Heather as if she were their Mother Superior from high school—a very recent memory for them, no doubt.

Of the four, only Griffin looked completely unfazed by Heather's appearance. But blasé was, of course, Griffin's natural state, and it would take more than getting caught playing poker with a couple of wide-eyed convent girls to embarrass him.

Ten years ago, when she'd caught him in the shower with her college roommate, not a single inch of his fully exposed body had so much as blushed. He'd even combed his hair and nicely knotted a towel around his waist before coming out to explain that Nicolette's arrival under the pulsing jet head had been a shock to him, too.

He strolled over now and retrieved the bottles for her. "Everything okay upstairs?" he asked pleasantly.

"Just fine," she answered, equally pleasant. "Hello, Troy. Hi, everyone," she added to the young women. "Don't mind me. I'm just getting a couple of new bottles ready for when the boys wake up. I'll be out of here in a flash."

Troy's color was returning to normal, and even Griffin's smile looked a little more natural. Returning the smile sweetly, she edged around him and went to the refrigerator, where they kept the prepared bottles.

She felt him watching her. But she went about her business, ignoring him. If he thought she was going to start ranting and throwing crockery just because he'd invited a couple of girls over, he was mistaken. She'd quit losing her temper about his sex life ten years ago, when she quit giving a damn what he did. She supposed, in a way, she had Nicolette to thank for that.

She popped the bottles into the microwave—fifteen seconds, she'd learned, was perfect. When it beeped, she pulled them out and, tucking them back under her arm, exited the kitchen with casual goodbyes all around.

She had reached the bottom tread of the staircase when she heard Griffin's voice.

"Heather."

She turned around.

"You forgot this." He held out Anna Mizell's chart.

"Thanks," she said politely, taking it. She smiled again and turned back toward the stairs.

"Heather. Wait."

She looked at him impassively. "Yes?"

"I just wanted you to know...Troy invited those women over here, not me. Troy and I were playing poker, and all of a sudden they were just there."

She smiled, remembering the drenched and defiant Nicolette. "Poor Griffin," she said. "That happens to you a lot, doesn't it? But don't worry. It's not a problem."

"Well, I didn't want you to think that I—I mean, it is your house, after all. I would have checked with you first."

That had occurred to her, too. Ordinarily she would have considered it fairly cheeky for a man to host a coed poker party in her kitchen without her permission. But she had to remember that she'd forced Griffin to spend the three weeks here at Spring House. His preference clearly had been to do the baby-sitting at his place. Now she could see why.

"It's really no problem," she assured him. "But

shouldn't you go back? They're probably waiting for you, don't you think?"

Griffin grinned. "I have a feeling Troy is enjoying himself just fine without me."

"Yes, I imagine you're right." She finally felt a prickle of the irritation Griffin had been expecting. "You know, now that you mention your friend Troy..."

"Yes?" Griffin looked curious.

"I guess it's none of my business, but something you said made me think that...well, isn't he—isn't he married?"

Griffin shrugged. "Apparently he's actually filed for divorce this time. Honestly, I never thought he'd do it, though he's been threatening to for years."

"Still." She tightened her hold on the warm bottles. "Filing for divorce and actually *being* divorced aren't exactly the same thing, though, are they?"

Griffin raised one eyebrow. "No, they aren't. But playing cards with a woman and committing adultery aren't exactly the same thing, either."

She felt herself flushing. She knew what that flat, amused tone meant. It meant that he found her to be insufferably uptight, a bourgeois bore who wasn't capable of understanding the sophisticated, elastic morality of jet-setters like Griffin and Troy.

"I couldn't care less what the state of Troy Madison's marriage is—or what his intentions are with regard to his fellow card players. My only concern is that he seems to have developed an interest in Mary Brady, and apparently he forgot to tell her that he's married.'' She stared at him unwaveringly. ''Mary is a very special person. I don't want to see her get hurt.''

Griffin looked surprised, but after a second he began to chuckle.

''Nuts. There may be a man somewhere in this world who could seduce Mary Brady, but I promise you Troy is not that man. He's not subtle enough. If he tried to make a pass at her, she'd chop him into little pieces and feed him to her brothers for lunch.''

''He may be more subtle than you think. Mary called me just a while ago. I don't think I've ever heard her so excited. Troy gave her a ride home tonight, and when they got talking, he expressed an interest in her writing. He wants to look at some of her stories. You know how much she's always wanted a future as a writer, Griffin. She's positively breathless at the prospect.''

Griffin made a silent *oh* with his lips.

''That is different,'' he said. ''And a hell of a lot more perceptive than I'd have given Troy credit for being.'' He chewed his lip thoughtfully. ''You know, I'm actually not sure he *was* being clever. He might just really be interested.''

''He might be.'' She let her skepticism show in her voice. ''Or he might just see it as the perfect pickup line. In which case it's doubly unkind. He will end up dashing her hopes twice. Once about him, and again about her writing.''

Griffin looked as if he might be going to argue, but

he apparently decided against it. "Okay," he said slowly. "I get it. I'll talk to him."

A burst of high-pitched laughter exploded from the kitchen. Griffin smiled. "See? I told you they'd be fine without me." He hesitated for a brief moment, then went on. "You know, I could come up with you now and help you feed them. I wasn't exactly dying to play cards. I had meant to get some sleep. It's just that Troy came over, and I—"

"You really don't need to explain anything to me," she said, but she said it without any sting. She felt rather mellow toward him, actually—at least for now. He had taken her criticism of Troy well, and now he was almost as good as admitting he'd rather be upstairs with the Stewberts than down here with the bimbos.

Which she'd suspected anyhow. They weren't his type.

"You do whatever you want with your free time, Griffin. If you want to rest, fine. If you'd rather play cards, or shoot pool at Lucky's, or go skinny-dipping on Mars, that's fine, too."

His eyes twinkled in the crystal light from the stairwell chandelier. "Skinny-dipping on Mars... Now there's an interesting i—"

"Whatever." She pointed one of the bottles at him in mock severity. "Just make darn sure you present yourself at that nursery door at midnight. Or I'm sending in the baby brigade to break things up down here."

Grinning, he straightened himself to stand at full attention, then raised his palm in a crisp salute. She couldn't help smiling back. She had forgotten just how devastatingly attractive he could be when he let that facade of sardonic cynicism slip for even a minute.

"Yes ma'am, General Delaney, ma'am," he said. "Any further instructions?"

"Just one thing," she said as she turned to go back up the stairs. "I've seen you play poker. Don't keep drawing to an inside straight."

CHAPTER EIGHT

THE CANDLELIGHT CAFÉ WAS so crowded Tuesday morning that Griffin, Troy and the Stewberts had to squeeze themselves into one of the tiny back booths. The chaos actually worked to their advantage, because all the noise and movement fascinated the little boys, who sat happily in their baby seats without making a peep.

Breakfast was always a bustle at the café. Theo Burke, the owner, made blueberry pancakes so light they flew into your mouth. But that wasn't what had drawn the crowd today.

Today the chamber of commerce was meeting to discuss the possibility of starting a new Firefly Glen tradition: a Carnival of Spring.

Granville Frome, who owned most of the downtown buildings and didn't ever let anyone forget it, was the chamber president this year. He didn't let anyone forget that, either.

He had set up a computer presentation tracking tourism figures, and he was talking the group through past years with painstakingly detailed slides and graphs and pie charts.

He had made it as far as 1937 when Bourke Waitely

finally stood and shook his elephant-tusk cane in the air.

"For God's sake, Frome, shut up! Who cares about all that? The only real question is whether Ward Winters will *let* us have a spring festival. You know how the meddling old fool acted during the Ice Festival last winter!"

"Now, Bourke, you just calm down," Granville said, though he didn't look very calm himself. Granville's temper was legendary in Firefly Glen. Griffin nudged Troy, alerting him to the potential for a good geriatric fistfight. Frome's face was red under his silver hair, which was one of the signs he was about to come unglued.

"Ward Winters doesn't call the shots around here." Granville puffed out his chest. "I do!"

"Well, now, I don't know about that," Alton Millner said, standing up from the back of the room. "As the mayor of Firefly Glen, I think I can honestly say I call the shots around here."

"Sit down, Alton," Hickory Baxter chimed in, his mouth full of pancakes. "Don't be such a jackass—"

"Well said, Hickory," Griffin whispered to Troy, grinning. Both Stewberts grinned, too.

Troy clearly didn't see the humor. "Griffin, pal, you've got to get out of this town. You can't really know—or care—which of these bad-tempered old coots runs this backwater burg." He gulped his coffee, scalded himself and grimaced. "Can you?"

"The real question," Hickory went on, wiping his

mouth with his linen napkin, "is how in hell we could possibly persuade tourists to come here in the spring. Summer, sure, they'll come boating and hiking and whatnot. Fall's kind of pretty. And winter, we've got the best powder in three states. But spring? Hell, gentlemen, it rains every goddamn day until June. We could offer nude mud wrestling, I guess, but short of that—"

"You volunteering, Hickory?"

"I'll buy a ticket to that!"

A few wolf whistles passed through the room, followed by a lot of laughter, including a couple of whoops from the Stewberts. Then there was just the clinking of silverware against plates as the chamber members returned to their pancakes.

Finally accepting that no one was going to pay attention to him, Granville huffily flicked off his computer and sat down with a grunt.

"Aw, too bad," Griffin said, disappointed, tickling one Stewbert's chin playfully. "Hickory has defused another bomb. And here I was, hoping to show you we're not such a sleepy little town after all. Those old boys really know how to mix it up."

"I'd have thrown them all out on their thick heads," Theo Burke said as she carefully set the pancakes in front of them. "Men! Bunch of thugs, that's what."

"Not all of us, Theo." Griffin picked up her thin, heavily veined hand and kissed it with a flourish. He knew she loved that kind of thing.

The angular spinster scowled at him, growling, but

she couldn't hold out. "Oh, yes, you are," she said gruffly. "Some of you just come gift wrapped." Clucking, she reached over and tousled his hair as if he were ten years old.

As she walked away, Troy stared at Griffin, his brown eyes wide with horror. "Cahill, let me get you out of here. Right now, before the soles of your shoes grow roots."

Griffin tossed his hair back into place and picked up his fork. "Can't. You know that. Not yet. Isn't that right, Stewbert?"

"Come on. You need to start working again. When was the last time you took a picture?"

Griffin smiled. "I just agreed to take some for the new chamber brochure."

Troy rolled his eyes. "I'm telling you, buddy, I can see it happening. If you stay here, it'll get hold of you. One day you'll wake up and you won't know where your life went. Or your hair."

Griffin held out his forkful of pancakes, steaming and aromatic. "There are worse things that could happen," he suggested.

"Name one."

Griffin looked at him. "I could wake up one day and discover that I didn't really like my wife or know my kids. I might realize that I hadn't been home in six months. That I didn't, in fact, even really have a home."

"That's low, Griff." Troy ducked his head and began fiercely carving up his pancakes. "Anita's having an affair, damn it. You make it sound as if it's my fault for being gone so much.''

''Well? Isn't that possible? Seems kind of naive to think any relationship is going to succeed without a little hands-on effort.''

Troy drew his brows together hard and stabbed a triangle of pancake. ''Oh, so now you're the expert on relationships?''

''I'm the expert on how to ruin them,'' Griffin responded easily. ''And believe me, ignoring a woman is the second most effective way to lose her. Comes in just behind the old tried-and-true, number one method—cheating on her.''

He leaned back, dangling his fingers for Stewbert to play with. ''And kids. Well, I'm just a beginner at this part, but from what I see, kids need you every damn second of every damn day.'' He smiled down at the baby. ''And don't you dare go home and make 'damn' your first word.''

For a minute, Griffin thought Troy might be so angry he couldn't speak. He stared into his coffee cup, his jaw tightening until a pulse pounded in his neck. But then, finally, Troy looked up, and Griffin could see that his friend was actually fighting back tears.

''Yeah, well, when they're little, they do need you,'' Troy said, staring hard at his Stewbert, who made a low, cooing sound and smiled, appreciating the attention. ''That's the good part, when they are so small and helpless, and they look at you, and you feel—''

Troy cleared his throat roughly and took another

breath. "Hell, Griffin, everybody likes babies. But then they start to grow up, and they don't need you so much anymore. Nobody does. And if you have to work, you have to be gone a lot, and they get used to you not being there."

"Troy, you know they don't—"

"Yes, they do. They get used to it, and they start to like it. Vicky is fifteen, Griff. You can't imagine the looks she gives me if I ask her to get off the phone so I can use it. And Mark is fourteen. He won't even talk to me. It's all grunts and rolling eyes, or silence."

Griffin hardly knew what to say. "Maybe it's just that they're teenagers. I remember being kind of—"

"They talk to their mother. It's not their age. Anita feels the same way. I'm just an inconvenience when I'm there. They never come right out and say so, but they wish I'd hurry up and leave again so they can go back to being normal. All they want from me is my signature on the mortgage check."

Griffin drank his coffee, then adjusted Stewbert's sock, stalling for time. How could he argue with anything Troy was saying? He knew it was possible—perhaps even likely—for a marriage to deteriorate into just such a hell. He'd seen it a million times.

The first time he'd seen it had been in his own home.

Against his will, he could suddenly hear again the ugly arguments that had so often filled the air in the Cahill house, poisoning it until the little boy Griffin had found it difficult to breathe.

"You frigid bitch," his father had said one memorable night, his ironic, well-modulated voice as sharp as a diamond cutter. Griffin's father never yelled. He was much too well-bred, too *intelligent* to raise his voice. Trashy people yelled, he explained. Stupid people yelled.

"You frigid bitch. If you could think of a way to get hold of my bank account without ever having to see me, or talk to me, or, God forbid, *touch* me, that would make you happy, wouldn't it?"

And his mother's voice had come back, acid with elegant cruelty, "Blissfully happy, Edgar. Do you suppose it could be arranged?"

Griffin felt a little dizzy. He put down his coffee cup and stared numbly at Stewbert. Where had his brother Jared found the courage to marry at all? Katie was great, but...didn't he remember their own parents? Didn't he read the papers? Didn't he know how heavily the odds were stacked against a successful marriage?

And how would anyone dare to create these helpless beings, innocents who would ultimately suffer the most when their parents began slicing each other into pieces?

"You know, you're right," he said suddenly, transferring his gaze to Troy.

Troy blinked. "I am? About what?"

"About how my advice is worth absolutely zip. I don't know the first thing about marriage, thank God, except that it seems to be the most deadly battleground on earth. So I say if that lawyer can get you free, Troy, go for it."

HEATHER LOOKED AT the empty plastic pocket on the door to Room Four.

She turned back toward the central common area, where the office staff were working. "Where's the chart for four?" she asked, trying not to be impatient. But this was such a beginner's mistake. She didn't have time for mistakes today. They were already running behind schedule, and it wasn't ten o'clock yet.

The nurses looked at one another and shrugged.

"Don't know," Tawny said without looking up, carefully touching a swab to a strep test strip. "Maybe there's not really anyone in there."

The coded flags above the door indicated otherwise. But one mistake was no more likely than the other, so Heather opened the door to find out.

To her surprise, the person sitting on the examination table, fully dressed, hands folded in her lap, was Mary Brady.

For one tense moment she wondered whether Mary really was a patient. Could she need…? Could she be…? No. She couldn't be… *not Mary.*

This had to be some kind of joke. And unfortunately, Heather didn't have time for jokes today, either.

She folded her arms, pressing her stethoscope against her chest and raised her eyebrows. "Yes?"

"Don't look like that," Mary said firmly. "I made an appointment. I knew I'd never get ten minutes to talk to you otherwise."

Heather frowned. "Don't be silly," she said. "You can talk to me anytime."

"No, I can't. I really can't. Haven't you noticed how overworked you are?"

"Mary." Heather sighed. "If you're going to complain about Griffin and the Stewberts again, I just don't know what to tell you. I promised I'd help and—"

"It's not Griffin." Mary held up her hands, protesting her innocence. "I've already told you how I feel about that, and I'm not going to nag. Well, not much, anyhow. And not now. Now I want to talk to you about business. About this office."

She took a deep breath, as if she needed it for courage. "I want to talk to you about how you absolutely, positively, *must* start looking for a partner."

Heather backed up a step. "Nonsense," she said. "We're just going through a busy spell. It'll calm down. It always does."

"No, it won't." Mary looked as stubborn as a mule, her brown eyes narrowed, her delicate jaw squared. "I just took three new patient appointments today. All pregnant. We're double-booking, Heather, just to get them all in. You always said you didn't want to do that."

"I don't." Heather put her hands in her lab coat pockets and toyed with the otoscope she kept there. "There must be something we can do to avoid that. Would it help if I took evening appointments? Or maybe if we stopped closing early on Saturdays for a while..."

"Oh, great. Then when will you have time for a real life? Your personal situation is already pretty pathetic, if you ask me, Doc. You haven't had a date in four months. And, believe me, a midnight rendezvous in the nursery for a strained-bananas cocktail with Playboy Cahill does not count.''

Heather stiffened. ''Mary, you run my medical office. You are not my social secretary. When I feel the need to spice up my personal life, I'll deal with it myself.''

They stared at each other in silence for a long second.

Mary blinked first.

''Okay, boss, you asked for it.''

Mary stood up, the stiff examination table paper crinkling as she moved. ''Here's the truth, plain and simple. If you aren't interested in having any fun, so be it. But the rest of us *are.*''

What? But as the message sank in, Heather felt herself flush, washed by a sudden sense of shame at having been so selfish.

''Look,'' Mary said, softening instantly. ''We love you. We love working for you. But we don't want to work all day and all night, too. We don't want to work Saturdays. Nobody does.''

She picked up a stack of manila folders from the shining stainless steel countertop. She held them out formally to Heather, both hands extended, like a butler offering a tray filled with cut-crystal decanters.

''So here's a bunch of résumés you've already received in the mail, just unsolicited inquiries from doctors who are curious about the possibility of coming to work in Firefly Glen."

Heather took the stack reluctantly. "You're kidding. All these people have already contacted us?"

"Right." Mary patted the top folder. "So here's the deal, Doc. You can hire a whole new office staff, assuming you can even find a crew of robots out there who want to work twenty-four-seven."

"Mary," Heather murmured. "I'm so sorry—"

Mary smiled. "Or—and I vastly prefer this idea—look through these applications. Find a doctor you like. And then, for God's sake, *hire him.*"

GRIFFIN PUSHED THE STROLLER through the double doors of City Hall, well aware of the stir he was going to create. But he didn't have any choice. It was his shift. Where he went, the Stewberts went.

And he had postponed this particular errand long enough.

Luckily the Stewberts were in good moods this morning. They babbled happily to each other as he moved through the walnut-paneled corridors, making his way to the mayor's inner sanctum. Along the way, he passed about a dozen city employees, all of whom had to stop and admire the babies—and rib Griffin.

"Why, I never thought I'd see the day!" "Will wonders never cease!" "Can this be true? Griffin Cahill pushing a baby carriage?" Griffin began to lament the Glen's lack of imagination. Did everyone have to say the same damn thing?

But then he ran into Suzie Strickland, a high school junior who worked part-time at the sheriff's office next door. Suzie sported orange-tipped black hair, heavy black Buddy Holly glasses, a green eyebrow ring and a neon-purple backpack, quite a statement here in Firefly Glen, where most teenagers wouldn't be caught dead in anything but Polo khakis and Hilfiger pullovers.

Suzie, thank God, could usually be counted on to see things a little differently.

"Hi, Suzie." Griffin paused, giving her plenty of time to take her best shot. She was sitting Indian-style on the floor, eating wheat germ straight out of the bottle, which put her nearly at eye level with the Stewberts.

The babies were, for once, completely silent. Suzie studied them phlegmatically.

"Gross," she pronounced finally, tilting herself another mouthful of wheat germ. "They look just like Cahills already."

Griffin grinned. Thank God for Suzie. "Yeah," he agreed. "We ordered them that way. We thought about asking for the Kennedy look, but we decided no. Great hair, but a little too much tooth, don't you think?"

"Totally." She crunched on her wheat germ a while. "So do they always do that?"

"Do what? Drool? I'm afraid so."

"No." In spite of herself, Suzie smiled. "No, I mean do they always look like whoever their father is?"

"Not always." Griffin wondered what had prompted

this odd curiosity. "But they might, so you probably would want to take that into consideration when you're deciding who should get the job."

"God, not me." Suzie shuddered dramatically. She eyed Griffin, obviously deciding how much she ought to say. "No, I'm just hoping that when Justine Millner comes back to town with her baby, it looks just like whatever dumb jock fathered it."

Griffin's curiosity deepened, especially since he thought he'd detected a break in Suzie's voice at the end there, on the word *fathered.*

"Why?" He kept his voice level. "What difference does it make?"

She glared at him with suspiciously shining eyes. "Because Mike Frome thinks it might be his, that's why. She told him it wasn't, but he keeps thinking maybe, and it's eating him alive. That's why."

So that was it. Griffin had heard that Mike Frome, who was a pretty nice kid on the whole, had gotten mixed up with that minx Justine, but he hadn't really followed the local soap operas very carefully.

Watching Suzie now, he realized there was a far more interesting subplot. Shocking Suzie had a crush on Conventional Mike, who unfortunately was still at the age when he'd rather be bored to death by a girl with big breasts than intellectually stimulated by a girl with a big brain.

"That's tough for Mike," he said carefully, not sure how to proceed. Suzie wasn't ordinarily the weepy type, but if she started crying here, that would probably get the Stewberts going, and then all hell would break loose.

"Yeah, well, he brought it on himself, the big idiot." She scowled, and the shining had disappeared from her black-lined raccoon eyes. "Maybe it'll teach him not to stick his finger in any old light socket, if you know what I mean."

Griffin, who considered himself a fairly sophisticated fellow, was momentarily speechless.

Luckily, at that instant, Alton Millner stuck his head out of his office. The front receptionist had obviously alerted him that Griffin was on his way back.

"Cahill? Are you coming in or not? I've got a meeting in twenty minutes."

"Yeah. Sorry," Griffin said, starting up his stroller. "So long, Suzie."

"Bye," she mumbled, her mouth full again. She cast one last look at the babies and shook her head. "God. Totally gross."

Alton shut his door firmly. "That girl is damn strange," he said to Griffin. "And the way she dresses! I wish Harry would get rid of her."

"Really? I like her," Griffin said. "She may be one of the few kids around here who actually knows how to think."

"Justine knows her. Justine says she's a freak."

Griffin smiled. "That's a coincidence. I think Suzie has a word for Justine, too."

"Don't you dare repeat it," Alton said loudly.

Griffin held back a chuckle. He enjoyed watching

Alton's eyes bug out, as if he were going to pop with indignation. He knew which word had come immediately to the man's mind. It was a word no father should associate so quickly with his own child.

"Actually, I think she referred to Justine as a 'live wire.'" He propped himself against Alton's desk, nudging the stroller back and forth with his foot. "Something like that, anyhow."

Alton had retreated to his big leather desk chair, and was trying to collect himself by shuffling papers into pointless piles. "Did you have something to talk to me about, Cahill?"

"Yes, I did. I want you to bring Heather Delaney's zoning variance request up for a new vote at the next council meeting."

"What?" Alton made a sputtering sound. "Why the hell would I do that?"

"Oh, I don't know," Griffin said, picking up Alton's paperweight shaped like a gavel and toying with it. "Maybe because it's the only fair thing to do?"

"The hell it is."

Griffin gazed calmly at the mayor. "Or maybe because, if you don't, I'm going to lodge a formal ethics complaint against you."

"What?" Alton stood furiously, his chair rolling back so hard it hit the wall. "Are you crazy? On what grounds?"

"On the grounds that you engineered the defeat of that variance because you harbor a personal grudge against Heather Delaney."

"That's—" Alton slammed his fist against the desk. "That's slander."

"No, it isn't." Griffin smiled. "You're such an ostrich, Alton. You think no one knows about the day Justine brought Heather Delaney home with her, because she was afraid to face you alone? You think no one knows how you went nuts because Heather dared to defy you, suggesting that Justine be allowed to remain in Firefly Glen, allowed to have her baby at home, surrounded by friends and family? In a town like this, Alton, everyone knows everything. They probably knew Justine was pregnant before she knew it herself. They *undoubtedly* knew it before you did."

Alton was purple with fury.

"You'll never make a charge like that stick. Not in this town. Nobody threatens Alton Millner!"

"This is not a threat," Griffin said quietly. The Stewberts didn't like angry voices. Griffin had already learned that. So he wasn't surprised when they began to whimper. "It's a simple statement of cause and effect. Did you ever take Logic? *If this, then that.* If you don't bring it up for a vote, then I will file an ethics charge. And whether it sticks or not, it will keep the whole town buzzing for weeks."

"This was that woman's idea, wasn't it? I knew she was cooking something up." Alton tugged on his tie, as if it were choking him. "Don't listen to anything she says, Cahill. Cahill? You know she's just—"

Millner probably said other things, too, but Griffin

couldn't hear him. He was already halfway out the door, and besides, the Stewberts, who might be only babies but obviously knew a bad guy when they saw one, completely drowned him out.

CHAPTER NINE

SWEET APPLES, the farmer's market at the edge of town, opened early on Sunday mornings, so Heather began dressing the Stewberts as soon as they woke up. She wanted to get there before all the best vegetables were gone.

She put the boys in something simple—soft blue sweatpants and blue-and-white-striped knit tops. At first she had been enchanted by their elaborate sailor suits and brand-name tailored rompers. But she'd quickly learned that the boys weren't dress-up dolls. They were active little people who wanted to be comfortable while they played.

Plus, what with one accident or another—at one end or another—they each went through about five changes a day. Heather had learned to judge an outfit by one standard only: how easy was it to get on and off?

One Stewbert found the dressing process highly amusing today. As he sat on the changing table, he was flailing his arms and squealing his pleasure.

"Shh," Heather said softly. "How is Uncle Griffin going to sleep if you keep making so much noise?"

"He's not," Griffin said dryly from the doorway.

"Luckily, he wasn't trying." He sauntered in, cup of coffee in hand. "Need any help?"

Griffin, whose shift had just ended, looked tired, but he was wearing a jacket, and his coffee was in a to-go mug, so obviously he was telling the truth. He wasn't planning to sleep. He was going out.

"That's okay," she said, glancing down at the Stewbert who was still on the floor, waiting his turn. "They're loud, but actually they're being cooperative this morning. Besides, you had them all night. Aren't you ever going to grab some sleep?"

Griffin shook his head, bending over to hand the baby his new favorite toy, a yellow plastic car with bug eyes that wiggled rather salaciously when the wheels rolled. They had privately named it Alton.

"Not yet. I've got to take some pictures. I agreed to get some spring shots for the chamber. Granville Frome is about to have a stroke because May tourism has been declining in Firefly Glen for six-point-three straight years."

Heather wrestled Stewbert's arm into his sleeve, then kissed the fat little fingers as they emerged. "Oh, really? And is that a big problem?"

"Apparently. Granville devoted ninety minutes and seventeen full-color charts to the subject at the last chamber meeting."

She laughed. Both Stewberts looked up at her and smiled. They were always ready to share a good laugh.

"Well, let's see. Spring..." she mused, trying to finesse a sneaker onto Stewbert's foot, which was difficult because he kept mischievously curling his toes. "I know! I'm headed over to Sweet Apples, and Mary told me that their orchard is absolutely spectacular this year. Why don't you go with us?"

Even before she saw the guarded look come over his face, she regretted making the suggestion. Of course he didn't want to go.

In fact, he had been markedly distant these past few days. The baby transfers were made with the minimum amount of interaction. When Heather arrived, Griffin didn't linger. He didn't chat, or stay for one last game of peekaboo with the Stewberts, the way he once had. He just filled her in on pertinent details, and then he left.

Probably he was just getting tired of the whole thing, and restless to get back to his normal life. But she couldn't help wondering if this new distance might be her fault. The other night, the night of the childbirth class, she had been tense and overwrought. When he made a simple gesture of concern, offering her a shoulder rub, she had stupidly overreacted.

Several times, she had considered apologizing. But his cordial distance never seemed to invite serious conversation. His laughing eyes didn't hold mockery, exactly—that would have been rude, which Griffin never was—but rather the *potential* for mockery. Somehow that was equally effective at warding off unwanted intimacies.

"How silly of me," she said, concentrating on Stewbert's shoe to cover her discomfort. She laughed lightly. "I don't know what I was thinking. Naturally, the last thing in the world you'd want during your free time is to get stuck with the babies again."

She thought quickly. "You could go to the falls instead. They're probably gorgeous right now, with the spring thaw."

He looked surprised. "You mean Silver Kiss Falls?"

"No, of course not." She took a breath. "I mean yes, you could go there if you wanted to, of course. I just meant that there are quite a few lovely falls around here, I wasn't particularly thinking of Silver Kiss."

Oh, God, she must be crazy. She was making it worse and worse. She should never have mentioned waterfalls—she should have known he'd think first of Silver Kiss, though it wasn't the showiest or best-known falls in Firefly Glen.

All young lovers had a special place. Silver Kiss Falls had been theirs. They had made love there for the first time—and the last time, too, though of course they hadn't known that then. As they stood beneath the tumbling water, surrounded by rainbows, they had still believed it would last forever.

She almost never went to Silver Kiss anymore. She could always hear things in the whispering spray. The ripple of his laughter. The splash of her tears.

Suddenly, the yellow car rolled out of Stewbert's grasp. Not good yet at judging distances, he reached over to pick it up, lost his balance and tumbled hard onto his nose. Indignant, he began to cry.

The baby on the changing table puckered up, too,

his face growing hot red. Heather braced herself for an earsplitting, stereo display of frustration. But suddenly Griffin scooped the wailing baby off the floor and lifted him high onto his shoulders in one smooth swoop.

Shock silenced both Stewberts immediately.

"Wow," Heather breathed. "Great reflexes."

Griffin grinned at her from under Stewbert's fat fingers, which were plastered awkwardly across Griffin's eyebrows. Gurgling happily, the baby tilted forward, pressing his open mouth to the crown of Griffin's head.

"On second thought, I think we'd better go to Sweet Apples together," Griffin said, shutting his eyes in silent martyrdom as Stewbert began to make soft sucking noises against his hair. "I'm not at all sure it's safe to let these little monsters outnumber you."

THE LIGHT AT THE ORCHARD was perfect. Sometimes a photographer had to use a polarizing filter to create the illusion of a sky so blue, or grass so green, but Griffin wouldn't need any such tricks today. May itself had done the work—with a little help from the April rains.

And to think he almost hadn't come. It was as if fate had given him a shove in the back, saying, hurry, go today. Yesterday the orchard could have been a degree too skimpy. By tomorrow it might have begun, ever so slightly, to droop.

But today was perfect. The apple trees, which stood in tidy lines running back from the Sweet Apples roadside stand, were as dressed-up as debutantes, showing off white gowns of a thousand frothy blossoms.

Granville would be thrilled with the pictures. Spring in Firefly Glen looked pretty darned romantic from here.

While Heather browsed the market tables, which were heaped with plump fresh vegetables, Griffin and the Stewberts gathered his equipment. He let each of the boys hold an empty plastic film case. They gnawed happily on the cylinders, while above their damp fists their bright eyes curiously watched Griffin's every move.

On impulse, he tossed a blanket across the handle of the stroller. And he slipped his waist-level viewfinder into the pack, too. If he saw a lucky picture of the boys, he wanted to be able to get a good, low angle on it without slithering around on his stomach.

By the time he joined Heather, her cloth shopping bag was filled to bursting. She expertly pinched a shiny red tomato, then slid it into the sack, somehow finding another inch of space.

"Got anything in there we could munch on?" Griffin parked the stroller off to the side of the aisle. "I thought you and the boys could picnic while I work."

She pointed to the cashier's desk, where large, softly browned homemade muffins spilled enticingly out of a grapevine basket. "I bought half a dozen of those, and a small jar of jam, too. They have free coffee over by the parking lot. We'll feast like kings."

They weren't the only ones who had come up with the picnic idea. The orchard was spotted with blankets and tablecloths. Griffin claimed a quiet spot, as far from the others as he could get.

The air was sweet back here, away from the street, and the light was a soft, Easter-egg yellow that would photograph perfectly. He moved around, taking a few easy shots, metering the light and exploring angles, while Heather fluffed open the blanket and unhooked the Stewberts from their seats.

Then she pulled out the muffins and the coffee and began arranging them on the blanket, like a little girl setting up a tea party. He smiled, the photographer in him appreciating the way the sun set off golden sparks in her auburn hair.

He slipped off a couple of pictures of her, though she didn't realize it. The waist-level viewfinder was useful that way. It allowed you to look down as you approached a shy animal, never making that conspicuous, threatening gesture of raising and pointing the camera.

She looked wonderful. The breeze blew tiny red-gold wisps of hair around her face and tickled shining strands against her slender neck. Watching her through the viewfinder, Griffin was caught unprepared by a sudden, heavy throb of desire, a tiny kick of intense arousal.

He lowered the camera and took a deep breath. God, this was familiar. How many years was it going to take to get past this knee-jerk, mindless sexual reaction? Ten obviously hadn't been enough. How about twenty?

Maybe the rotten truth was that he'd *never* be able

to look at her without wanting to make love to her. He felt like some fiendish science experiment. Erotically programmed by circumstance. She'd been his first lover, and he was doomed forever to lurch helplessly at the sight of her.

He dropped his camera to his side, went over and plopped himself down beside her on the blanket.

He gestured toward the muffins. "One of those for me?"

"All you want," she replied, holding out the biggest muffin and a napkin. "The Stewberts don't like them. They just crumble them up and toss the bits around."

"Oh, but that's the sign that they *do* like them," he corrected with a smile. "Their enthusiasm can be measured by square feet of destruction."

"Oh, yeah. I forgot." Heather leaned back on her elbows, lifting her face to the sun. The Stewberts were climbing across her legs, as if she were their private jungle gym, but she obviously didn't mind.

She sighed. "How lovely it is this morning! I've been spending too much time inside lately, I think."

"It's nice, isn't it?" Griffin carefully avoided agreeing with the second part of her comment. If he chimed in, it would feel like pressure, the same pressure he'd always applied—stop working so hard, come out and have fun, enjoy the world with me.

"I just never seem to have any free time. But that may change." She reached down to stroke Stewbert's hair. "Did I tell you that I'm interviewing for a partner?"

"No." He was surprised. Very surprised. "What made you decide to do that?"

"Mary." She laughed softly. "She explained that my staff would stage a mass walkout if I didn't get some help. I think I had resisted the idea because, once I bought Spring House, money was so tight. And now if all those expensive renovations have been for nothing..."

Her voice dwindled off, as if she had lost herself in her musings. Watching her, Griffin had an intense desire to wipe that troubled look off her face. He could tell her about his visit to Alton. But he held back. Better not to get her hopes up until he was sure the mayor would do the right thing.

In a few seconds, though, she rallied on her own. How silly he'd been to think she'd need him to comfort her. She hadn't ever been the type to brood.

He'd never forget how, the day after she broke off their engagement, she had aced a chemistry final. He, on the other hand, had spent two full days in bed with a bitchy blonde and a killer hangover and a rather vicious attitude toward life in general.

"Well, anyhow," she went on, "when I thought it through logically, I realized that if there's demand for another gynecologist in town, sooner or later someone will show up." She smiled. "So, basically, the new guy can either come in as my partner or as my competition. Partner sounded better."

"Sounds like good strategy. Any real candidates yet?"

"One. He's coming up tomorrow for an interview and a look around. He works in the city, but he was born in a small town, so I'm hoping he won't be too appalled by our little dollhouse community."

"Maybe he's tired of the big city. Tired of the rat race. It can get old."

She looked at him quizzically. "Can it?"

A couple of bluebirds had lighted in the tree just beside them. Griffin began to make a quick switch to his eye-level viewfinder. "Well, sure it can," he said as he worked. "Sometimes you just have to get away for a little while. Change the scenery. Take a breather."

She didn't even blink. She didn't interrupt her steady stroking of Stewbert's hair. "Well," she said blandly, her voice perfectly even, "if he's just looking for a breather, he'd better not look here. I have no interest in taking on a *temporary* partner."

Griffin paused, his camera halfway to his eye, and looked at her carefully. Did this conversation have a subtext? What exactly was she trying to say?

He hesitated just a moment too long. The fickle birds flew away again, the apple blossoms shaking slightly in their wake. Griffin lowered the camera, wondering how he should respond.

But Heather had bent her head to the babies, who were almost asleep, leaning up against her like book-ends.

"So," she said, "tell me about your photography."

Her voice expressed only a perfunctory interest. She didn't really care. She was clearly just trying to change the subject. Her primary focus seemed to be the Stewberts. She was gently combing their silky hair with her fingertips.

''What about it?''

She looked up. ''Anything. I know you're helping Granville with his tourism brochure right now, but what do you have planned after this? You take mostly travel pictures, right? Anything interesting coming up?''

''A couple of things are on the table. Troy's trying to talk me into a trip he's excited about. But I may be in the mood for something different.''

She laughed. ''I would have thought everything you did was 'different.' I've seen some of your pictures in travel magazines, and I can't even pronounce half the names of the places you've been.''

''Yeah, I pretty much wake up every morning wondering where I am.'' He poured himself a cup of coffee. ''Until this year, anyhow.''

She didn't look at him. She developed a sudden interest in the trees, which had begun to rustle in a stiffening breeze.

''And this year that you've been home,'' she said, still giving him her profile, ''are you just taking a...a breather? I mean, I've always wondered. Why *did* you come home after all these years?''

At first, he didn't say anything. He toyed with his camera, wondering which version he should give her. The official dinner-party version, guaranteed to get a well-bred chuckle: *I work in the rain forest and the*

Riviera. When I want a vacation, I have to come home. Or the teasing deflection offered to golf partners or bar buddies: *I ran out of film.* Or the polite but equally meaningless version, reserved for nice, sincere people: *I had some personal business to take care of.*

Always twenty-five comfortable words or less. No one ever got the strange, confusing truth.

Which was that he'd come home because one day he found himself sitting in the Munich airport, a ticket to Finland in his hand, listening to them call his flight. They had kept calling. *First call. All passengers. Last call...* but he hadn't moved.

He'd just sat there, like a man in a trance. And when the Finland flight had roared past the window, and finally shrunk to a speck in the twilight sky, he had stood up, approached the reservation desk, and traded in his ticket for one that read "New York."

It wasn't something he ever talked about. And he hadn't looked too far into the future. Hickory Baxter had wheedled him into sitting on the city council, which locked him in until summer. After that...

Well, he just assumed he'd stay here until one day he bought a ticket that said something else.

"I've been setting up some photography scholarships," he said, settling for a more prosaic truth. "I discovered there aren't very many of those around. I'd like to see a few gifted, underprivileged kids go to college and get some serious art training, really make something of their talent."

She chuckled softly. ''Are there any underprivileged kids in Firefly Glen?''

''A few. In fact, Mary Brady's younger brother Tucker has applied for one of them, although he warned me he hasn't told Mary yet.''

Heather looked pleased. ''Oh, he should tell her! She'll be thrilled. Is he going to get it?''

Griffin shrugged. ''Maybe. He's pretty good.''

Finally Heather's smile looked genuine. ''You know...'' She paused. ''Establishing those scholarships was really a generous, worthy thing to do, Griffin. I had no idea you—''

''Ever did anything worthy?''

She shook her head. ''No, I was going to say I had no idea you were so passionate about your career.''

He didn't want to talk about this. He looked up, aware that the light had been changing as heavy clouds moved toward them, filled, no doubt, with one of their famous spring rains. Pure sunshine had a white cast, but an overcast day would photograph as slightly blue. It might lend drama to the apple trees, which tended to be a little too anemic in their demure prettiness. But he knew that Granville would prefer bland and pretty. So he picked up his camera.

''We might be getting a storm,'' he said. ''Mind if I take a few pictures while the light's still good?''

''Of course not. I'll pack up here.''

She moved the Stewberts aside carefully, arranging the sleeping boys on the blanket without waking them. Griffin walked a little distance away. He looked at the apple trees, which were lovely. And then he looked at Heather.

Her body, as she knelt protectively over the boys, was fluid and graceful. The wind pressed her light green spring dress against her curves, her breasts, her thighs, her hips. And her face, as she freed Stewbert's little hand from an awkward position, was focused and tender—and incredibly beautiful.

So, self-indulgently, he turned his camera on her instead. To hell with Granville.

As he kept clicking, finding new secrets in her face from every angle, he lost all interest in the apple trees. They would be here tomorrow, next week, and every spring into eternity. They were rooted in place, always accessible.

He had learned, as a nature photographer, that it was more important to seize the unexpected moment. Like a skittish deer, which will give you only one fleeting instant of heartbreaking eye contact before bolting away, Heather was a rare, elusive beauty.

After this week, Heather would never be his to photograph again.

"Hi, there, son. How about if I take a picture of the whole family for you?"

Griffin looked up. An elderly man wearing madras Bermuda shorts, a Disneyland cap and a Spending My Kid's Inheritance T-shirt was standing at his elbow. The man's wife, whose own T-shirt read 70 Is Sensational, was over near Heather, smiling eagerly.

"Yes, do let Fred take one, dear. Someone always

gets left out of these family photos. You'll want at least one picture of both of you with your darling little ones!"

"Family photos?" It took Heather a second to catch on, but then she flushed and shook her head. "Oh, no, we're not—"

"That would be terrific," Griffin interrupted quickly, smiling at the elderly man. "Just let me show you how to work this camera. It's tricky."

"You go on over and put your arm around your pretty wife, son," the old man said, waving Griffin away. "I wasn't always a hundred years old, you know. I used to build skyscrapers. I think I can figure out a little old Nikon."

Griffin handed over the camera with an apologetic smile, then crossed to the blanket, where Heather was giving him a glare that would have turned him to stone if he let it.

"Isn't that nice, honey?" He knelt beside her and slipped his arm around her shoulders. "Fred is going to take our picture with our darling little ones."

"Oh, yes," she said between her teeth, smiling a broad, fake smile. "Very nice. Especially since it will be the last picture ever taken of you alive."

But he didn't really believe she was angry. A little embarrassed, perhaps, but no worse than that. He winked at her, then turned to offer the camera a grin just as Fred clicked the shutter.

Still smiling, Heather tried to pull away immediately.

"One more, one more," Fred called out. "This time,

son, why don't you give your lovely wife a big, lovely kiss?''

Heather's shoulders turned rigid under Griffin's arm. ''Do it,'' she whispered, ''and you die.''

''But you already told me I'm a dead man anyhow,'' he whispered back, taking her chin in his hand and dipping his head toward hers. ''So I really have nothing to lose, do I?''

Her skin was like creamy satin under his fingers, and her green eyes were dazzling up this close. Her rosy lips were full, and her breath touched him in warm waves of cinnamon and apple blossoms.

His own breath was tight with a desire so intense it startled him. And he realized that, even if her threat had been real—even if the cost of kissing her right now *was* death—he would probably do it anyway.

''Come on, lovebirds, I'm an old man! Don't dawdle!''

''Griffin...'' Heather's troubled gaze searched his, and a delicate pink stain was forming on her ivory cheeks. ''Griffin, we—''

He smothered the rest of the sentence with his lips. As he found her, he felt his heart grow very still, then begin to race. Oh, yes, God help him, he remembered this. This beauty, this sweetness, this heat.

''Perfect! Damn, I'm good, if I do say so myself. You're going to love that one!''

But Fred's excited voice seemed to come from a million miles away, and Griffin ignored it. He slid his hands into Heather's hair, pulling her close, then closer.

For a moment her lips were tight, but gradually, as he moved across them, they softened and fell open, releasing the tiniest of moans.

''Will you look at that! I think we started something.'' Fred was laughing loudly. ''Boy oh boy. We may need to turn a hose on these two, Mona.''

Somehow, long after he knew he had passed the bounds of good manners, Griffin found the willpower to pull away. He kept his arm around Heather's shoulders, which were trembling.

He managed to smile at Fred.

''Thanks for your help,'' he said. ''That was a great idea.''

''Certainly appeared to be.'' Fred handed Griffin the camera, grinning with irrepressible mischief. ''I guess we can see how you two ended up with those pretty little babies.''

Griffin glanced at Heather, whose head was bowed, her auburn hair falling forward over her equally auburn cheeks.

''Well, thanks again, Fred. Have a great day.'' He did appreciate the old guy's help, but he very much wished that Fred would give it up now and go away.

Griffin needed to talk to Heather. Maybe he needed to apologize. Maybe he needed to kiss her again.

''Fred,'' Mona said, clapping her husband on the back. She seemed better at reading hints. ''Come on. Let's go.''

''But we just got here.'' Fred eyed the blanket, as if he were looking for a spot to plant himself. ''I mean it, Mona, aren't those babies cute? Twins, right? What are their names, anyhow?"

Griffin smiled pleasantly. "Actually, we're not sure."

Beside him, Heather made a small, strangled sound.

Fred frowned. "What do you mean you're not—"

"You see, they're not our babies."

"What?"

Griffin fought down a chuckle, somehow keeping a straight face.

"Oh, Fred, you're such a dope," Mona said tartly, yanking on her husband's arm. "For God's sake, shut up and let's go home. Can't you see the boy wants to be alone with his wife?"

The old man harrumphed as he turned away.

"*Wife?* I'll bet you dimes to dollars that red-haired floozy is not his wife."

At which point even Heather couldn't handle it. She looked at Griffin, her mouth working desperately. She buried her face in his chest, her shoulders shaking.

"Floozy," he whispered. She batted him weakly with her fist, her eyes streaming with merriment. And finally the two of them collapsed in a heap onto the blanket, smothering their helpless laughter in the soft blue cotton like a couple of very naughty—but ridiculously happy—children.

CHAPTER TEN

OKAY, RUSSELL BRADY, listen up. I'm sure Tad Halliwell is a laugh a minute when he's knocking back shots, but the rest of the time he's a first-class fool. Tad's life is going to hell on a rocket, and you know it. You hop into that bucket of bolts with him Friday night, and you just may go with him.

Mary gnawed on the end of her pen, frustrated. She was going to have to do better than this. Russ was twenty-one now, and the number had gone to his head. Technically he didn't have to *Listen Up* to anyone, as he was fond of telling them all.

Humor was the best way to reach him, but ever since she had heard that his idiot friend Tad was setting up a Friday night drag race through Vanity Gap, she hadn't felt much like laughing.

Oh, well, it was only Monday. Maybe something would come to her.

She put her pen down on the kitchen island and, picking up the paring knife, carefully started taking the peel off a fat red plum. She was baby-sitting the twins for a couple of hours, while Heather attended the emergency city council meeting, which had been called just this morning.

Apparently Heather's rezoning request had been put back onto the agenda. Mary wondered whether that might be Griffin's doing. He had promised Heather he'd help, but Mary hadn't set much store by that. Playboy Cahill had a convenient way of forgetting his promises.

Still. She wasn't an unfair woman. She'd give him credit if and when he proved he deserved it. But if he let Heather down again…

Mary traded for a larger knife and karate-chopped a banana into neat little slices. No. He wouldn't dare.

Surely Heather would come home with good news. In the meantime, Mary was going to make some plum-yummy for Robert and Stewart. It was her mother's recipe, and babies always loved it.

She had just dumped the fruit into the blender when someone knocked at the kitchen door. Wiping streams of plum juice from her hands, Mary opened it with her wrists.

It was Troy, who looked adorable this morning, in his tight blue jeans and flannel shirt. Of course, she was a sucker for a man with shaggy hair and buff biceps. It must be her earthy logger roots.

"Hi," she said, smiling. "Griffin's not here." She left the door ajar, returning to the blender. "He's at the council meeting. I thought you might have gone with him."

Troy came in and shut the door behind him. "Good God, no. Why would I do that? It's not safe. Those old men are lunatics."

Mary laughed. A couple of them were, and that was no joke. "Anyhow, Griffin will be coming back here when the meeting's over. His baby shift starts right after lunch. Want to grab a Coke and wait for him?"

"Sure." Troy got his drink, then settled on one of the kitchen bar stools, resting his elbows on the marble-topped island. He looked down at her papers, which she had foolishly left out. "What's this? Some of your writing?"

She wished she could snatch it away before he read a single word, but she had just turned on the blender, and she didn't dare leave it unattended.

"That's nothing," she said, but she knew he couldn't hear her over the pureeing plums. He had already read the half-finished *Listen Up* letter and had moved on to the pages behind it.

Oh, darn, she had forgotten about those. There were several other *Listen Up* letters, earlier lectures to Russell that she'd brought along to make sure she didn't repeat herself. And something else too, she remembered, groaning. At the bottom of the pile were a couple of her Littletown Adventures, which she'd brought over to work on in case the meeting ran late.

Troy was reading Littletown now, and he was smiling. What did that mean? Was that good or bad?

Oh, this was awful. It was as embarrassing as having him catch her naked. Worse, because frankly she didn't give a damn what he thought of her body. And for some stupid reason, she cared a lot, a whole lot, what he thought of her writing.

When the plums were finished, he was still reading. "I'm going upstairs to check on the boys," she said stiltedly. "They should be waking up any minute."

He nodded, gesturing goodbye with a preoccupied hand without lifting his gaze from the pages. She hesitated, bowls of plum-yummy in hand. She tried to read his expression, tried to guess what exact part of the story he was reading right this minute. What was making him smile like that?

Oh, what difference did it make what he thought? She stuck the bowls in the refrigerator, then exited the kitchen and stomped up the stairs, furious with herself.

Robert and Stewart were just waking up. She refused to call the poor kids the Stewberts. Typical of Cahill to think that was funny. They might be just babies, but they still deserved names of their own. She had arbitrarily dubbed the one with the cowlick Robert, though, to her eternal annoyance, neither one ever answered to anything but Stewbert.

She changed Robert's diaper first, because Stewart was always the more patient of the two.

"It doesn't matter what he thinks, does it, Robert?" She found the baby powder and shook it all over the baby's bottom. "*You* like my Littletown Adventures, don't you? You loved the one about Prince Dudley Do-nothing, didn't you?"

But Robert was on a mission to capture his big toe and eat it. He was folding himself in half, trying to get his foot close enough to chomp. This made diapering tricky, and Mary felt herself getting annoyed.

"Come on, Robbie, you're not even listening." She jiggled him a little. "Robert." She sighed, scowling. *"Stewbert!"*

The baby looked up, his wet, questing mouth still open, his leg still over his head. "Bee!" he said. He smiled his silly two-tooth grin. "Buck speet."

Mary had to laugh. She slid the diaper under his soft little fanny and pulled open the tape.

"Fine. I'll take that as a yes," she said. "'Five Stars,' raves famous *New York Times* book critic Stewbert Cahill. *The Littletown Adventures* are the best children's stories to come along in decades.'"

"Aw, shucks," Troy said from the door. "He stole my line."

Mary looked over at Troy. He had clearly heard everything. She decided that she'd have to kill herself on the spot. But because the nursery had been babyproofed, there wasn't a sharp object in sight. Just her luck.

"I love them," he said, coming toward her, holding out the sheaf of papers. "I absolutely love them. All of them."

"You don't have to say that," she said, refusing to meet his eyes. She traded Stewberts and began diapering the second one. "You don't have to say anything. I didn't leave them out so that you'd read them, you know. I didn't have any idea you were coming over today."

He was standing at her elbow. He stepped on the

pedal of the diaper pail at the perfect moment, so that she could drop the soggy one in.

"I love them," he repeated slowly. "You're a very talented woman, Mary Brady. And Littletown is a wonderful creation."

She just looked at him, mute with idiotic delight. She hated herself for feeling so thrilled. She especially hated the overeager questions that came thronging to her lips. *Do you really like it? What's good about it? What exactly do you like about Littletown? Did you recognize Prince Dudley Do-nothing? How could I make the stories better? Do you think I could ever, ever, get them published?*

"Mary, I want to show them to my agent. She represents all kinds of authors, not just travel writers. I think she'll be as excited as I am."

Mary had to work just to swallow. Her throat felt suddenly dry. He sounded sincere, but she mustn't believe in this. The disappointment would be terrible if he didn't mean it. If he didn't follow through.

And he was Playboy Cahill's best friend, after all.

Scooping Stewbert into her arms, she turned to Troy.

"That's a very generous offer. And I'm not saying I wouldn't be thrilled. But I'm not going to thank you by sleeping with you." Her fear made her sound tough. But that was okay. She'd rather sound bitchy than pathetic. "I just thought you'd better know that at the outset."

"It hadn't crossed my mind," he said, grinning. "Tricks like that wouldn't work with a woman like you. After all, did Princess Cerulean kiss Count Fribbleslag just because he threatened to lock her puppy in the tower? Of course not. She nearly drowned him in the moat for suggesting such a thing.''

He really had read them. In spite of herself, Mary smiled back. ''In that case, if you're sure it's what you want to do… I mean, if you really think that the stories are…''

She took a deep breath and started over. ''I would be absolutely, positively thrilled and grateful.''

Troy nodded, businesslike. ''Good. If you'll give me six or eight of your best stories, I'll send them first thing in the morning.''

It was all Mary could do not to kiss him. He didn't look a bit like Count Fribbleslag, who had been based on a lazy, middle-aged millionaire who summered here years and years ago, back when Mary had been a housekeeper at the hotel. One day, the jerk had suggested that her tips might improve if she were a little friendlier. She had found it necessary to dump her full bucket of slop water on his lap.

Luckily, her foolish impulse to plant a big, sloppy, grateful kiss on Troy's cute mouth was short-circuited by the sound of footsteps running up the stairs and Heather's voice calling, ''Mary! Mary, where are you?''

The meeting must be over.

Mary held her breath for a long second, praying. Well, as she had already admitted, she was better at being bitchy than being pathetic, so her prayer sounded more like a *Listen Up* letter, but she assumed that God was used to that. *You'd better tell me Cahill did the right thing today, because I know how you feel about murder.*

"Mary!" Heather burst into the nursery, breathless. "Mary, you should have been there! We won!"

Mary began to breathe again. She didn't need the details—it was enough to see Heather's face. She had never looked so joyous, her smile electrically radiant, her green eyes as bright as the crystal ones on Stewbert's stuffed bunny.

Though Heather had been her usual stoic self about the whole mess, Mary knew how much this decision meant to her. Owning Spring House, living here and working here, had been Heather's dearest dream.

Mary also knew that buying the house had shoved Heather's finances right to the brink. If the rezoning hadn't gone through, Heather would eventually have had to sell it. She might as well have sold her heart, with her left arm thrown in for good measure.

But now, thank God, the house, and the dream, were safe. No wonder Heather was walking on air, her usual overbred, uptight restraint thrown to the winds.

Mary, who was definitely underbred, pumped her fist in the air jubilantly. "Yes!" She hugged Heather hard. "You did it, girlfriend!"

Heather shook her head. "No. Griffin did it. He won't tell me precisely *how,* but—"

Griffin, who obviously had followed Heather up the stairs at a more leisurely pace, appeared in the doorway, his grin cute and cocky, the kind of grin Mary usually wanted to knock off his face. But right now it didn't bother her one bit.

"I told you. I didn't really do anything. I guess Alton Millner finally grew a conscience, that was all."

Mary snorted. "Grew a conscience, my foot. You can't fool us. He could just as soon grow another head." She grinned evilly. "No, wait. The man already has two faces, doesn't he?"

Everyone laughed, including the Stewberts. Heather hugged Mary again, and Troy clapped Griffin on the back, smiling. "Congratulations, pal. You did good."

Silently Mary and Troy exchanged a smile. What with her own excitement about Troy's reaction to her stories, and now Heather's victory, there was so much happiness floating around this nursery Mary was surprised the room didn't lift right off the house and fly away.

Still softly laughing, Heather picked up one of the babies and twirled him in circles, her lab coat swirling around her like a ball gown.

"Oh, this is a wonderful, wonderful day," she told the little boy. "Uncle Griffin is a miracle worker, Stewbert." She brought the baby up to Griffin. "Tell your uncle what a very good thing he's done today."

"Flam!" the baby cried excitedly, waving his arms. "Greek!"

Griffin chuckled, but Heather kissed the baby's chubby cheek. "That's right, Stewbert. Now tell Uncle Griffin how very, very grateful I am."

Griffin held Heather's gaze. "Why don't you tell me yourself?"

Heather hesitated, her cheeks flushing.

''No, no,'' Troy remonstrated playfully. ''Ixnay on at-thay, bro. You'll spoil everything if she thinks you had an agenda. You're not allowed to ask for anything in return for a favor. Ask Princess Cerulean. Ask Count Fribbleslag.''

Griffin smiled, though he didn't take his gaze from Heather's. ''But I'm not Count Fribbleslag, Troy. I'm Prince Dudley Do-nothing.''

Shocked, Mary laughed nervously. ''How the heck did you know that, Griffin?'' She scowled. ''Besides, so what? Prince Dudley Do-nothing isn't allowed to blackmail anybody, either. Especially not for doing something he should have done the first time around anyhow.''

''It's not blackmail, Mary,'' Heather said quietly. ''He already did his good deed, and he never asked for anything in return. This is...'' She smiled up at Griffin so sweetly Mary thought she might yak. ''This is different.''

Mary sighed. ''Oh, well, if it's *different,*'' she said, rolling her eyes. ''Then by all means give the hero a hug and get it over with.''

But Heather hadn't waited for Mary's permission. When Mary looked back, Heather was in Griffin's arms, her head resting on his chest, the baby snuggled between them.

Griffin lay his cheek against Heather's shining hair. His lips moved. Mary wasn't quite close enough to hear, but she thought he said, ''You're welcome.''

"GRIFFIN CAHILL! The very man I wanted to see!"

Emma Tremaine Dunbar grabbed Griffin as he entered the door of the Paper Shop and whisked him to the custom-order counter in the back of the store.

Griffin groaned. "I was afraid of this," he said sadly, allowing himself to be dragged by the sleeve. "One kiss, and you were hooked. You know, you're just going to have to forget me somehow. Your husband has a very big gun, and—"

"Shut up, Griffin." Emma gave him a dirty look as she plopped him onto a chair behind the counter. "Your kisses aren't nearly as amazing as you think."

"They aren't?" Griffin gazed up at her, offering her his best wounded expression. "You mean all those other women were..." he swallowed hard "...lying?"

Emma glared at him. Then her blue eyes softened and she crinkled her nose. "Oh, probably not," she said. "Damn your conceited soul. Probably not."

She glanced around the store, as if checking for eavesdroppers. Only one customer remained, a teenager looking at birthday cards over by the door.

"But that's not why I'm so happy to see you," Emma said, lowering her voice. "I've been hearing the most astounding gossip about you, and I want to know if it's true."

"Probably," he said equably. "Although if it's that thing about me and Justine Millner's baby, it's a dirty lie."

Emma grimaced. "Nobody's fool enough to think you'd touch a hair on Justine Millner's little airhead. Why, you're old enough to be her—"

"Be *very* careful."

"Older brother." Emma shoved a stack of card samples out of the way and hiked herself up onto the edge of the counter. "But quit trying to change the subject. Here's what I'm hearing—you and Heather Delaney are living together at Spring House, parenting a couple of babies you *say* are your nephews. You and she were seen smooching in the orchard behind Sweet Apples Sunday morning. And best of all, you first buried her rezoning request and then, for no apparent reason, revived it in an emergency council meeting in the predawn hours yesterday."

Griffin whistled softly. "Damn, Emma. You just got back from your trip late last night, right? Where did you come up with all that?"

"I'm connected," she said smugly. "And this is Firefly Glen, remember? Home of the high-speed grapevine. Just tell me if it's true."

"Okay. Yes, no comment and sort of."

Emma folded her arms. "Details, damn it. I want details."

"Consult your grapevine, then. You're not getting them from me."

Emma pressed her lips together irritably, which made Griffin want to laugh. God, Harry really had his hands full with this stubborn wife of his, didn't he? Emma was trying to bore her intensely blue Tremaine eyes into his soul. She probably had a rack in the back office, where she tortured information out of people like him.

He took it for a minute. Then he yawned broadly, tilted his head and smiled at her. "Give it up, Em. It's not working. Besides, you haven't even asked me why I'm here."

Emma grinned. ''You said it yourself. One kiss, and you're addicted. But you're going to have to get over me, Griff. My husband has a big gun.''

''I know. That's why I've come, not as a lovelorn home wrecker, but as a paying customer.'' He smiled at her look of surprise. ''So. You might want to be a little nicer to me, huh?''

She grinned again. ''Probably not.''

He took a piece of paper from his pocket. ''Good thing you're the only stationery store in town. Here. I need a hundred copies of this printed out on something nice, and I need them by this afternoon. Can you handle that?''

Emma took the paper from him and scanned it. It was an invitation to a surprise party Friday night, to celebrate the opening of Dr. Heather Delaney's new offices at Spring House.

''Oh, my gosh,'' Emma breathed. ''It's true! Heather got her zoning variance!''

''A hundred copies,'' Griffin reiterated patiently. ''This afternoon.''

Emma's eyes glinted. ''So that means the rest of the rumors must be true, too. You and Heather—''

''Are you listening, Emma? A hundred copies by two-thirty. No later than three. I want them to go out in today's mail.''

The bell over the shop's front door tinkled, announcing another arrival.

''Oh, for Pete's sake.'' Emma looked up, growling. ''What now?''

''They're called customers,'' Griffin said. ''I hear some stores actually encourage them.''

But this wasn't just any customer. This was Mary Brady. Griffin watched her approach with resignation, the way he might watch an incoming storm.

Completely absorbed in some sheet of paper she held, Mary was striding purposefully toward the custom-order counter, where Griffin and Emma were huddled. She didn't look up, and consequently she was almost on top of them before she realized that Emma wasn't alone.

"Emma, can you do these up for me ASAP? They're the announcements of Heather's new offices, and we need them—"

Her reaction to the sight of Griffin was so dramatic it was almost comical. "You?" She recoiled, almost dropping the paper. "You? Here?"

Griffin sighed, realizing how it must look, the two of them tucked away behind the counter. Especially to Mary, who was always ready to believe the worst of him.

"Yes, me. Here." He pushed aside a sample book of wedding announcements and took Mary's hand in his. "But, please, you must promise not to tell anyone. You see, Harry has this terribly big gun."

Mary snatched her hand away. "God, Cahill, every time I think you couldn't go any lower—"

Emma was looking confused. "What on earth is the matter with you, Mary?" She glanced from Griffin to Mary, then back to Griffin. "Oh." She frowned. "Oh, good grief, I'd almost forgotten. Has everyone heard about it?"

Griffin shrugged. "Firefly Glen. Home of the high-speed grapevine."

Mary was sharply folding up the paper she'd brought in. "I'll just come back another time, Emma," she said stiffly. She turned around to exit the store, her shoulders rigid and squared, the picture of silent disapproval.

Watching her, Emma chewed on her bottom lip, tapped her fingernails on the wood counter rapidly and finally hopped down with a sigh.

"Darn it, Mary," she called out. "Wait."

Mary turned around slowly. "Really. I'd rather come back later."

"Yeah, well, I've got something to tell you, and I want to tell you now."

"You don't have to do this, Em," Griffin said quietly.

"Yes, I do," she said. She went over to Mary and put out her hands. "Mary, listen to me. You've probably heard that Griffin and I were sneaking around, having this hot, illicit thing, and Harry caught us together. Is that about right?"

Mary flicked a hard glance at Griffin. "That's the edited version," she said tightly.

"And now you think he's some kind of coldhearted, black-hearted bastard who sneaks around with married women, right?"

Mary lifted her eyebrows. "That's the edited version."

"Okay. But here's what really happened." Emma took a deep breath. "Harry and I were having some problems. I didn't know what to do, so I asked Griffin to help me make Harry jealous. He didn't want to, but I pretty much forced him into it. We staged a kiss, Harry saw it, and it worked. Now Harry and I are back together, and everything's fine. That's the whole stupid, humiliating story.''

Turning to Griffin, she smiled weakly, running her fingers through her short, black hair. ''I'm sorry, Griff,'' she said humbly. ''I don't know why you didn't just tell me to go straight to hell.''

Griffin smiled back. ''Because you were already there, sweetheart. Personally, I don't get it, but apparently for you life without that goofy husband of yours *is* hell.''

Emma's eyes were suspiciously bright, but bravely she turned and faced Mary again. ''I asked Griffin to keep it a secret because I was embarrassed, but now I see how selfish that was. He shouldn't have to look like a cad just because I don't want to look like a fool.''

While Emma was explaining, Griffin could see Mary's indignation fading. The puffed-up disapproval seeped out of her like air from a leaky balloon.

''Well,'' she said uncomfortably. ''Well, I don't know. I honestly don't know what to say.''

''Don't say anything,'' Griffin suggested, suddenly afraid that they were rapidly approaching a tearful denouement. Standing knee-deep in wedding announcements with a couple of weeping women was not his idea of the perfect afternoon. ''Don't let the sentimentality of the moment carry you away. I'm still Prince Dudley Do-nothing, remember? This wasn't my only sin.''

''It was your worst, though,'' Mary said grudgingly. ''I mean, your worst lately.''

Griffin cocked his head. ''Mary,'' he remonstrated.

''Tell the truth, now. What about Heather and the Stewberts?''

Mary glowered. She made an irritated sound with her tongue against her teeth. ''Okay, fine, you're absolutely right. I admit it. When I saw Heather in your arms yesterday, I thought I was going to have to—''

''What?'' Emma grabbed Mary's arm. ''Oh, my gosh! Come behind the counter. You have to tell me everything!''

Dear God. Griffin extricated himself neatly from the counter area and headed for the door. ''I'm afraid,'' he said politely, ''that this is where I came in.''

''Griff, wait—'' Emma was grinning. ''Don't you want to hear what Mary has to say about the rumors?''

''Emma, my love,'' Griffin said, opening the door. ''I'd rather have your darling Harry's gigantic gun pointed straight at my cold, black heart.''

CHAPTER ELEVEN

HUMMING TO HERSELF, Heather slathered water all over the back of the eight-foot strip of prepasted wallpaper and then climbed on the ladder to press it in place. It went on perfectly, as if it were eager to cooperate.

As she smoothed the air bubbles out, she could just barely hear the deep, bonging tone of the grandfather clock out in the hall. Just one note? Was it already one in the morning? Good thing she was almost finished.

She climbed down and was preparing to wet another wallpaper strip when Griffin stuck his head through the doorway.

"I thought I heard noises. It's late, you know, especially for a doctor who has to wake up at five in the morning. Don't pregnant women get nervous when their obstetricians fall asleep in the middle of a delivery?"

He was right, of course. She ought to leave this for the workmen to finish when they came in the morning. She needed to get some sleep.

But the truth was, she had too much pent-up energy, and she had to do *something* with it. Wallpapering the last examination room in her beautiful new office was as good as anything else.

Besides, she enjoyed the work. She loved creating beauty and order in this wonderful place. Now that she knew Spring House was truly hers, that she would never have to sell it in order to pay rent on some concrete block office she hated...

She smiled. "I just want to finish this wall. Then I'm going straight to bed, honestly."

He surveyed the half-papered room. She wondered if he liked her choice in wallpaper—a soft green abstract swirl that she had hoped was both attractive and calming. But she didn't want to ask. His taste was so sophisticated, so masculine. He probably thought it was too frilly.

"Tell you what," he said. "The Stewberts are sound asleep. How about if, until they wake up, I pitch in down here?"

"There's no need," she insisted. "Really. I'll be fine."

"But I've been wanting to show you the orchard pictures. I was hoping you'd tell me which ones you think Granville would like."

She hesitated. Griffin was in his official sleeping uniform—though as far as she could tell he never slept more than a couple of hours at a time. He wore a loose pair of navy sweatpants, a butter-yellow T-shirt and not much else. And still he looked disgustingly elegant. Must be that long, low waist, and those broad shoulders. Made everything look like a tuxedo.

Heather thought of her own glue-spattered cutoffs and sticky sweatshirt and grimaced.

He came in, his bare feet slapping softly on the hardwood floor. He set a stack of photographs, all color eight-by-tens, on the examination table.

"Here. You look at these, and I'll put the next strip up for you."

Reluctantly she put down the brush. Probably he didn't need her approval of his photographs any more than she needed his approval of her wallpaper. Still, it was nice of him to ask.

"Okay." Picking up the pictures, she hoisted herself onto the table and began to study them.

The first two were innocent enough. Griffin had found an interesting perspective that hinted at an endless angled row of apple trees, blooming ever smaller, into eternity. The next was a close-up, just the intricate patterns and textures of brown branch and white blossom.

But the third one stopped her. It was a picture of Heather herself, sitting on the picnic blanket, leaning back on her elbows. Her face was lifted, open to the sun, her breasts pressing against her flimsy dress.

Heather tightened, barely holding back a gasp of displeasure. Had her dress really been that revealing? Had she ever posed in such a flagrant display of sensuality?

This wasn't one of Griffin's "spring" pictures—unless spring was merely the symbol for fertility. The sun was ripe, the trees were ripe, the woman was ripe. Even the babies that sprawled against her were as fleshy as sweet peaches that had become too heavy for the branch and rolled to the ground.

She supposed it was a good picture. Sensual, creative, well composed. And very flattering of her, in its way. But even so...

Looking at this woman, who was Heather and yet was not Heather, made her feel strangely edgy. And a little angry with Griffin, who seemed to be implying that he knew things about her, things she didn't even know about herself.

"I didn't realize you were taking pictures of me," she said. She tried to laugh casually. "At least I guess it's of me. This must be a kind of trick photography. I hardly recognize myself."

He paused, the brush in his hand. "It's no trick. It's what they call a candid shot. Candid, as in un-posed. Without pretense." He raised one eyebrow. "Or defense."

Looking back at the picture, she realized that he was absolutely right. What made her uncomfortable about this photograph was how utterly defenseless she looked.

Without question, this woman was prettier, softer, more accessible than Heather. But she was also more vulnerable. Unarmed and unaware, the woman in the photograph was weak.

The perfect prey.

She glanced at Griffin, who was standing on the ladder now, smoothing the strip of wallpaper into place. His back was to her, his long, powerful body outlined by the well-worn cotton. His hands, moving across the green swirls, were deft and sure. He was strong, supple and focused.

The perfect predator.

And the most alarming thing about it was that, somehow, looking at him, at the beautiful, coherent strength of him, made her feel, just for a moment, that perhaps things *should* be this way.

It made her believe that perhaps power *should* meet surrender. Thrust should meet yield. Take should meet give.

No! Her anxiety level rose like mercury in the sun. That was *not* what she believed. Oh, maybe she had made a terrible mistake, getting this close to him again. She had to get him out of this room—and, as soon as possible, out of this house—before she began thinking like a victim.

His victim. And just one of many.

She put the pictures down carefully and stood, though her legs felt strangely uncertain, as if she had caught some weakness, like a flu, from the woman in the orchard.

She moved toward the last precut strip of wallpaper. "I think I'll get started on this one," she said brightly, as he climbed down from the ladder. "That way we'll be finished sooner."

"Okay," he agreed, clearly unaware of the turmoil inside her. "I'll be working on the bottom, so if you start at the top, we shouldn't get tangled up."

But suddenly she was all thumbs, which was absurd. She was a doctor—her hands were unusually steady, trained to be skillful and quick. She'd already hung a dozen strips of this same paper without a single mistake.

This piece, however, was different. It had been cut wrong, for starters. Either that, or the ceiling was suddenly off plumb. Pleats, wrinkles, air bubbles and lumps rose up everywhere. She growled under her breath. What an unholy mess!

Determined to start fresh, she peeled it off, but the darn thing began to fold over her, over itself, like a crazy, limp accordion.

She reached over her head, and her hands met a wet mess of glue.

"Damn it," she mumbled, trying to back away without losing her toehold on the rung of the ladder. The paper was sticking to her hair now, and, no matter how she twisted it, the glue side was always against her skin.

Finally she lost her cool. Indifferent to whether she preserved the wallpaper, she began to wad up every inch she could reach. "Get—off—me, you diabolical—"

Maybe she couldn't see a thing, but she could hear just fine. Griffin was clearly chuckling. She turned, ready to blister him, but she almost lost her balance. And then, thank heaven, she felt his solid steadiness just below her on the ladder.

"Hang on a minute," he said, repressed mirth altering his words. "Just hold still, and I'll get it off."

She stood there, fuming, while he slowly worked her

free. He gradually unearthed her head, peeling her hair loose strand by sticky strand.

And, as she emerged, she met the amusement brimming in his blue eyes. "It's not funny," she said.

"Sure it is," he retorted, grinning. "Why, come to think of it, it's almost as funny as the sight of a grown man getting sprinkled by a naked baby."

She scowled, recognizing the echo. Okay, so she'd been insensitive that day. She should have known he'd pay her back with interest.

"Seriously, are you all right?" he asked.

"No." She really, really hated looking like such a fool. "The damn thing tried to eat me."

"It's okay." He smiled. "It's nothing that can't be fixed."

He led her to the sink, which, thank goodness, was already fully operational. He turned on the warm water and put her hands under it, scrubbing softly with his own to dissolve the glue. Then he urged her forward and splashed the water along her forearms.

"Thanks." She cast him a half-grudging look from beneath her lashes. "I could do this myself, you know," she said, but not very forcefully, so she wasn't surprised when he didn't let go.

"I've got it," he said cheerfully. "You just relax."

He must be kidding. She couldn't remember when she had felt this agitated and uptight. Maybe she was overreacting, but she suddenly realized that, for her, just standing this close to him was dangerous.

They had almost made it safely through their tricky

three weeks together. She mustn't let herself start thinking stupid thoughts now.

He massaged between her fingers, working off the glue. It was efficient, and effective. But it felt oddly sensual.

She wondered if he had meant it to. She slanted another glance at him, but he looked perfectly businesslike. She must be imagining things.

"Okay. Now the rest of you." Griffin led her to the examination table. Circling her waist with his hands, he lifted her up onto it. "You wait there," he said, turning back to the sink. "And don't touch anything."

As she sat there, on this table made for patients, she felt strange, as if her body were trying to contain two overwhelming and contradictory urges. One was the frantic impulse to run—just bolt, without warning, without explanation, without apology.

But the other was the absurd, self-destructive desire to have Griffin go on touching her.

He found several clean white washcloths beneath the sink. When he had them nice and damp, he lay them on the padded mattress beside her.

Her legs dangled over the side of the table, so he parted them slightly, making room for him to come in very close. Her knees settled softly against his hips. Self-conscious, she tightened her muscles, holding her thighs a fraction of an inch farther apart.

He didn't seem to notice one way or the other. But she did. With his sexy body tucked between her legs like this, she could hardly think straight.

"Face first," he said, chuckling as he tilted her chin, letting the brilliant overhead light shine on the rapidly hardening streaks of glue. "Although, I don't know. You're kind of cute when you're covered in paste. Takes me back to our kindergarten days."

"I didn't even know you in kindergarten," she said, glad of anything to take her mind off the way his hard, lean hips shifted against her knees whenever he moved. "I only had eyes for James Loughlin. Now he was a *real* man. He actually ate the paste. *And* he had a Spiderman lunchbox."

Griffin grinned, taking one corner of the towel and addressing her eyebrow, which had glued itself to her hair. "The girls really go for that, do they?"

"You bet. It's the kindergarten equivalent of a Ferrari."

He chuckled, but he didn't say anything further, seemingly intent on his work, though surely she couldn't have absorbed that much of the paste. But she didn't complain. The cloth was warm, like the pampered, scented towels at an expensive spa, and he draped it over his hand like a glove.

He worked slowly, systematically, beginning at the brow. Then her nose and cheeks and chin. He took the most time with her mouth. He traced the outline of her lips first, then smoothed across the surface. Then, with a smile, he lightly pinched a fleck of paste from the soft, dipping curve of her upper lip.

Finally, with his forefinger, which was carefully

shrouded in warm, wet cotton, he reached back and stroked the sensitive skin behind her ear.

''Now the rest of you.'' He traded for a fresh towel and, spreading it wide open, moved it up and down her throat, rubbing lightly. He found a spot of flaky paste on her collarbone. He worked it free, then slid the edge of the towel lower, just slightly below the neckline of her sweatshirt, to get the rest.

She felt a strange tingling in her midsection, as if this were a new and slightly kinky kind of foreplay. Idiotically, she began to obsess about the towel, about the wet warmth that left cool shimmers in its wake, about the slightly scratchy fibers that awakened each nerve ending separately.

And then she began to think about how all this would feel without the towel. He still hadn't touched her with his bare hand, and she realized that every inch of her body strained for the moment when he would.

Suddenly, out of nowhere, she was shivering. Goose bumps spread across her skin like dominoes falling. She crossed her arms, hugging herself.

He stopped immediately. ''Are you cold?''

She shook her head. ''Not really,'' she said. But she kept her arms wrapped protectively, clutching her elbows so tightly it almost hurt.

''What is it?'' His voice was deep. ''Heather? I didn't hurt you, did I?''

She shook her head, not trusting herself to speak. This was ridiculous. But that was the power he had over her. The power to make her weak. To make her ridiculous. She shut her eyes, and was horrified to feel a damp warmth seeping from the corners.

With a low, concerned murmur, he caught her tear in the towel. Touching her chin, he tilted her face toward his. "Sweetheart, what's the matter?"

She looked at him helplessly. "I don't know," she said. "It's just all so—" She blinked, forcing herself not to cry, which would be unbearably pathetic. She never cried. "I think I'm just tired. And a little bit confused."

He gently touched the towel to her other eye, absorbing the tiny drop of wetness. "About what?"

"About everything. About you. I don't understand why you are being so…so nice."

He smiled. "Well, thanks a lot."

"You know what I mean. You just keep doing things that are—"

He waited.

She didn't know exactly how to go on. She couldn't just say, *Without even trying to, you're turning me to jelly. You're seducing me, and you don't even know it. You don't even care.*

But she had to say something. "You've done too much. The vote yesterday was all your doing, no matter what you say, and—"

"I told you I'd try to help with that. After all, you're doing me a huge favor with the Stewberts, aren't you?"

"Yes." She tried to clear her mind, but it was difficult. He was still stroking her cheek softly with the warm towel, and it was painfully distracting. ‘‘And that should settle it, it should make us even. But you keep doing things, little things, but they add up. Like the night you helped with the class, or the times you’ve let me sleep through part of my shift. Or that picture, in the orchard. Or tonight, with the wallpaper…’’

She swallowed hard. This was the important part, the only really honest part. ‘‘And now, the way you’re touching me—’’

She paused, expecting him to jump in, protesting, explaining, wielding his glib eloquence to dazzle or deflect.

But he didn’t. He just watched her, his eyes dark and intent.

‘‘What about the way I’m touching you?’’

‘‘I don’t know.’’ She took a deep breath. ‘‘I guess I’m not sure what you want, what you expect from me. I’m…I’m feeling things, things I never wanted to feel again. I don’t even know whether you’re doing this deliberately, or if I’m just trapped in some ten-year-old…’’

She felt her voice rising, and she reined it back down. ‘‘I guess I just don’t know what your agenda is.’’

‘‘I don’t have any agenda.’’ He was half smiling, but his eyes, for once, looked somber. ‘‘Hasn’t it occurred to you that maybe I’m trapped, too? That maybe we’re both caught up in something we can’t control?’’

‘‘No,’’ she said flatly. ‘‘Not you. I’ve never seen you lose control, never in your whole life.’’

"Of course you have. You just never understood what you were seeing." He dropped the towel on the table beside her, and he put his hands, his hard, bare hands, on her shoulders.

"I lose control every time I see you, Heather. It's been that way since I was seventeen. It's that way now. I'm very much afraid it will be that way forever."

She looked at him, at that dark, determined look she knew so well, and for a moment her vision blurred again, splintering the bright light into a field of broken crystal.

Sex. He was talking about sex.

For him, the magic of their relationship had always been entirely physical, hadn't it? He had never understood how much more than that it had been to her. He'd never realized that, for her, his laughter fired up the yellow torch of the sun. His lips lit the silver candle of the moon. His smile tamed demons, summoned angels, made every day worth living.

He would have laughed at such maudlin sentimentality. For him, "love" was easy, fun and simple—and as multiorgasmic as possible. It was wet, possessive kisses, hard, hot passion, shivering sweat and sweet, satisfied exhaustion.

It was, in short, just good sex. And lots of it.

And yet, maybe her indignation here wasn't quite honest. She had to admit that she had always understood that part, too. She had often felt that pulsing, liquid heat rising up, like the subtle pump of an interior, invisible volcano, just because Griffin Cahill had entered a room.

She felt it now, in fact.

And he knew it.

"But you asked for answers, Heather, and you deserve them." His blue eyes scoured her face with a kind of hunger that was both a ghost from the past and a devil from her dreams. "It's really very simple. You asked what I expect from you. I expect nothing. You asked what I *want.* I want everything."

"Everything?" she echoed helplessly. Everything... But that was too much. That would leave her, when he left, with nothing.

"Everything." He hooked his hands beneath her knees and dragged her slowly toward him. "I want you to wrap your legs around me and never let go. I want to kiss you until neither one of us can breathe."

He brought their bodies so close together that she had to reach back, planting the heels of her hands on the soft table, to balance herself. The heat of him was a piercing ache between her legs.

"I want to look at you." He bunched the fabric of her sweatshirt in his hands and lifted it almost to her throat, baring her breasts to the light, which was terribly bright, bright enough for a doctor to work by.

She inhaled sharply. He had always loved her breasts. And she had loved the way he loved them.

"I want to touch you." He slid one hand between their bodies, setting off a sparkle of colored lights sizzling through her veins.

"And taste you." He lowered his head, and grazed his closed lips over the tingling tips of her breasts. She moaned lightly, wishing he would take her into his mouth. That hot, hungry mouth. She would remember his mouth, she thought, when she'd forgotten everything else in the world.

"And I want to make you call out my name, the way you used to do."

His breath was hot against her skin. "Do you remember that, sweetheart? Do you remember how my name was always the last thing you said? The last thing you whispered? Right before you began to scream..."

She tightened her legs around him, her body answering with a truth more compelling than words. She remembered everything.

"Do you want that, too?" He touched his tongue to her, and she twisted helplessly. The world was fading, narrowing to two people, one hunger. "Tell me, Heather. Tell me that you want it, too."

"I want it," she said hoarsely, as if she'd already screamed his name till her throat was raw. "I want you. I—"

But the world had not really gone away. It roared back at that moment, like an enemy that had retreated briefly, only to regroup and attack again.

Right under his hand, on the waistband of her shorts, her pager suddenly went off. The buzzing noise, so close it felt as personal as a slap, was horrible. Loud, electronic, malevolent.

He yanked the pager free with a disbelieving curse.

He stared at it for a long, numb, silent moment. And then he looked at her.

"I don't suppose there's any chance you won't answer it," he said.

She blinked, horrified to realize that, for one heedless moment, she had considered exactly that. Her feet had been wrapped around the small of his back, and she let them fall gracelessly away. She scooted back from him, farther onto the table.

She had to think. She had to breathe a little. Clear her head.

"It must be a patient," she said thickly, pulling her shirt down to cover her breasts. "Only my service knows the number."

Stepping back politely, he handed the pager to her. She looked at the digital display. Of course, it was her service. Only in a carefully scripted happily-ever-after fairy tale would it have been an error, a carelessly dialed wrong number, a glitch in the tiny little wiring.

She forced her weakened legs to carry her across the room. She picked up the telephone, called her service and listened, saying little.

It was Anna Mizell. She was in labor. Probably false labor, but she was at the hospital, in a panic, blood pressure skyrocketing, begging for Heather to come.

Heather hung up the telephone. As her mind cleared, she told herself this might be a blessing in disguise. She needed time to think.

She was under no illusions about what would have happened next. She would have become Griffin's lover.

Again. And this time he wouldn't even have had to bother with the whole messy pretense of an engagement. He could have departed next week with a thoroughly satisfied libido, and a conveniently clear conscience, as well.

She couldn't deny she wanted him. Who wouldn't want him? He was six-feet-three-inches of raw sexual magnetism and breathtaking expertise. But did she want him that much? Enough to break her heart for him all over again?

"I have to go," she said with a fairly good approximation of professionalism and control. "I have to change. I have a patient in labor."

She had expected him to be furious. But though his face was etched with tension, to her surprise he merely nodded.

"I know," he said levelly. "It's all right."

She hesitated, but what else was there to say? She nodded, too. And then she took a deep breath, smoothed the wrinkles from her shirt and moved toward the door.

In spite of herself, when she reached him, she stopped.

"I'm sorry," she said. "But, you know, maybe this is for the best. Things were getting a little out of control and this will give us time to—"

"Don't kid yourself, Heather," he interrupted gruffly. He was holding himself stiffly, as if his body hurt when he moved. "If ten years of waiting haven't put out this fire, the next ten hours aren't going to do it.''

''Yes, but, if we think it over, we—''

With a low growl, he pulled her into his arms and shut her up with a very hard, very hot kiss.

''Accept it, sweetheart. This isn't over. It's just postponed.''

CHAPTER TWELVE

ALL RIGHT, GRIFFIN CAHILL, listen up. If you think I'm suddenly going to start believing you're Mr. Nice Guy, just because you're making a big deal over Heather's new offices, think again. Just because you're going to a lot of trouble, and expense, and planning this swell party just to make her happy, well…

Mary stopped, abruptly aware that this *Listen Up* letter, which she'd been composing in her head, wasn't going at all the way she'd intended it to. Annoyed, she fiddled with the lacy edges of a beautiful tablecloth, just one of many available for rental at Temporarily Yours, Firefly Glen's most exclusive party shop.

She tried to talk herself back into her customary disdain. But it wasn't working. The truth was, Griffin *had* begun to redeem himself in her eyes.

A little.

He really was going all out with this surprise party. He had asked Mary and Troy to come here, to Temporarily Yours, to arrange for all the elegant necessities, like china and silverware, tables and chairs, linens and lighting.

And he wasn't just dodging the hard work, either. Griffin himself was over at the florist right now, Stewberts in tow, coordinating about a zillion dollars worth of flowers.

"Hey, what do you think about this?" Troy was standing next to a huge fountain, in which a curvaceous naked woman rode a dolphin that ejected a continuous spray of champagne out of its grinning mouth. "Griffin said get whatever we wanted, spare no expense."

She shook her head, shuddering. "I also heard him tell you nothing tacky."

Troy leaned his head against the statue's shoulder and gave Mary a piteous look. "Hey, that's not nice. I had one of these at my wedding."

"I guess that explains why you're divorced."

Mary moved toward the chafing dishes. If all one hundred people—and their dates—accepted Griffin's invitation, which they probably would, the caterer was going to need a lot of help.

Troy gave the statue's bottom a friendly goodbye pat and strolled over to the alcove where architectural features were displayed.

"So do you think we ought to get some arches, or maybe some columns? Now don't tell me they're tacky, too, because I've seen them at some pretty swanky parties. They fill 'em up with fake roses and little white lights and stuff. They look great."

Mary eyed the tall, plaster-of-Paris columns, the white latticework arches. "Still too kitsch," she decided. "You've seen Spring House. It's so ornate, with all that Victorian stuff going on everywhere. It really doesn't need a lot of extra froufrou, you know?"

Troy pouted. "Fine. I'll just go sit in the corner and let you decide."

Mary smiled. "Fine."

Troy wasn't the type to sulk for long, though. In less than five minutes, he was up again, joining Mary at the champagne glasses. "So, Mary, have you ever been to Nepal?"

She laughed. "I haven't ever been anywhere." She held up two glasses, a classic and a continental. "Which one do you like?"

He frowned at them. "The fat one." When she looked surprised, he rolled his eyes. "I mean the skinny one. Who cares? After a couple of drinks, they all look exactly the same anyhow, right? Kind of like women."

She made a rude sound and kept walking. Maybe the frosted glasses would be nice...

"Well, as I was saying. Nepal is really exciting," Troy went on as if she'd never interrupted. "Even more exciting than a Friday night surprise party in Firefly Glen, if you can believe such a thing."

She ignored him. But he kept hovering at her elbow, fidgeting in a way that seemed almost nervous. She began to wonder whether this conversation might actually have a point.

"Yeah, and...?" she prompted him.

"And." He paused. "And, well, I'm probably going to have to miss this party, because my plane for Nepal leaves Friday afternoon." He sounded a little embarrassed. "I just wanted to tell you that ahead of time.

You know, so you wouldn't rent an extra champagne glass on my account.''

Mary was quite pleased with the way she kept her cool. She glanced at him casually. ''Why? All the Saturday planes to Nepal were full?''

''No, nothing that easy to fix. There are time elements involved. People. Events. Deadlines. Stuff like that. I don't really have any choice.''

''Oh.''

She picked up one glass after another—etched ones, plastic ones, pink ones, black ''Over the Hill'' ones. She made absolutely certain that none of her irrational disappointment showed on her face.

Because what right did she have to be disappointed, anyhow? Troy Madison was just another rich guy blowing through their quaint little town. He had never even hinted that he might stay.

And besides, what difference did it make to her when he left? A couple of weeks ago, she hadn't known he existed. In a month or two, she wouldn't even remember his name.

Except that, darn it, she liked him. Not in that fluttery, romancy way. But as a friend. He was smart, and he was easy to be with, lighthearted and funny.

Most of all she respected him as a writer. She liked reading his work and letting him read hers. She liked talking to him about the craft, about the business. It had been very exciting for a little Firefly Glen wannabe. He knew so much, and she knew almost nothing.

But it was over, and that was that.

She picked up a deceptively simple crystal continental champagne glass, one of the most elegant and expensive styles in the store.

"This one, I think," she said. "It's pretty, and—even better—it'll put a serious dent in Griffin's budget."

She had a sudden horrible thought. She turned to Troy. "Wait just a minute. Is Griffin going with you?"

She was sizzling mad at the very thought of it. If Griffin Cahill arranged this party, and then didn't show up for it... If he jetted to Pakistan—or India or Timbuktu or wherever the heck Nepal was—she'd have to hunt him down like a dog and beat him to death with his own expensive camera.

"I've been trying to talk him into it," Troy said with surprising candor. He must have missed the bloodred fire in her eyes. "But so far I'm not having much luck. He takes this uncle business pretty seriously."

"Damn good thing," she muttered.

Troy wrinkled his brow. "Why? I thought the more miles there were between you and Griffin the happier you were."

"It's complicated," she said. And it was. She wasn't even sure herself why she wanted Griffin to stay. A blind Martian could tell what was happening between Griffin and Heather these days. Whenever they were in the same room together, the sexual tension was so thick the rest of the people could hardly breathe.

All that edgy, uptight, panting, blushing, coy little touches. It made Mary want to yak. But she knew what it meant. It meant Heather was going to let Playboy Cahill break her heart all over again.

So did it really matter so much whether he broke it before Friday night, or after?

Yeah, actually, it did. She didn't know why, but it did.

She plopped the champagne flute on the counter so hard the crystal rang through the large showroom like a church bell. "Okay, that's glasses, china, linens and tables. All that's left is to decide on the chairs."

She had just about picked one out—the most expensive, of course—when Griffin came through the double doors of the store, rolling the tandem stroller in front of him.

The Stewberts seemed to be in high spirits. But the one on the left had a couple of slobbery yellow daisy petals stuck to his lips, as if he'd just eaten a canary.

Mary opened her mouth.

"Don't even ask," Griffin said wearily. "Suffice it to say that my bill at the florist will be slightly higher than anticipated."

Mary chuckled. *Way to go, Stewbert,* she thought, giving him a mental high five. Between them, they were going to make Griffin pay big time for the chance to impress their dear, deluded Heather, weren't they?

"So what flowers did you decide on?" Mary knelt down and extricated the petals from the baby's mouth. "Daisies?"

"No, daisies were Stewbert's choice. But I vetoed that. I picked something the florist called the Splendor of Spring, which, though its name sounds a little hysterical, is actually quite pretty. It's mostly violets and lily of the valley."

"Lily of the valley?" Mary stood up slowly. She gave Griffin a suspicious look. Had the son of a gun just gotten lucky? Or did he really remember little details like that? "Heather loves lily of the valley. It's her favorite flower."

Griffin smiled. "Yes," he said. "I know."

"Well." Mary squinted at him. "That should make her very happy."

"Yes," he agreed. "It should."

"Which is what she deserves," she added pointedly.

Griffin nodded.

"Yes," he said, in a tone Mary decided to interpret as a promise. "It is."

IT WAS THE PERFECT DAY to interview a potential partner. Heather had never felt more certain that she needed one.

Actually, the *perfect* day would have been yesterday. Then she would have had someone already on staff, prepared to take over for her this morning.

And then maybe she could get some sleep.

Heather smothered her tenth yawn of the morning and tried to focus on the handsome, twenty-nine-year-old doctor who sat across the desk from her, explaining why he wanted to leave New York City and move to Firefly Glen.

Poor guy. He kept having to repeat himself. He must think she was very stupid—or very hung over.

Her eyes were red-rimmed and scratchy, her whole body slowed down by fatigue. She'd been up all night with Anna Mizell, making sure it was truly a false alarm. She had finally released her at 8:00 a.m.

But that meant Heather hadn't slept all night.

And she wasn't going to sleep today, either. Apparently sleep was a luxury single practitioners couldn't afford.

That's where...what was his name? She sneaked a peek at his flawless résumé. *Adam Reading.* That's where Adam Reading came in. Would he think it was odd if she hired him on the spot, told him his first patient was in Room One, and then curled up and took a nap?

Oh, well. It was a lovely fantasy.

"I've talked to your references," she said, looking down at her notes. "They were highly complimentary. Everything looks great on paper. But a partnership..."

She decided to be candid. She was too tired to bother sugarcoating things right now. "Sharing a practice is a very intimate relationship, a lot like a marriage. Frankly, I'm still not sure I'm ready to take anyone on, and if I did..."

He smiled. He had a very warm smile. And he looked like a very young Gregory Peck. The patients must love his bedside manner.

"If you did," he said, "you'd want to be sure it was the right partner. You'd want to be sure we saw eye to eye on all medical issues—and a lot of personal issues, too."

She nodded, glad that he didn't seem to be offended that his sterling credentials and Ivy League education didn't necessarily guarantee anything. Good doctoring wasn't done on paper. It was done on people.

"I'd also want to be sure that you were approaching this as a long-term commitment. Small towns aren't always as delightful as people think. And we're slow to integrate strangers. If you didn't stay, I'd have a difficult time persuading my patients to accept another new doctor anytime soon."

"I can imagine," he said, clearly unfazed. "But I love small towns. I was born and raised in one just a hundred miles from here. I wish they could use another ob-gyn, but they can't. My dad doesn't plan to retire for at least thirty more years."

So his father was a small-town doctor, too. Heather felt herself warming even more to this slightly old-fashioned young man. Though he was only a few years younger than she was, he seemed so serious and innocent. It was actually very appealing.

He leaned forward, his long, strong-boned face growing even more serious. "I am looking for a permanent position. I'm finished with big-city medicine. My wife and I have done a lot of soul-searching and a lot of research. Firefly Glen is the perfect place for us."

She raised her eyebrows. "Your wife?" She didn't know if this was good news or not. It would depend on the woman. Firefly Glen wasn't crazy about glitzy women. And vice versa. "Does she like small towns, too?"

"She doesn't know very much about them," he admitted. "She was born in New York. Sally was a dancer. With the City Ballet."

Uh-oh. Heather didn't want to stereotype anyone, but a ballet dancer? She knew from tough personal experience that if people yearned for excitement, travel, adventure, crowds, culture...then Firefly Glen couldn't hold them for long.

"*Was* a dancer," he repeated, stressing the past tense. "She quit five years ago. She gives dance lessons now. And...well, we found out a few months ago that we're going to have a baby. In the fall." He finally smiled again. "That's what finally decided us. It's our dream to start our family here, in a place like Firefly Glen."

Heather hesitated. She had planned to cut the interview short, considering how exhausted she was. She had expected to thank Adam Reading, then send him on his way, with promises of a follow-up call sometime soon.

She wasn't an impulse kind of person. She liked to think things through, make careful decisions after weighing all the elements. But everything was a little weird today. And suddenly her instincts about this honest, gentle man were so strong she couldn't imagine dismissing him according to plan.

"Tell you what," she said impetuously. "Why don't you spend the day with me, here at the office?"

She stood, smiling invitingly. The waiting room was full. What better way to see if she liked him? What better way to see if he'd fit in—in her office, in her town, in her life? "Meet some of the patients, get a feel for what you'd be doing. Then come to my house tonight and have dinner. We've got a lot to talk about."

"I'd be honored." Adam was obviously surprised, and deeply pleased.

Heather was pleased, too. It all made perfect sense. He was by far the best candidate. She had liked him on sight. Getting to know him better right away would expedite the decision and *maybe* prevent a mass walk-out by her staff.

And the fact that Adam's presence at dinner tonight would keep Heather and Griffin from picking up where they'd left off...

Well, that was just a lucky coincidence.

DINNER, WHICH THE THREE OF THEM ate by candlelight on the side porch, where the wisteria smelled the sweetest, was a huge success.

By the time they reached the peach cobbler, Griffin and Adam Reading were the best of buddies. They liked the same plays, vacationed at the same resorts, read the same books. Griffin had even, it turned out, seen Adam's wife dance once, a few years back. He must have said all the right things, because Adam's smile was so profoundly grateful it moved Heather almost to tears.

Of course, that wasn't hard, given how exhausted

and surreal she felt by then. She'd been up and working for thirty-seven hours straight.

Amazingly, the men didn't seem tired at all. The night was clear and starry, the spring breezes mild enough to encourage them to linger. So they poured another glass of wine and settled into a comfortable discussion of teething.

Heather had to smile. Griffin Cahill talking about teething. It was like seeing the sun set in the east.

Declining a refill—she'd already had two glasses—she stretched out on the porch swing just a couple of feet away, listening but too sleepy to participate much. She shouldn't have had the wine, not on top of two weeks of sleep deprivation. She felt as limp as overcooked spaghetti.

She used to be able to weather all-nighters better than this, she mused dreamily. But then, she hadn't ever had so many jobs before—doctor, civic militant, renovator of historic houses, mother to twin babies.

Not that she really was a mother, but...she felt like one. At least for the moment. A temporary, very tired, mommy. She rested her head against the arm of the swing, thinking, somewhat irrelevantly, how extraordinarily warm babies were. How their smiles lit up your heart.

Yes, they were exhausting. But having that sweetness in your life was probably worth it, she thought, closing her eyes just for a moment. It was probably worth whatever it cost.

She woke to the sound of rain, and the cool, earthy

scent of wet grass. Confused, but too drowsy to care much, she burrowed a little further under her blanket.

But then a cold drop of water hit her cheek. At the same time, she felt a warm hand on her arm.

"Heather," Griffin's voice was saying. "Wake up. It's time to go to bed."

She sat up, vaguely anxious. Time to go to bed? What time was it? Even more disturbing, her bed shifted weirdly under her when she moved. But it wasn't her bed. It was the porch swing.

She pushed her hair back from her face and looked up at Griffin groggily. "Did I fall asleep out here?" She frowned. "What time is it?"

"It's about three," he said, taking the quilted blanket and placing it around her shoulders. "Come on in. It's storming."

"Three?" Vague anxiety gave way to real alarm. She felt in her pocket for her pager. Oh, God—all that wine! She almost never drank. She was always on call. So she had no head for it.

Oh, how foolish! What if one of her patients had needed her?

"I've got it," Griffin said, holding out the little black box. "I was afraid you wouldn't hear it, so I took it with me when I went up to feed the Stewberts. It didn't go off."

But she had to check anyhow. She scrolled hastily through the stored numbers. He was right. For once, nobody had called. Not even Anna Mizell.

Still, the fog in her head wouldn't quite go away.

She tried to piece together the evening. She'd brought the new doctor home for dinner, and...

"Oh, no. What about Adam?"

Griffin smiled. "He finally left about midnight, but I practically had to throw him out. He was so fascinated by the Stewberts he could have stayed up there playing with them all night."

"He met the Stewberts?"

"They woke up—you didn't hear that either—and he was so excited. He begged me to let him help. He's trying to learn everything he can about babies." Griffin widened his eyes angelically. "I generously allowed him to learn all about the diaper-changing process."

Groaning, Heather leaned her head back against the swing. "Great. My best prospect for a partner, and I pass out in the middle of dinner, leaving him to the mercy of a total stranger and a couple of bawling infants." She sighed heavily. "He probably thinks I'm a drunk and a lunatic."

Griffin smiled. "He thinks you're a cross between Florence Nightingale and Mother Teresa. He couldn't stop raving on about how great you are with your patients." He tugged on the blanket. "*I'm* the one who thinks you're a lunatic. Any chance we could talk about this inside? I'm getting wet."

"Of course. I'm sorry." She stood, still heavy-headed and slightly groggy.

The blanket fell onto the swing. Griffin gathered it up and once again arranged it around her shoulders.

"Come on, Mother Teresa," he said. "Let's get you to bed before the Stewberts wake up again."

"The Stewberts...oh, no, Griffin—my shift!" She groaned one more time. Was there no end to the ways in which she'd been inept tonight? According to the schedule she had herself concocted, she was in charge of the Stewberts from eight to midnight. "I slept right through it!"

"No problem," he said lightly, holding the blanket under her chin and smiling down at her. "I had Adam to help, remember? The man has done his homework, I'll say that for him. Their baby's not due until October, and he already knows five complete verses of 'Little Bunny Foo-Foo.'"

Heather felt a little wobbly. Now that her anxiety was subsiding and the blanket was warming her up again, she realized she was still very, very sleepy.

"Five verses," she said, trying to keep her eyes open and her head upright. "Wow."

"I know. He'll make a great father. He has an almost godlike patience for 'This Little Piggy.'"

All of a sudden she gave up. She let her head fall forward, coming to rest against his chest. "I hate 'This Little Piggy,'" she confessed to his shirt.

Chuckling, he stroked her hair gently. "Me, too. I say give me peekaboo any day."

"Absolutely," she said seriously, as if they were discussing strategies for world peace. "Peekaboo is much better. It makes the Stewberts laugh."

He tugged on her earlobe gently. "You know, sweetheart, you're going to catch pneumonia if you don't come in out of the rain. Can you walk, or do you want me to carry you up to bed?''

Sweetheart. She loved the sound of his voice saying that word…

Sweetheart? Oh, no. She suddenly realized that the moment she'd been fearing had arrived. They were alone. Together. And she had pretty much fallen into his arms.

''Griffin,'' she said, tilting her head to look up at him. ''I don't think we should— I know you said it wasn't over, but I'm just not ready to—''

He shook his head gently. ''Don't worry, I'm not going to try to seduce you tonight. We've both had too little sleep to do it justice, don't you think?''

''Absolutely,'' she agreed, weak with relief. She let her head fall against his chest again. ''And, I'm afraid, too much wine.''

She could feel his lips curving against her hair. ''Actually, my hopeless innocent, wine is one of the internationally recognized staples of seduction.''

''Well, of course, I know that, but—''

He chuckled softly. ''I said don't worry. I like my women wide-awake. And frankly, your adoring young doctor's rhapsodies are a little too fresh in my mind. *No one* makes a pass at Mother Teresa, sweetheart. Not even me.''

CHAPTER THIRTEEN

"SO WHAT DO YOU THINK, Stewbert?" Griffin angled his cards so the baby, who was crawling around on the floor beside him, could see them. "Should I raise or call?"

Stewbert grabbed for the cards, eager, as always, to sample anything new and different. But Griffin held them out of reach. "No way, pal. This is the first decent hand I've had all night, and I'll be darned if I'm going to let you eat it."

Troy, who was also on the floor, growled as he tried to peel apart a mess of sticky notepaper. "Damn it. Did we decide the green Post-it notes were five or ten?"

Griffin sighed. "Try to concentrate, won't you? The greens are one. The pinks are five. The yellows are ten." He placed a yellow Post-it in the central pot. "It's really very simple."

"It is *not* simple," Troy said, ripping free a pink "chip." He tried to toss it into the pot, but it stuck to his fingers. "It's crazy, that's what it is. Sane people do not play poker on the floor. Sane people do not bet with Post-it notes. Sane people do not show their cards to slobbering infants and ask for their advice."

Griffin yawned. "Get over it, Troy. You don't care where we play. You'd play poker on top of a coffin if you had to. In fact, we did that, didn't we, that time in Louisiana?"

Troy was still trying to shake off the pink Post-it. "Yeah, so? There wasn't anybody in it."

"So, my point is you're not bugged because we're on the floor, or because we've had to hide the real poker chips from the Stewberts. You're bugged because you're losing."

Troy glared at him. "Actually, Einstein, I'm bugged because I can't make you come to Nepal. I'm bugged because I'm going to have to do the story with some other photographer, who won't be half as good. I'm bugged because you're playing nanny to these babies, when you know darn well you could hire somebody else to do it for you."

He leaned against the wall, ignoring the Stewbert who was attempting to unclasp his watch with his one tooth. "I know you, Griff. You could get bored covering the Apocalypse. You're a gather-no-moss, itchy feet, adrenaline-rush kind of guy. You've got to be going absolutely bonkers, stuck in this burg for a whole year. And now this baby-sitting gig…I'm actually starting to worry about you, bro."

Griffin shrugged. In theory, Troy was right. Griffin asked himself every day why he wasn't going crazy. Why had he been more or less content to spend almost three weeks puttering around Spring House, doing odd jobs to expedite the renovation, tending the Stewberts, waiting for Heather to get home from work?

And the pictures he'd been taking... A few nice shots of Spring House, which he intended to give Heather when their Stewbert job was over. Some cute pictures of the babies that would undoubtedly please Jared and Katie. A few chamber of commerce photos for Granville Frome. Hardly Griffin's usual stuff.

"Maybe I needed a break from the road," Griffin said, drawing two new cards. "A hotel room can get pretty boring, too, you know."

And lonely.

"Not *your* hotel room." Troy wiggled his eyebrows like Groucho Marx. "So what's really going on here? You and I have been talking about this Nepal trip for years. Your brother is coming back Monday, right? You'd only have to leave your nephews three lousy days early."

"I promised I'd take care of them, and I'm going to. Just play cards, why don't you?"

Troy apparently hadn't even heard him. "It's Heather, isn't it? You've traded the international Parade of Pulchritude for the chance to play doctor with one ravishing redhead."

Griffin grimaced. "Do all writers talk in cheap alliterations, Troy, or is it just you?"

"All of us—but I'm the best." Troy smiled self-deprecatingly. "And don't try to change the subject. I think I might be onto something with this new theory. I think I've caught the scent."

"Your theory stinks, so that might be what you're smelling." Griffin grinned suddenly and pointed toward Troy's pile of Post-it notes. "Plus, I think you're being robbed."

Troy looked, and then he cursed. Stewbert had sat in Troy's stash of poker "money," and now was crawling away toward the playpen, colorful little pieces of paper stuck all over the bottom of his diaper.

"I give up," Troy said, slamming down his cards. "All I can say is thank God I'm out of here tomorrow. I'm warning you, Griffin. You should come with me, or the next Stewbert running around here just may have your name on it. And that'll be the end of the road for you, my friend."

"Oh, relax," Griffin said irritably. "The Nepal assignment is good, but there will be others. I'll go next time."

"Griffin?" Heather's voice came floating toward them. Griffin looked up and saw that she had opened her bedroom door a crack and was peering out. "Can I talk to you for a minute?"

"Sure."

"Thanks." She shut the door.

Troy gazed knowingly at Griffin, nodding slowly in an extremely annoying I-told-you-so way. He leaned back against the wall and shut his eyes.

"End of the road," he intoned mournfully. "The absolute end of the road."

Griffin resisted the urge to knock Troy's head off as he passed. He scooped up one of the babies, instructed

Troy to watch the other one and headed for the door to Heather's room.

He wondered why she wasn't asleep. Her shift had ended over an hour ago, and she had to get up early. Had they been too noisy? But these old houses had thick walls. He certainly couldn't hear anything that went on in the nursery when he was asleep in his room, which was on the other side.

Heather was sitting on the edge of the bed, waiting for him. She wore a long white cotton nightgown with green sprigged flowers. A matching robe lay across the foot of the bed, on top of a lacy white bedspread.

Griffin came in and pulled the door shut behind him carefully.

"Hi," he said softly. "We weren't keeping you awake, were we?"

She shook her head, smiling at the baby.

"Hi, sweetie," she said. She patted the bed beside her. Griffin understood that the invitation was purely for Stewbert, but after he brought the baby over and propped him up against the pillows, he sat down, too.

"Everything okay?"

"Yes, of course. I just forgot to tell you that Stewbert had been crying a lot earlier—teething, I think. I gave him some Tylenol about eleven, and I didn't want you to accidentally give him another dose."

"Okay," Griffin said, though he felt a little skeptical. Wasn't that the kind of thing she could have called across the room? Surely it didn't necessitate a private, middle-of-the-night chat.

Not that he was complaining. In spite of any warning Troy might have to offer, Heather could call Griffin into her bedroom anytime she wanted.

He watched her now, as she bent over Stewbert, kissing his tummy and murmuring an endearment. He'd like to have a picture of this moment, he thought. The slope of her back was so graceful. And in the honey light from her bedside lamp, her hair, which fell loose across her shoulders, looked almost golden.

He felt a strange twisting sensation in his chest. God, she was beautiful. Sometimes, when she was suited up in her intimidating lab coat, with her hair tightly bound and her manner strictly professional, he almost forgot how fine and fragile and feminine she really was.

Oh, hell. He was waxing as alliterative and ridiculous as Troy. It must be something about the intimacy of the hour, the shadowed light, the simple beauty of her slim, ivory-pale bare arms and the supple curve of her breast under the cotton gown.

Or maybe he was just horny as hell.

He breathed slowly to steady himself. Good thing he'd brought Stewbert with him, or who knows what he might have done now.

He'd been in Heather's bedroom before, of course. The exchange of baby shifts had required lots of moving back and forth through the three-room suite. And he had sometimes even let himself indulge in a fantasy or two…fantasies about what it would be like to sleep in that solid four-poster walnut bed, under that white, lacy spread.

Or rather, *not* to sleep.

But ever since that night in her downstairs office, when they had come so close to making love, the fantasies had been absolutely out of control. He couldn't look at her without desire flaring up like the blue fire of a gas jet. He walked around with a tension in his gut that wouldn't go away. The rope was so tight right now he felt half-bowed from the pressure of it.

At this moment, he would have given every Post-it note he owned for the right to make love to her one more time.

"Well," he said, struggling to be practical, "I guess Stewbert and I should get going. Let you get some sleep."

She turned toward him, her hand still resting protectively on Stewbert's tummy. "But there was one more thing," she said. "Something else I wanted to talk to you about."

He nodded. "I thought there might be. What is it?"

"I—" She looked uncomfortable suddenly. "I'm sorry. I didn't mean to eavesdrop, but I heard a little of what Troy was saying to you just now."

Griffin smiled. "Troy's a writer," he said. "He talks nonsense just for the joy of stringing words together. Don't pay any attention to him."

She smiled back, but she didn't look convinced. Oh, hell, Griffin thought. Troy and his big, unstoppable mouth. He wished he could remember exactly how far Troy had gone. He groaned inwardly, remembering that bit about playing doctor.

"I heard him talking about an assignment. Something special. Something you've been wanting to do for ages. And apparently you're going to miss it because you have to stay here with the Stewberts. Is that right?"

"More or less." Griffin shrugged. "But if there's anything I've learned through the years, it's that there's always another assignment."

Stewbert had begun to fuss, so Heather picked him up and held him comfortingly against her breast.

"Maybe," she said as she stroked the baby's head. "But I want you to know that it would be all right with me if you wanted to go with him. It's only a few days until Jared comes back, and I could manage the Stewberts until then."

"No, you couldn't," Griffin said. "What if one of your patients goes into labor?"

"It's only three days," she argued reasonably. "Mary could stay over to baby-sit. And actually Adam Reading is staying on for a week or so, too. We're seriously talking about a partnership. He's wonderful with the patients, Griffin. His skills are excellent. So he could always pitch in if the emergencies got out of control."

Griffin looked at her, too surprised to speak. She meant it, didn't she?

He knew he should be grateful. Objectively, he could see what a generous offer it was. And yet he didn't feel grateful at all. He felt strangely raw, and irrationally resentful that she could so easily toss aside the last three days they had together.

Maybe the last three days they'd ever have.

Sometimes, when he was caught in one of those self-indulgent fantasies, Griffin told himself that maybe a love affair of some kind wasn't out of the question. Heather obviously felt the same sizzling chemistry that was burning away at him. Maybe, he dreamed, maybe when the twins were gone, if she really hired a partner, she would travel somewhere with him—somewhere exotic, somewhere romantic.

The Bahamas, maybe. He'd been wanting to photograph that one last waterfall for the book he was proposing. Yes, that might appeal to her. She liked waterfalls. Silver Kiss Falls had always been their favorite secret place.

So why not, the fool with the fantasy always insisted? Just because they were too different to create a permanent life together...surely that didn't mean they couldn't share something wonderful for a little while, something they'd both remember forever.

But then the fantasy would pop like cheap bubble gum. Heather wasn't the traveling type. And she damn sure wasn't the temporary fling type. Their differences had driven them apart ten years ago. And during those ten years their lives had twisted even further in opposite directions, like divergent vines growing out from a common root and ending up on different planets.

So realistically, what were the odds that this little

oasis, this temporary truce, could last even five minutes beyond the departure of the twins?

No, these next three days were all they'd ever have. And he didn't intend to give up a minute. Not for Troy, or Nepal, or anything else on earth.

"I appreciate that, Heather," he said finally. "But I really don't have any interest in going to Nepal. And besides, I couldn't run off now. I can't leave you to break the news to Katie that I've mixed up her precious Stewberts."

"Oh, that's right." Heather smiled at him over the baby's now-sleeping head. "But actually that moment might go more smoothly if you're *not* here."

She put her hand on his arm. "Honestly, Griffin, it's all right if you go. I really can manage."

"I'm sure you can," he said softly, resisting the urge to touch her, too. Instead he reached out and traced the incredibly fragile labyrinth of Stewbert's tiny ear.

"But I don't think you understand me, Heather," Griffin said. "I'm staying because, for the next three days, there's nowhere on earth I'd rather be."

MARY WENT TO THE AIRPORT with Troy the next morning, even though she really couldn't spare the time. It was Friday, and the preparations for Heather's surprise party at Spring House were reaching a fever pitch. They couldn't begin until she left for the office, and they had to be finished before she came home at night. It was bedlam.

Even so, Mary simply decided to *make* the time. She didn't want to lose her last few hours with Troy.

Typically, the plane was late, so they sat companionably on the uncomfortable airport seats, watching people trundle luggage back and forth. It was peaceful, not having to chitchat just to fill the air. And it made Mary feel particularly cozy because, though neither of them said a word, she knew they were both inventing histories for the interesting characters who walked by.

That was what Troy had given her, she thought warmly. A sense that she was not weird, living so much in her imaginary worlds. A sense that she was not alone.

She wished that she could give something back to him. But the only gift she had to offer was advice, and she felt pretty sure he wouldn't welcome it.

Oh, well. It wasn't her way to hold back.

"All right, Troy Madison," she began impulsively. "*Listen up.*"

He grinned at her. "Yikes," he said. "That sounds ominous."

"Yeah, well, I've got something to say. And you know how I am when I've got something on my mind."

He nodded emphatically. "Yes, ma'am, I definitely do."

"Okay, so here it is. I know this trip to Nepal is important to you. It sounds absolutely fantastic. I wouldn't dream of suggesting you turn it down. But when it's over, I want you to do something for me."

He frowned quizzically. "Oh, yeah? What?"

"I want you to go home."

Clearly he hadn't been expecting that. He pushed his shaggy hair off his forehead and looked blankly at her. "Home? You mean to my wife? To Anita?"

"Yes. To your wife Anita and your daughter Vicky and your son Mark." When Troy turned his head away, symbolically rejecting the very notion, Mary took his chin and pulled his face back toward hers. "I mean it, Troy. Go home. It's not too late to sort things out."

He laughed unpleasantly. "Yes it is. You don't know Anita."

"No, but I know people. I know women. And if you ask me, that so-called affair of hers was nothing but one great big stick of dynamite set off for the express purpose of grabbing your attention."

"Bull." Troy's face was stony. "It was my best friend, Mary."

"Which made it almost inevitable that you'd find out, right? Is Anita stupid?" She saw his eyes flicker. "Okay, then I rest my case. Look, maybe you can't work it out. But you don't know that. You haven't even gone home since you heard about the affair. She probably thinks you don't give a damn."

Troy's jaw was tight. "She saw the divorce papers, didn't she? That ought to tell her I give a damn."

"Men!" Mary let her head fall back. "I swear, there isn't enough brainpower among the whole lot of you to run a flashlight. Listen to me, Troy, and listen good. Filing for divorce tells her you're mad. It tells her

you're offended and furious and you by God refuse to share your own private female with anybody. What it does *not* tell her is that you give a damn about *her*."

Troy squinted at her, obviously irritated. But he shifted uncomfortably. Her message was getting through. That was one of the many things Mary liked about Troy. He might hate the truth, but he didn't refuse to look it in the eye.

"So I'm just asking you to think about it. Think about going home and getting to know your family again. A lot of this is your fault, you know. Common sense ought to tell you it's hard to keep a family together if they're always apart."

"Wow," Troy said, almost smiling. "I'm actually getting my very own *Listen Up* letter."

She ignored him. She had heard the flight attendant announce the preliminary boarding for his flight, and they didn't have much time.

"Hush up," she said. "I knew there was a reason I always did this in writing. It's impossible to get a man to listen for more than five seconds at a time."

He folded his hands in his lap and waited meekly.

"Okay, well, anyhow, I firmly believe that you can find a way to mend the broken places. But you'll have to stay put long enough for the glue to set. You know what I mean?"

He nodded slowly.

The darn, insensitive flight attendant called for Troy's row. He glanced over, then looked back at Mary. Finally he stood up.

"I know," she said. "Just promise me one more thing. If I'm right, if you guys really do find a way to patch things up, you can thank me by inviting me to your next book signing."

He tilted his head, giving her that cute grin she had already grown so fond of.

"And you can invite me to yours," he said. He held out a little piece of paper. "Take this. It's my agent's name and telephone number. She wants you to call her."

Mary stared at his outstretched hand. "What?" She didn't dare touch it. This felt decidedly too good to be true, and she was afraid the paper would poof into fairy dust. "Why?"

"Women," Troy said, laughing. "They don't have enough brainpower among the whole lot of them..."

He picked up her hand and pressed the paper into it. "Because she thinks you have a future as a writer, dummy. In fact, she's pretty sure she can sell one of the syndicates on the idea of a hot new advice columnist with an in-your-face, no-nonsense, big-sister tone."

Mary felt lost. "An advice columnist?"

Troy nodded. "Yep. *The Listen Up Letters,* they'd call them."

Mary opened her mouth. Then she shut it.

"She has feelers out about *Littletown,* too, although she said that might take a lot longer. The children's fiction market's pretty hard to break into, but she wants to give it a try."

Mary shook her head, disbelieving. "I never thought you really meant it," she said numbly. "I thought you just wanted to sleep with me."

"I did, of course." Troy hoisted his carry-on over his shoulder, then leaned over and kissed her on the cheek. "But I knew you weren't falling for it. Besides, what would that have done to my chances with Anita?"

Mary squeezed his hand. She tried to smile. He kissed her cheek one more time, and then he was gone, leaving only the one magical piece of paper behind to prove he'd ever really been there.

She went to the picture window and realized she was so sad or happy or something that she was about to burst into tears.

Well, that would be ridiculous, wouldn't it?

All right, Mary Brady, she began firmly, touching the cool glass with her fingers as Troy's plane taxied toward the runway. *Listen up.*

CHAPTER FOURTEEN

ON FRIDAY AFTERNOON, Heather's last two patients of the day canceled. Though that was unusual, she was secretly relieved, because it meant she might actually be able to catch up on some of this paperwork.

But she had barely settled into her chair when Mary came bursting into the room, a dry-cleaner's dress bag slung over her shoulder and her most determined, militant gleam in her eye.

"Put those charts away," Mary commanded. "You've got a dinner engagement with your new partner and his wife in less than an hour. So lay down that pen and change into this."

Heather looked at her watch. "You know I can't go anywhere, Mary," she said. "I've got baby duty at six."

Mary had that dangerously stubborn look, as if she might actually start wrestling Heather out of her clothes single-handedly, so Heather tried to think fast. "Maybe I can scrounge something up to feed the Readings at Spring House. I might have some of that pasta left."

Mary tossed the dry-cleaning bag on the desk. "You are going out," she said. "Dr. Reading wants you to meet his wife. He wants to take you somewhere nice.

You are not going to offend this guy, do you hear? He's perfect. We want him. Get dressed.''

Heather still hesitated. She was tired, and besides... ''What about Griffin? Is he okay with this? He was supposed to have the evening free.''

Mary put her fists on her waist and narrowed her eyes. ''He's okay with it.''

Heather smiled in spite of herself. ''As if you gave him any choice in the matter.''

''Whatever. They're his stupid Stewberts, anyhow, aren't they? He's okay with it. Now hurry up. Dr. Reading's wife has made a long trip. She's pregnant, she's tired, and she is still eager to meet you. The least you can do is hurry.''

Heather recognized defeat when it stared her in the face. She put down the pen. ''Okay, Mother. What am I wearing?''

Smiling happily now that she had emerged victorious, Mary ripped the plastic covering off with a flourish. ''Behold! Your best dress.''

Heather frowned. It was her green silk, very simple but very dressy. It had a fitted bodice, almost no back and clasps of silver rhinestone bows at the shoulders. ''God, Mary, where are we going? The castle ball?''

Mary beamed proudly, as if she'd made the dress herself. ''Remember, Sally Reading used to be a ballerina. We have to show her that Firefly Glen has style.''

Heather sighed, fingering the cool silk. She hadn't had much opportunity to wear this lately. She'd been working so hard her social life had practically disappeared.

"Style, my foot. She'll probably just think I'm a vulgar show-off who has no idea how to dress for an ordinary Friday night dinner."

But Mary was starting to look cross again, so Heather abandoned the argument. Sighing, she picked up the dress, and the little case of accessories—underclothes, makeup, panty hose, black pumps and handbag—that Mary had brought along as well. She'd even brought a matching silver headband for her hair.

Wow. Mary sure did want to impress the Readings, didn't she? Good thing Adam was married. Mary probably would have instructed Heather to sleep with him just to show him how great the sex was in Firefly Glen.

"Okay," Heather said, "but I'm going to tell her the truth. I'm only ridiculously overdressed like this because my bossy assistant picked out my clothes."

Mary made sweeping motions with her hands, shooing Heather toward the full bathroom adjoining her office.

"Oh, for God's sake, stop whining and just put the dress on. I promise you, you'll thank me for it later."

But as she shut the bathroom door, Mary grinned in a way that made Heather suddenly feel nervous, as if she were being costumed up for some kind of sacrificial ceremony.

Heather stuck out the heel of her hand, jamming the door so that it wouldn't quite shut. She gave Mary a piercing stare through the narrow crack. "You're not cooking up something dumb here, are you, Mary?"

Mary frowned, all innocence, as if the comment bewildered her.

"You know what I mean," Heather said firmly. "I'm not going to get to this restaurant and find only Griffin, a big vulgar bottle of wine, and some smarmy violin player waiting there, am I?"

Mary snorted. "Get real. Do I look like I spend my time hand-delivering chicks to Playboy Cahill?"

But Heather was no fool. She knew that Mary hadn't quite answered the question. She held the younger woman's gaze steadily.

Mary sighed, wounded. "God, have a little faith, would you? I swear to you, straight out, on my honor as a Brady. Griffin Cahill is at home with the Stewberts. He is *not* going to be waiting for you at the restaurant."

Heather breathed deeply, relieved. "Okay, then. Sorry. I'll hurry."

But as the bathroom door fell shut, she caught one last glimpse of Mary. And darned if the woman wasn't grinning all over again.

EVERYTHING WAS READY.

The purple and white color scheme looked great against the existing Victorian decor of Spring House. The florist, particularly, had created a work of art. The Splendor of Spring arrangements of lily of the valley and violets were gorgeous. Silver bowls of them graced every table, and deep green leafy garlands of the flowers swung from the staircase banister and along every mantel.

As for the food, Griffin had left the decisions to Theo Burke, asking only that she use a Victorian theme. When she arrived an hour ago, she had insisted on showing him every canapé, every hors d'oeuvre, every sauce and every pastry. The food looked wonderful—orange-rosemary chicken, mushroom bisque, chocolate-whiskey cake, quince-almond tarts, hazelnut truffles. And it smelled even better.

People began showing up around six. Of the one hundred he'd invited, only five had declined. An amazing percentage of the guests were delighted to come, particularly considering how short the notice had been.

Most of the Glenners who accepted honestly wanted to celebrate Heather's victory. She'd lived in Firefly Glen all her life, as had her father, the town's only obstetrician for decades, and she was much loved.

A few of the others came for more selfish reasons, lured by Theo's food or the chance to tour the beautiful historical Spring House. Griffin had tried to weed out the vultures who would be attracted only by the aroma of fresh gossip. He hadn't invited people like Bourke and Jocelyn Waitely, who would just love to see Griffin and Heather together so that they could test the temperature of every touch, dissect the meaning of every glance, and perhaps make nasty little predictions about how long the aloof Heather Delaney could hold out against Playboy Cahill.

But he wasn't naive. He knew that everyone, even the nicest people, would be curious. They'd all be watching. For Heather's sake, he'd have to be careful.

Maybe he could start by hiding his impatience a little better. By six-thirty, he'd already glanced at his watch six times. But where was she?

Suzie Strickland, one of the few teenagers who had been invited, appeared at his shoulder. She actually looked pretty good tonight. She'd toned down her eye makeup and removed her eyebrow ring, probably because she'd heard Mike Frome was coming, too.

She couldn't bring herself to be completely conventional, of course. Her dress was the color of radioactive owl puke, but Griffin decided not to comment.

"So you honestly believe that not one soul in this town spilled the beans to Dr. Delaney?" Suzie surveyed the decorated room phlegmatically, making sucking noises on some kind of candy drop. "Sorry. Echinacea and zinc. I'm getting a cold. Want some?"

Griffin declined with regret and addressed her earlier question. "I hope no one told her. Why? Do you think they did?"

Suzie considered, sucking loudly. "Naw. Probably not. They were getting a kick out of the cloak-and-dagger stuff. Makes their petty little lives seem important, I guess."

Griffin smiled. "I know it has done wonders for mine."

"Oh, your life isn't little," Suzie said. "You're an artist. You got loose. You went places. I've gotta give you props for that. As soon as I can, I'm going to bust out, too.'' She frowned. ''But I'm *never* coming back.''

Griffin looked at her. Never? Well, maybe. Maybe she was absolutely right. Maybe she'd hit Vanity Gap running, and she'd never look back.

But maybe not. *Never* was a long time, and the world was a very strange place.

''She's here!'' Hissing whispers went up all over the house. Griffin hadn't been sure what ruse Mary would employ to get Heather to stop by Spring House on the way to her imaginary dinner with the Readings. But obviously Mary had prevailed, because Heather's car had just pulled up in the front driveway.

Only the dim hall sconces and the lights in the upstairs nursery had been left burning, so that the house would look completely normal. Everyone fell utterly silent as Heather's footsteps crunched across the oyster-shell driveway.

Finally her key scratched in the lock. He could hear the collective intake of breath. Then Heather opened the front door, and assigned guests all over the first floor flipped switches. The whole house was suddenly ablaze with sparkling white light.

''Surprise!''

Two hundred voices all shouting at the same time packed a rather intense punch. Heather, who had been laying her keys on the hall table, froze so completely she looked as if she were made of wax.

From his spot near the staircase, Griffin saw Mary coming up the porch behind her friend. She paused, quickly surveying the entire scene, from the cascade of lily of the valley to the huge banner that read Congratulations, Dr. Delaney.

Mary's eyes met Griffin's. And slowly, almost grudgingly, she began to nod. *Imagine that,* Griffin thought with an internal smile. He had finally done something that Mary Brady approved of.

Now if only Heather felt the same.

But he was going to have to wait to find out. The guests had swarmed the hallway, crowding around Heather, laughing and hugging and offering their happy congratulations.

As the crush pushed past, Sarah Tremaine ended up at Griffin's side. ''Why don't you shove your way through?'' She was holding a champagne flute filled with water, which she was resting on her rounded tummy as if it were a table. ''The party was your idea, after all.''

Griffin watched Heather for a minute. She was flushed and smiling, gorgeous in green silk.

''I can wait,'' he said.

But even as he said it, he knew he couldn't wait forever.

''Hey. Stop flirting with other men,'' Parker Tremaine said playfully, coming up to wrap his arms around his wife. ''You know it makes me jealous.''

Sarah leaned her head back against her husband's shoulder as if it were her favorite pillow. ''Nonsense. I was just telling Griffin that this party was his idea. He should get the first kiss.''

But he had already done that, Griffin thought silently. Heather Delaney had given him her very first kiss, years and years ago. He could remember it still. It had tasted of strawberry-flavored lipstick, the kind all the fifteen-year-old girls were wearing that year, the tinny hint of braces, and terror. It had turned him on so hard and fast he almost fell down. He'd never, in his whole life, been so helplessly aroused by any other single kiss.

Parker chuckled, watching his friend watch Heather.

"I think," Parker said to his wife, "that Griffin may be a little like me. He doesn't care who gets the first kiss. Just as long as he gets the last."

TWO HOURS LATER, when Heather was dancing with old Ward Winters, Griffin finally cut in.

She'd been wondering if he'd come to her. She'd gone to him, right at the beginning, and tried to thank him for the wonderful surprise. But there had been so many people around, and someone had whisked her away almost immediately. All night long, she'd been fed and feted. She'd been kissed and congratulated, twirled and teased and toasted.

Surrounded by a chorus of oohing and aahing, she had opened a hundred wonderful presents—all the little office extras she hadn't been able to afford after renovating the house.

Mary and the staff self-servingly but sensibly gave her a coffeemaker for the office. Parker Tremaine gave a gift certificate for free legal service to draw up a partnership contract. Emma Dunbar donated a year's supply of free printing from the Paper House. Hickory Baxter sent a thousand pink tulips, and the man-hours to plant them in the side yard.

Others had been equally thoughtful, giving according to their means. She'd opened magazine subscriptions for the waiting room, toys and video tapes for the children's corner, gift certificates for medical supply stores, and, from one of the teenagers, batteries for her pager.

It was the most impressive outpouring of goodwill she'd ever witnessed. She would easily have the most splendid medical offices in the country.

But though she had enjoyed seeing all her old friends, she had often found herself looking around for Griffin. When she spotted him, he always seemed very busy, playing host, taking care of the party, tending bar and tending the socially insecure. He had kept Granville and Ward from getting into a fistfight, and he had even managed to get artsy Suzie Strickland and superjock Mike Frome to share a couple of dances.

Nice of him, but it meant that somehow, through it all, Griffin and Heather hadn't had a single minute to really talk. Not a single minute alone.

Until now.

Ward Winters grumbled, but Griffin wasn't budging, so he finally relinquished her. Heather grinned at the crusty old man, who was one of her favorite people in the world, kissed him goodbye, and then turned to Griffin.

"Hi, there," she said with a smile, feeling his arms come around her waist. "I've been looking for you. I wanted to thank you properly. Everyone tells me the party was entirely your idea."

"Yes," he said politely, his hands warm against the small of her back. "It was."

"Well, it was a wonderful idea, simply heavenly. But you really didn't have to do anything like this, you know." She sighed. "Didn't I tell you not to be so nice? Didn't I say you'd already done too much?"

"Yes," he agreed, his lips against her ear. "I believe you did."

She pulled away a little and smiled into his handsome, sardonic face. "You're not, by any chance, trying to impress me, are you, Griffin Cahill?"

"Yes," he said, smiling back. "I believe I am."

She sighed again. "It's working," she said helplessly. She rested her cheek against his shoulder. "I'm afraid it's working far too well. I'm within an inch of believing that you may actually have a heart."

He did, of course. She could feel it thudding hard beneath her cheek.

"Is that so? An inch?" He rubbed his chin slowly against her hair, which sent little goose bumps shivering down her spine. "Tell me, Dr. Delaney. What would it take to get you to go the rest of the way?"

He wasn't really kidding. She knew that. But she tried to sound jocular. It wouldn't do to show now, in front of all these people, how completely he had destroyed her resistance.

"Hmm," she stalled. "Let me think."

She closed her eyes and breathed deeply, taking in the familiar, exciting scent of him. Her body seemed to be molding itself into his.

"You don't need to think about it, Heather," he said, his voice low and insistent. "Tell me. What would it take?"

"I don't know," she whispered as his hands subtly caressed the curves of her hips. The silk seemed to melt to nothingness beneath his fingers. She turned her face into his crisp white shirt. "No, that's not true. I do know. Not very much, I'm afraid. All you'd have to do is ask."

IT WAS TWO IN THE MORNING.

The guests had all gone home. Griffin's housekeeper, Mrs. Waller, who had been baby-sitting during the party, had gone home, too. The Stewberts were bathed, fed and put back to sleep. Heather had taken a shower, washed her hair and carefully hung up her pretty green dress.

She ought to be exhausted. But she wasn't. She felt, in fact, as if she might never sleep again.

She stood by the window, watching the dark rain that had been falling heavily for the past hour. In the shining orbs cast by the landscaping lights, she could see flowers bending, leaves quaking, grass drowning in the silvery flood. The Stewberts should sleep well tonight. They loved the soothing grumble of a storm.

Finally, at almost two-thirty, she heard the sound

she'd been waiting for. Griffin's low knock on her door. He must have been trying not to come, she thought. He must have been trying to resist.

But she could have told him it was futile. This night had been ten years in the making, and neither of them was strong enough to stop it from coming.

She opened the door and let him in.

"Hi," she said softly. She didn't pretend to be surprised to see him. She had been waiting, ticking off the seconds one by one. Surely he knew that.

He was still dressed, although he had taken off his tie and unbuttoned his white shirt at the throat. His sleeves were unbuttoned, too, and shoved up almost to his elbows. She felt awkward, suddenly, in her sleeveless cotton nightgown, her hair damp and streaming carelessly over her shoulders.

"Hi," he said. He held out a flat box wrapped in green paper and tied with silver ribbon. He had taken a sprig of violets, probably plucked from one of the staircase garlands as he came up, and he had slipped it under the ribbon. "I brought you a present."

She took the box, which was surprisingly light. "What is it?"

"Well, everyone else gave you a gift at the party," he said with a small smile. "But I thought you might prefer to be alone when you opened mine."

Her nerves had begun to hum. She moved to the bed and sat carefully on the edge. She freed the violets and set them on the white sheets. Then she tugged at the silver ribbon, which fell open easily.

It was a small stack of letters, maybe only eight or ten of them, neatly tied with another silver ribbon. Holding her breath, she took the packet out of the box, but she knew what they were without even looking. They were her teenage love letters to Griffin.

"I can't believe you've kept them all these years," she said slowly, turning them over and over in her hands.

"I couldn't destroy them," he said simply. He was still standing at the far side of the room. "They're all there, just as I promised. The one about the falls is on top."

Oh, yes, the one about the falls. She had almost forgotten that he had offered to return these to her, back when he was trying to persuade her to help him with the twins. That seemed so long ago now. She couldn't imagine him needing to bribe her to participate. These had been the most gratifying three weeks of her life—and in some ways the most exciting. She would not have traded them for anything on earth.

She looked at him, wondering if it were possible to say any of those things. But she couldn't find words that made sense. She just opened the packet, unfolded the top letter and began to read.

Her first impression was astonishment—the handwriting was so girlish. She had imagined herself so grown-up at seventeen, had firmly believed that falling in love had made her a woman overnight. But this gawky, looping script could almost have belonged to a child.

And the infamous ''vow'' now seemed absurdly tame. Silly, even. ''All right, I promise,'' she had written at his insistence. ''I will stand under the falls—naked—while you take my picture. But you must never show anyone, Griffin. That's what you have to promise me. I couldn't bear for anyone to know the things that you can make me do.''

And the rest of the letter—which had seemed so daring and X-rated at the time—it was just a collection of dreadful, unimaginative clichés.

''Your hands are made of fire.'' ''When you touch me, I feel as if I am the waterfall.'' ''I am a flower, Griffin, and you are my sun and rain.''

But, back then, they hadn't been clichés, not to her. She remembered writing this letter, and she knew how it had felt—as if she and Griffin had *invented* love. Like young pagan gods, they had created passion with nothing but the power of their bare bodies. Every metaphor of fire and flood and flowering desire seemed to have been born fresh the day he touched her.

''Oh, Griffin,'' she said sadly, folding up the letter. ''I can hardly believe I was ever so young. So foolish.''

''You weren't foolish,'' he said huskily. ''You were the most beautiful thing I had ever known. I couldn't believe I was allowed to touch you. To make love to you.''

The shadow of a smile crossed his lips. ''I think that's why I wanted that picture. Because I wanted something to keep, something to prove it had all really been true.''

"It *was* true," she said, laying the letters on the bed beside her, next to the sprig of already drooping violets. "I can still remember how it looked, standing there under the falls. I can remember every rainbow, every note the water sang as it hit the rocks, every gauzy plume that tore off in the wind and blew away."

She looked at him. "And I can remember how it felt. Can't you?"

For a moment he didn't even move. Then, slowly, he walked toward her and sat beside her on the bed. Reaching out, he took her hand and placed it against his heart.

"Heather, listen to me." He tightened his hand around hers. "Tonight, when we were dancing, you told me—" Shaking his head slightly, he started over. "You said that all I had to do was ask. Did you mean that?"

"Yes," she said. And then again, on an unsteady exhale. "Yes."

His eyes were very dark. He put two fingers under her chin and tilted her toward him.

"I'm asking, Heather." He lowered his head to hers. "I don't have the right, but, God help me, I'm asking."

She swallowed, hypnotized by his lips, so near she could feel their warmth.

"You know what the answer is, Griffin," she said. "The answer is yes."

"Yes," he echoed, like a prayer. And finally he kissed her.

His lips at first were gentle, but the fire caught

quickly, as if the years had left both of them parched, dangerously easy to spark. They fell together on the bed, as eager and hungry as they had ever been—trying to make their questing hands find every thrilling place at once, murmuring sounds that were more than words, kissing hair and skin and cotton alike, struggling with buttons and zippers and sheets.

But finally, when they had shed their clothes and bared each other to the moonlight, he seemed to force himself to a slower pace. He took time to put on a condom. Then he knelt before her on the bed, gazing down at her with glittering eyes, and she knew, she knew with a sizzling thrill, that this time would be very, very different.

They weren't children anymore. His body was stronger, the muscles trained into sharp definition. And he held himself with a new, mature control. She knew that the desperate, impetuous boy was gone forever. This powerful, virile man knew exactly what she wanted—and how to give it to her. And he could make it last longer than the moon could hang in the sky.

But the real difference was deeper than that. It was in his eyes, in the new shadows there. The shadows spoke to her, told her that these past ten years had taught him some of the same hard lessons. He, too, had met loneliness. He, too, had forged a fragile truce with regret.

And they both had learned something about the ephemeral nature of joy. A night like this wasn't to be devoured thoughtlessly, as they once had done. It must be cherished, second by agonizing second. Such a night might never, ever come again.

All those truths, and more, were in his hands and lips and eyes as he stared down at her naked body.

"Yes, Heather, I do remember how it felt," he said, lowering his mouth to her breasts. It seemed a lifetime ago that she had asked the question. She shivered as his breath drifted warm across her flesh.

"I dreamed of it for years. I dreamed of parting your thighs under the water and sliding into you." As he spoke, he nudged her trembling legs apart. He touched between them with gentle fingers. "Every night, it was the same dream. Me, moving through the cold water into the incredible heat of you."

Desire knifed into her, following his fingers. Her heart was pumping so fast she could hear it in her ears.

"Do you still dream of it?" She looked at him, wondering if he could see the ache that pulsed through her like a second heartbeat. "Do you still dream of making love to me?"

"I had finally taught myself not to," he said, stroking her softly and watching her, as if he could read what her body wanted in her eyes. "But then I came home, and it began all over again. I dream of you all the time, Heather. I dream of this. Even when I'm awake."

He shifted then, removing his wonderful fingers, and she shut her eyes, trying to hold on to the feeling. He rose above her, his hard, ready body touching her, and though he tried to hold back, she knew that he had waited almost as long as he could.

"It's all right," she whispered. "Come to me, Griffin. The answer is still yes. The answer will always be yes."

With a low moan of relief, he entered her. It was a hard, passionate claiming, fierce and swollen and oh, so familiar. "Griffin," she said helplessly, and in answer he began to move.

Instantly she felt deep, slow ripples of building passion. She clutched his shoulders. This was not memory. This was not a dream. This was Griffin.

He put his hands behind her hips, arching her back, controlling every stroke, every rhythmic ebb and flow of pressure. Within minutes, she was lost. It was too much. He was too sure. He knew everything, and she could hide nothing.

He shifted, a conscious friction. The tiny movement blinded her.

And suddenly it was washing over her. She caught her breath as the misty past surrendered to the flooding now. Her throat made a small, raw sound, a sound so full of fear and joy it might as well have been a word.

She knew that word, just as she knew his body moving ever faster, harder, into her. It was the word that meant yes. Still, yes. Always and forever, yes.

And, oh, Griffin, Griffin, help me. It was the word that meant love.

CHAPTER FIFTEEN

FOR ONE CONFUSED and wonderful split second when he woke up that radiant Saturday morning, Griffin Cahill felt—

Young.

He felt young. Buoyant, eager, brimming with the mindless physical joy a nineteen-year-old takes for granted. As if life and the world were full of pleasure, and all of it belonged to him.

Stretching on soft cotton sheets, he smelled lily of the valley and smiled. Only half awake, without even opening his eyes, he knew exactly where he was. He was in Heather's prim Victorian bedroom, in Heather's prim Victorian bed.

Heather. His body tightened, remembering the long, amazing, anything-but-prim Victorian night, and instantly wanting more, needing more, knowing with a hazy, sensual delight that he could never get enough.

But he was ready to try.

He turned and reached for her, murmuring her name. But the place beside him was cool and empty.

Heather was gone.

He sat up, brushing his hair out of his eyes, and looked around the room. Her nightgown, which had tumbled to the floor last night in an abandoned heap, was nowhere to be seen. His own clothes were folded neatly on the dresser.

He could smell the damp sweetness of a recent shower floating in from the adjoining bathroom. And then he knew. She wasn't just briefly gone, in the next room checking on the babies, or on the sleeping porch watching the clean spring morning come to life.

She was *gone.*

He looked on the nightstand by his side of the bed, and saw with relief that she had left him a note, and, thoughtfully, his cell phone. If she needed to call him, she wouldn't want to call the house line—it was noisy and often woke the Stewberts.

He picked up the note.

Mrs. Mizell again, it read. *I'm sorry. Back soon.*

The cell phone buzzed, and he picked it up before it could finish the first ring. "Tell me you're on your way home, damn it," he said gruffly. "I'm already going crazy without you."

There was a hesitation on the other end, and finally a young woman's voice said tentatively, "Mr. Cahill? Is that you?"

Griffin almost laughed out loud, recognizing the voice of his agent's young secretary. Damn, he really was nineteen again, wasn't he? That was such a classic idiotic teenager's faux pas.

"Yes, Jeannie, it's me." He cleared his throat, trying to sound awake. "What's up?"

Jeannie took a couple of minutes to recover from the

shock of his greeting, but finally she relayed her message. It was good news. The best. His agent had a terrific offer on a book he'd proposed last year—a photographic essay of the world's most beautiful waterfalls. He'd been hoping someone would bite.

And now, he thought, punching the off button and disconnecting the poor, bewildered Jeannie, now maybe he could take Heather with him. He closed his eyes, briefly lost in the fantasy. Okay, maybe he was jumping the gun, assuming that she'd be willing to leave Firefly Glen. But she had already decided to get a new partner—that must mean something, some shift in her life outlook.

And last night.

Well, that had meant a lot. Maybe, he thought… maybe it had meant enough.

The cell phone buzzed again. This time he was more careful, preferring not to embarrass himself again. He looked at the digital display, though that really wasn't much help. It wasn't one of his preprogrammed numbers. The readout simply said, "Unassigned."

Maybe she was calling from the hospital…or Anna's house…or anywhere. He kept hoping it was Heather, right up until he heard his sister-in-law's voice.

"Griffin? Is that you? You're still alive? The twins haven't killed you yet?" Katie sounded happy and playful…and, though he knew you couldn't always tell for sure, she sounded *close.*

"Not quite," he said. "But they haven't given up yet. They've still got a couple of days to work on me."

''No, they don't!'' Katie laughed merrily. ''That's why I'm calling. I'm in Firefly Glen, and I'm coming to save you, Griff. And Heather, too. Like the marines, right? I'm marching right in to the rescue.''

He sat up straighter. This wasn't supposed to happen today. She was due to pick the boys up on Monday. He and Heather were supposed to have two more days.

Heather, he thought again, instinctively knowing how difficult this was going to be for her. He had to call her. He had to warn her. If Katie took the boys away while Heather was at work…

He tried to think it through. ''You're here? You're coming? When?''

''I'll be there in less than an hour. So you'd better hurry, Griff. Go wake those bad little boys up and tell them their Mommy is home.''

What could he say but yes? He hung up the phone and stared at the nursery door. And right on cue, as if they'd heard everything, the Stewberts began to cry.

FINALLY, FINALLY, Anna Mizell was consoled, comforted and convinced.

Heather had never before found it so difficult to maintain her professional serenity. But somehow she managed. Yes, she assured Anna. Her backache was normal. Her baby was fine. The baby's head had engaged, so she might go into labor soon, within the week perhaps. But it would not be today. Definitely not today.

As soon as Anna left the room, Heather turned to

Mary, who had come in ten minutes earlier to relay Griffin's terse message about the Stewberts.

"My next few appointments," Heather said urgently, pulling off her stethoscope and laying it on the counter. "Are any of them emergencies?"

But Mary was way ahead of her. "They're rescheduling them as we speak. We can free up at least an hour, maybe more. Don't worry about any of it. Just go." She grabbed the otoscope from Heather's pocket. "Hurry."

It took Heather only ten minutes to drive from Main Street to Spring House, but today it seemed to take forever. She didn't speed, but she drove with focus, not even glancing at the lush spring flowers that grew in window boxes and pots and yards. Usually, spring in Firefly Glen delighted her, but today it was no more than a fuzzy kaleidoscope of pointless colors.

Still, though she didn't waste a second, when she got to the house a large red minivan was already parked in the driveway.

So she would have no time to say goodbye in private. But at least the Stewberts were still here. That was something to be grateful for.

The front door was unlocked. Dropping her purse on the hall table, she flew up the stairs. Her heart was pounding by the time she reached the nursery, so she forced herself to take a deep breath before entering.

"Hi," she said as she opened the door, smiling with her best approximation of casual good cheer.

The woman standing beside the crib looked up. So

this was Katie, Heather thought, coming into the room. The twins' mother was tiny, blond and beautiful. She had one of the Stewberts in her arms and was showering kisses on his bare back.

Griffin stood beside her, holding the other baby, who also wore only a diaper. He seemed to be in the process of packing a large blue duffel. That half-filled bag stopped Heather in her tracks. For the first time, she understood that the Stewberts were really leaving.

Katie beamed at Heather. "Hi, there," she said enthusiastically. "You must be Saint Heather. I've been dying to meet you. Thank you, thank you, thank you, for helping Griffin take care of my little monsters. Heaven knows what would have become of them if Griffin had been left to his own devices."

She grinned at Griffin. "They'd probably be smoking and cussing and whistling at big-chested women by now."

He smiled back. "How do you know they aren't?" He patted the baby's padded bottom. "Come on, Stewbert. Say something dirty for Mommy."

Oh, no. He had called the baby Stewbert. Heather held her breath. But Katie laughed, which apparently was Katie's reaction of choice.

"Stewbert? Is that what you call them? Like Stewart and Robert mixed together? That's too funny!" She leaned over and kissed the baby Griffin was holding. "Don't listen to him, Bobby. Give Mommy a kiss."

Bobby. Heather smiled, realizing that Katie hadn't had a moment's trouble separating the boys—and hadn't considered for an instant the possibility that anyone else had, either.

She should be glad. Griffin had dodged that bullet, at least. But, instead, Heather felt strangely wistful. It was sad, somehow, that now, when they were leaving, she was learning who they really were.

The one with the cowlick, the one who hated peas and always woke up when the telephone rang. That one was Robert.

And the other one, the one who could play peekaboo for hours, the one who tried to eat everything he could reach—that one was Stewart.

"Anyway, Heather, thank you so much. You were an angel to pitch in. I bet you could have killed me for being gone so long."

Heather shook her head. "No," she said honestly. "I loved every minute of it. The boys are absolutely adorable."

Stewart, who had been gnawing on his mother's top button, turned at the sound of Heather's voice. "Geep!" he cried in profound delight, holding out his hands and straining toward her. "Barn fink!"

Though it made her arms ache to repress the urge to take the baby and kiss his silly, wet mouth, Heather didn't know what to do. Surely, after three weeks away from her sons, Katie would not want to share their affection. But Katie merely grinned wryly.

"Well, I guess that's what I get for being gone so long," she said, handing the fretting, wriggling Stewart over to Heather with yet another smile. "He's obviously forgotten all about me. He's clearly fallen in love with you.''

Griffin was watching Heather with soft eyes. ''Yes,'' he said. ''They both did. I think Heather is what they call a natural.''

When Heather took him, Stewart stopped fussing immediately. He folded himself contentedly against her breast and began sucking his fingers as if he might go back to sleep.

Katie watched the two of them for a minute without a hint of envy. Heather marveled that the other woman could be so relaxed, so assured of her ultimate place in her sons' hearts. Heather held Stewart closer, trying to soak up this last warm, sleepy hug, trying to internalize it, so that she'd never forget how it felt.

Perhaps Katie's easy confidence was the special magic of being the real mother—instead of the temporary one. She'd never have a *last* hug. For Katie, there would always be another.

''Yeah, I'd say you've definitely got a flair.'' Katie tilted her pert blond head speculatively, then looked over at Griffin. ''Hey, make yourself useful, why don't you? I've left a suitcase out in the minivan, and I need it.''

Griffin smiled at his sister-in-law's autocratic tone. ''Yes, your highness,'' he said with a bow. ''Don't let her boss you around too much while I'm gone, Heather,'' he said, chucking Stewart's chin as he passed. ''She has definite slave driver tendencies. She makes Mary Brady look like an amateur.''

Katie glowered at him. ''Are you still here, Griffin?''

When his footsteps had receded, Katie turned back to Heather, obviously eager to take advantage of their privacy. ''So. Are you married, Heather? Do you have any children of your own?''

Well, that was subtle. Heather shook her head.

''No,'' she said, aware that a ridiculous stinging had started behind her eyes. How foolish it would be to cry. She had always known the Stewberts were not hers. Not really. ''No, not yet.''

''Well, you definitely should hurry up and have some. You'll love it. It's the best thing in the world.'' Katie smooched loudly against Robert's head, and the baby looked up at her, laughing. ''Although I have to say...I hope you're not counting on Griffin to be the daddy—''

''Katie, really, I—''

''Oh, I know, I know. He's gorgeous. And sexy as hell. But he's one hundred percent useless in the relationship department. Okay, so I know I'm butting in here, but you seem really nice. Just a friendly heads up. Do *not* bank on Griffin. I've never seen anyone so allergic to commitment.''

Heather couldn't help feeling Katie was being a bit too harsh. ''You know, he was wonderful with the boys. And even when he had the chance to leave, he didn't. He took this commitment very seriously.''

''Oh, dear. He's got you deluded, doesn't he?'' Katie looked sad. ''If he stayed, it was because he was enjoying himself.'' She eyed Heather anxiously. ''I didn't mean with you. I meant— Oh, I don't know what I meant. He makes me nuts. He's so frivolous, you know?''

Heather shook her head. ''I don't think you under—''

Katie was on a roll, though, and couldn't be stopped. ''And he'll *never* have children, I'll tell you that. He'd have to grow up first himself, and he has positively no intention of ever doing that.''

Her comments had a well-rehearsed quality, as if this was a frequent lament in the Jared Cahill family. *When will your irresponsible brother ever grow up?*

''Katie, really, it's all right,'' Heather broke in with polite firmness. ''I really was just doing him a favor. Griffin and I are just good friends. We've known each other since we were kids.''

Katie smiled in obvious relief. ''Oh, then that's okay. If you really know him, you know better than to count on him for anything important. I almost killed Jared when he told me he'd left the babies with Griff. Talk about a short attention span.''

She tickled her baby's ear playfully. ''Little Bobby can focus on one person longer than Uncle Griffin, can't you, pumpkin?''

Heather didn't answer, but Katie didn't notice. Her conscience cleared, she had begun rummaging in the dresser. Pulling out a red romper, she plopped Robert on the changer.

''But I hope you do have *someone* in mind,'' she babbled on as she deftly wiggled Robert's foot into the romper's leg. She seemed utterly oblivious to Heather's uncomfortable silence. "You really should get started pretty soon."

AFTER THE MINIVAN had pulled away—packed to the bursting point with toys and diapers, strollers and high chairs and cribs—Griffin and Heather walked back into Spring House slowly. Silently. Side by side, but not touching. Like people left behind after a funeral.

Instinctively they went upstairs. But the nursery, once a colorful hodgepodge of clutter and activity, was bare and silent. Heather could hardly stand to look at it, with its unbroken expanse of hardwood floors, one scruffy chest of drawers and a poignantly empty rocking chair.

She didn't like to go in her own room, either. Its memories were too recent, as well.

So she stepped out onto the sleeping porch. It had begun to rain again. She looked at the gray drizzle and hoped that Katie's minivan had antilock brakes.

It would have been kind of ironic, really, if it hadn't been so tragic. She wrapped her arms around herself, wondering how life could have managed to spring such a perfect and inescapable trap.

In the past three weeks, she had unearthed two long-buried truths about herself.

The first truth: With all her heart, she longed for a family. Children. Babies of her own.

And the second: With all her heart, she was still in love with Griffin Cahill.

The trap was that they were mutually exclusive. By choosing one, she would almost certainly give up the other. She could never have them both. She could almost hear fate laughing at her as she stood here, struggling in its cruel, shining jaws.

"Heather." Griffin had come onto the porch behind her. "It's all right. I know how much you're going to miss them."

"Yes," she said quietly. "I am."

He put his arms around her and rested his cheek against her hair. "I can't believe how quiet it is around here."

She nodded.

"But I have something exciting to tell you." He nuzzled her ear. "And something to ask you, too."

She didn't answer. She just watched the rain, which grew every minute more steady and dense, forming a silver curtain that she simply couldn't penetrate.

"I'm going to be leaving soon," he said. "I just got the call this morning. It's a photo assignment I've been negotiating for a long time, and it finally came through. I'll be going to the Bahamas, to shoot pictures of a waterfall there."

He tightened his arms. "I was hoping you'd come with me. You could leave your practice for a few weeks, couldn't you? Now that Adam Reading is here?" His voice sounded so eager, so full of anticipation. "I think you'd love it there. It's absolutely spectacular."

She felt a long, slow sinking, as if someone had

dropped an anchor in her heart. Not an hour had passed since the babies were in his arms—not twelve had passed since Heather herself had been there. And all the while he had been making these plans to leave.

A waterfall in the Bahamas...

How could she have been such a fool as to believe he had changed? He'd just been taking a breather from *real* life. Just proving to his skeptical, critical sister-in-law that he could do it.

Just playing house.

But Heather had forgotten it was just a game. She had watched him with the babies, and she had imagined that he was learning to appreciate the joys of domestic life, with a loyal partner by his side and laughing children at his feet.

Instead, he had been impatiently ticking off the days. She remembered the smile he had turned on the other men, the daddies in her birthing class.

I've only got two weeks left in my sentence, he had crowed proudly. You're in it for life.

He had meant those words. Everyone had known it but her.

He touched her shoulder now, as if sensing that she wasn't paying attention.

"Did you hear me, Heather? I'm asking you to go with me."

"I'm sorry," she said in a low voice. "I can't."

The tension in his arms was subtle, almost imperceptible. But she felt it. "Why not?"

"I have commitments here," she said. "I have a

home. I have a practice. I can't just dump my patients on a total stranger, no matter how pleasant Adam Reading may be. I don't approach life that way, Griffin. I couldn't just drop everything and go chasing after pretty waterfalls because you ask me to."

Griffin's arms slowly fell. He backed up a step. "Of course you could," he said concisely. "It's only for a couple of weeks. You could make it work if you really wanted to."

And he was right, of course. She could. It wouldn't be easy, but she could manage. She could leave Adam here, in charge of Anna Mizell and the others. She could pack a bag and follow Griffin blindly into a passionate, tumultuous affair. It would be hot and thrilling…and painfully brief.

And when it was over, she would be destroyed.

"Perhaps you're right," she said, trying to be honest. Surely she owed him that. She owed it to herself. "I guess the truth is that I don't really want to."

"Why not?"

"Because I think you'll break my heart." Heather turned and faced him, because, however painful, this was something that *had* to be faced. "Be honest with me, Griffin. Can you ever see yourself settling down? Having children? Staying with one woman for the rest of your life?"

He seemed to choose his words very carefully. "I can see us being together," he said slowly. "You felt what happened last night. It was magic. That's what we are together. I want more of it. I think you do, too."

She looked at his handsome, earnest face. "How much more? Another night? A month? A year?"

Griffin frowned. "How can I answer that? As long as it's good. I'm not sure I believe in forever, but I do believe that we could make each other very happy. We've got a fresh start, Heather. Let's not overthink it. Let's just see where it takes us."

She could see how it might look that way to him. No couple, when they first started out, could be sure where their relationship would end. They just played the cards and hoped for a winning hand.

She wasn't afraid to take an emotional gamble. But that was the important difference. With Griffin, it wasn't a gamble—it was Russian roulette with every chamber loaded.

Because he hadn't changed, not really. For him, the success of a relationship was still measured in months, not lifetimes. It was still measured in laughter and waterfalls and mind-shattering sex. The things she wanted terrified him. They had driven him away ten years ago, and they'd drive him away again.

"Come on, Heather," he said, frustration lacing his voice. "Don't let fear make you an emotional coward. You know last night wasn't enough for either of us. Let's go to the Bahamas. And then, when the trip is over, maybe then we can think about what comes next. About whether we want to consider…something else. Something more permanent."

"Marriage," she said tightly. "That word you can't say—it's called marriage. It's called commitment. You say I'm a coward. But I think you are. See how that word scares you? It scares you so much you can't even trust yourself to utter it."

"I uttered it once," he said, his voice suddenly very different, filled with a cold, impersonal amusement. "I got down on my knees, and I said it with tears in my eyes. I believe we both remember how that turned out."

That sardonic tone felt like a light whip, flicking carelessly against her heart. He hadn't taken that tone with her in a long time now. She'd forgotten how much it could hurt.

She turned away, fighting back the senseless tears it had stung into her eyes. There was another word he hadn't uttered.

Love.

And obviously he hadn't said it for one simple, fatal reason. He *didn't* love her. He wanted her, quite passionately. He clearly believed a few weeks in the Bahamas would be a wonderful way to satisfy his hunger. But love, for Griffin, simply didn't enter into it.

"I can't talk about this anymore," she said, and her voice was full of unshed tears.

He cursed, hard, under his breath. Perhaps at her, perhaps at himself.

"The answer wasn't yes for very long, was it, Heather? One day, and you're already back to saying no. No to any kind of risk. No to me. No to life."

When she didn't respond, he took her shoulders

roughly. "Damn it, Heather, talk to me. Why does it always have to be all or nothing with you?"

She turned, shrugging off his hands, which had too much power over her. She didn't trust herself to be strong as long as his hands were on her skin.

"Because," she said desperately, "if I give you one more day, that day will turn into a year. And that year will turn into another, just like it did before. And when you finally decide you're tired of me, that I'm not quite enough fun, that you'd rather visit your waterfalls with more exciting women, it will hurt too much."

His eyes were dark and full of anger. "Are you telling me it won't hurt if we end it now?"

"Yes," she answered honestly. "It will. But not as much." If he left her now, she could just barely survive it. Last night would become another one of those painful memories. But a year from now…or two.

"I'm not twenty-three anymore, Griffin. I'm making choices that will affect the rest of my life. If we end it now, I'll still have time to find the things I need. Roots. Commitment." Her voice faltered. "Children."

"And are those things so important to you?" He narrowed his glittering eyes. "Even if it means you have to find them with another man?"

"Yes," she said, although the word was almost too painful to speak. "Even then. I won't end up one of your broken toys, Griffin. I deserve to find a better life than that."

In spite of the dismal gray light, his eyes were as suddenly brilliantly blue as sapphires, and as impossible to read. He looked shockingly like a complete stranger.

"I see," he said politely. "In that case, I had better get out of your way and let you start looking."

CHAPTER SIXTEEN

FOR THE FIRST COUPLE OF DAYS after Griffin left town, Heather did very well, carried along by the steamy momentum of anger and pride. She would not crumble. She knew how to handle Griffin's absence. It should be easier, in fact, than handling his presence. She certainly had more practice.

She threw herself into her work. She saw fifty patients and dealt with a dozen emergencies. Anna Mizell came in three times in three days. It was almost time. Heather asked Anna to stay close to home, just in case.

Then she drew up a partnership contract for Adam Reading, who signed it with his usual quiet pleasure. When the two of them returned from Parker's office, they were greeted by Mary and the staff doing a noisy victory dance in the waiting room. When Adam took Heather's arm, she let him twirl her around without resistance—right in front of all the patients.

At home at night, Heather tackled spring cleaning. She intended to throw away all the faded party garlands, but she found herself pressing one sprig of violets between the pages of her current novel. And when she ran across a yellow plastic key covered in tooth marks, she didn't throw it away, either. She slipped it into her top drawer.

So technically she wasn't brooding. She wasn't crumbling. But she wasn't quite herself, either.

To Mary's shock, Heather even went on a date, dinner at the Candlelight Café with a local C.P.A. If she was going to start looking for Mr. Right, she might as well get started.

But, while her date was nice, he was just barely Mr. Maybe. He ate with his elbows on the table, which caused Theo Burke to scowl at Heather, as if she'd brought a cockroach into the restaurant on a leash. And when Suzie Strickland walked in, it prompted the man into a twenty-minute rant about the horrors of multiple piercings practiced by this younger generation.

Bored senseless, Heather wished she had Stewbert with her. He'd know what to do. He'd give the man a very loud, very wet raspberry, slap his hands on the table and shout, "Flam!"

The image made her chuckle, which apparently wasn't the appropriate reaction. Mr. Maybe looked deeply affronted.

"Can you fail to appreciate," he intoned, "how such hideous self-mutilation demonstrates her abysmal lack of self-worth?"

"Geep fink" obviously wouldn't suffice, although it was the first response that came to mind. Heather looked at him, and thought what boring babies he would make. He went from Mr. Maybe to Mr. Never in the blink of an eye.

''Actually,'' Heather said calmly, taking a sip of wine, ''I was thinking of piercing some body parts myself.'' She sounded, even to her own ears, a little like Griffin Cahill at his most sarcastic.

Mr. Not-in-this-lifetime looked horrified, as if she'd sprouted green horns. He suddenly remembered an urgent tax return he needed to file.

Gathering her purse contentedly, Heather smothered a grin. *Double flam.*

It wasn't all superefficiency and irreverent amusement, though. There were other times, tough times. The night of her date, she woke up in the predawn hours, reaching out for Griffin. She hadn't done that in ten years, and, when she realized she was alone in the huge house, she turned her face into the pillow and cried like a child.

The worst times were at work. Often her patients brought their newborns along to their postnatal checkups. In the past, Heather had been delighted, offering the expected admiration, but always comfortably detached.

Now, with every tiny, sleepy face, she felt a wash of longing. Why had she never seen before what a breathtaking miracle birth truly was? The mothers weren't just happy. They were stunned with joy.

Sometimes the fathers came along, too. They held their infants with a special, awestruck caution. It was as if their large, clumsy hands had been entrusted with the world's only spun-glass basket of unicorn eggs and fairy wings.

That Thursday afternoon, Heather closed the door to her office quietly. It was three days after Griffin's departure, and she had just finished one of those family-style postnatal examinations.

This time, though, she had been so humiliatingly undone by her emotions that she needed a few minutes to compose herself.

She put the heels of her hands on her desk and leaned over it, breathing deeply. Dear God, she had to get a grip.

She heard the door click behind her. "Heather?" Mary said quietly. "Are you all right?"

Heather nodded, but she didn't turn around. "I'm fine. I'll be right out."

She could feel Mary's concerned gaze on her back. And she heard the deep sigh of worry.

"Oh, hell," Mary growled. "I think there's something I'd better tell you."

Heather shut her eyes hard. "Not now, Mary." She turned around and tried to smile. "Honestly, this is really not the right time for a *Listen Up* lecture."

"It's not a lecture." Mary backed up against the office door, as if she intended to use her body to block intruders. "It's just... Well, heck, probably I'm sticking my nose in where it doesn't belong."

"You?" Heather shook her head wryly. "Surely not."

"Oh, hush up, and let me say it. It will be quicker if you'll stop interrupting. I just wanted to say that...I don't know exactly what happened between you and

Griffin. But I thought maybe...maybe you heard the rumors. About him and Emma Dunbar, I mean.''

''Oh, good grief,'' Heather said on a sigh.

''I just wanted you to know that they weren't true. He wasn't fooling around with her, no matter what anyone says. So if that caused any trouble between the two of you—''

Heather had to smile in spite of everything. ''For heaven's sake, Mary. You didn't actually believe those stories, did you?''

Mary lifted her chin. ''Yeah, I did. Why not? There was a time when I wouldn't have put anything past that man.'' She frowned. ''How did you know they *weren't* true?''

Heather laughed. ''Emma is my best friend,'' she said. ''I know how her wacky mind works. It was a colossally dumb scheme, but you've got to hand it to her. It worked.''

Mary looked thoughtful. ''If that's not the problem, what is? I thought you and Griffin might be getting back together. Not that I was so all-fired crazy about the idea, but, still, I thought so. Everyone did.'' She folded her arms across her chest. ''But suddenly he goes screaming off on an airplane, and you start moping around here like a month of wet Sundays.''

Heather drew herself up. ''I am not moping,'' she said indignantly. ''I've been very busy and productive. I work, I laugh, I hire partners.'' She gave Mary a steely look. ''I go out on dates.''

''*A* date,'' Mary corrected. ''With a tall, thick slice

of soggy bread who couldn't even take *my* mind off Playboy Cahill, much less *yours*."

"Mary," Heather said crossly. "I thought we were overbooked. Don't you have work to do?"

"Yes," Mary admitted. She put her hand on the doorknob. "But so, my friend, do you. And I don't mean those patients out there. I mean all that denial and confusion in here." She tapped the area near her heart with her fist.

"You'd better get yourself sorted out, Doc. Because the next time you burst into tears at the sight of a baby, we're going to start losing some business."

HEATHER HAD NEVER SEEN Silver Kiss Falls at dawn before. It was beautiful, like something in a dream.

The rising sun was dazzling, a silver-and-gold firecracker on the eastern horizon. Around it, the sky was white, as if it hadn't yet picked out what color it would wear today.

Heather worked her way down the ravine carefully, trying not to trample the lovely coltsfoot and columbine that grew in wide sweeping bands of spring flowers.

The falls were impressive right now, still swollen with spring meltwaters. Even from the top of the ravine, they had thundered so loudly she could hardly hear the morning song of the meadowlarks. Down here, at the foot of the falls, water roared in her ears, blotting out all other sounds.

The basin pool was alive, its bubbles spangled with

gold dawn light. She took off her shoes and sat on the rocky banks, dangling her feet in the cold, swirling water.

She wasn't quite sure why she had come here. It wasn't terribly sensible. She had to be at work in two hours, and already her clothes were littered with tiny fleabane petals. Her feet were dirty, and her hair was frizzy from the damp.

But Mary's warning had struck home. It *was* time Heather sorted herself out. And she had instinctively felt that she could do it better here than anywhere else.

Maybe she'd been wrong to avoid this enchanted place, where the air was full of rainbows and her heart was full of memories. Avoiding Silver Kiss was like avoiding a piece of herself.

She had spent ten years trying to run away from the passionate, vulnerable girl she had once been. But then Griffin had come home, and she had discovered that she'd only been running in circles. She had ended up right where she had started. In his arms.

So she needed a new plan. If she wasn't going to run anymore, what was she going to do?

Spending those weeks with the Stewberts had awakened something maternal in her—that much was obvious. It was as if some hormonal trigger had been activated, and now she was filled with yearning for children of her own.

But was it merely children she longed for? Or was it *Griffin's* children?

What about her instinctive recoil at the thought of

making babies with the sanctimonious C.P.A.? She didn't want his children, did she? She couldn't, in fact, think of a single human being whose children she *did* want.

Except Griffin.

And what about marriage? Wasn't that answer pretty much the same?

Her father had told her that an obstetrician needed a heart big enough to hold a lot of love, a lot of pain—and a couple of uncomfortable secrets. He'd been right, of course. As the Glen's baby doctor, Heather knew almost everything. She knew that Emma and Harry couldn't have children, which nearly killed Harry. She knew that Parker Tremaine wasn't the father of Sarah's baby, which didn't bother Parker in the least.

She knew which Glen wife had started taking birth control without telling her husband—and she also knew which wife had secretly stopped. She knew who greeted news of pregnancy with joy, and who shed tears behind the closed examination room door.

She knew, in short, that a big diamond wedding ring didn't guarantee happiness. And neither did a gleaming white cradle.

Nothing guaranteed happiness. Nothing.

But she knew one thing that came pretty close.

Love.

She smiled, remembering Griffin's beautiful young body knifing through this bubbling pool like a flashing golden fish. And his strong, knowing body finding hers in the moon-washed four-poster bed. And his sassy, upside-down smile, as he rolled on the floor with his nephews.

How could she have been so blind? It was the moments filled with love that were the happiest. Love might not be a guarantee. It might not be permanent. It might not even be safe.

But it was the only real, spontaneous, soul-searing happiness she had known in her whole, entire life. And she had been a fool to send it away.

Suddenly she heard footsteps on the slope of the ravine. She looked up, her heart holding its breath.

Someone was coming down to see the falls.

A man. A tall man. Slim, blond…

The man looked up, glimpsed Heather sitting there, and smiled politely.

Her heart ached once, then began its normal rhythm once again. Not Griffin. Of course not Griffin. He was in another country.

But suddenly everything seemed perfectly clear. She stood, brushing flower petals and soil from her slacks briskly. She had two choices. She could either sit here forever, searching for Griffin in her memories, in her dreams, in every blond stranger who happened by.

Or she could go to the Bahamas and find him.

CHAPTER SEVENTEEN

THE SUN WOULD SET in about an hour. Griffin knew that if he didn't head out to the falls soon, he'd miss the sweet-light, those extraordinary minutes right before the sun goes down when the angle of the light is most dramatic, creating interesting texture and depth.

Maybe it would help. God knows he needed something. He'd shot the falls four times already, but it had been a criminal waste of film. What insipid pictures. It was as if he'd been in such a hurry to leave Firefly Glen that he'd forgotten to pack his talent.

The sweet-light just might make the difference. He should hurry.

But instead of picking up his equipment, he stayed where he was, on one of the resort's deck chairs overlooking the bright blue pool, which overlooked the glimmering green ocean. He'd been here almost an hour already, holding but not drinking a very expensive glass of spring water and listening to the wind clicking palm fronds like castanets.

And trying to figure out what the hell was wrong with him.

This was his chosen life. The footloose photographer, traveling to exotic locales at whim, searching for the perfect picture.

And until recently it had suited him just fine. No strings, no complications, no boredom. Five-star resorts and perfect-ten women, a new one every time he got restless. And, of course, photography to feed his creative side.

The perfect life, right?

Wrong. It didn't feel even remotely exciting anymore. It felt like a puffed-up collection of dust—no substance, no meaning, nothing that wouldn't blow away in the first wind.

Suddenly it seemed that he had nothing, nothing that mattered, anyhow. No Heather, no Stewberts, no Firefly Glen. And absolutely no interest in sex, perfect ten or otherwise. Just a series of impersonal, monotonous hotel rooms and small talk with strangers. Bad food, bad mattresses and, worst of all, very bad pictures.

He told himself it was only temporary. It would pass. He'd get over it.

He could start by getting out to the damn waterfall before the sweet-light turned into utter darkness.

But he didn't go. He crossed his legs and watched the water.

After a few minutes, a young man sat down on the deck chair next to him. He had a baby girl on his lap, all dressed up in a starched pink dress, lacy pink socks and tiny patent leather shoes. A rather foolish big pink bow had been propped on her little bald head.

"Hi," the man said in a friendly voice. He nodded toward the ocean. "It's nice, huh?"

"Gorgeous," Griffin agreed, welcoming the distraction from his own thoughts. He smiled at the baby, who looked red faced, fussy and a little confused, as if she had been crying so long she'd forgotten why. "How old is she?"

"Four months," the man said. He jiggled the baby nervously. "I don't know why she's so grumpy. I've tried everything, but she just keeps crying."

Griffin could have suggested taking off some of those hot, scratchy clothes, but it wasn't any of his business, so he kept quiet.

Apparently Griffin provided a momentary distraction, because the baby stared at him fixedly, her damp eyes intensely curious. Griffin met her gaze pleasantly but without any overeager interest of his own. Babies, he had learned, liked to make the first overture.

Her mouth was open, drooling, and she was frowning slightly, as if he were some strange new species she had yet to catalogue and wasn't sure she approved of. Griffin had to fight back a chuckle. It was a pretty uppity look, actually, as if she were the Queen Mother instead of a little bald blob who couldn't even sit up yet without her daddy's chest to balance against.

God, children's faces were wonderful, their emotions playing on their features as clearly as the wind racing across the water. His fingers itched to take out his camera and see if he could capture that hilarious, endearing expression.

He was shocked to realize that this was the first truly creative urge he'd felt since he left Firefly Glen.

For no apparent reason, the little girl began to wail. Her daddy patted her back and bounced her gently on his knee, obviously beside himself with anxiety.

"She's usually pretty happy," he said to Griffin apologetically. "I just don't get it. I've changed her, fed her, burped her." He looked down at his yowling daughter. "Come on, Ginny, tell me what's wrong. We don't want to have to wake Mommy up. She really needs a nap."

But Ginny just arched herself furiously and cried harder. Poor kid, Griffin thought. It was hard to watch anyone in such inconsolable distress. She reached her little fist up and tugged at her ear—and the gesture triggered something in Griffin's subconscious.

"Could she be teething?" The Stewberts had tugged their ears like that when their teeth were hurting them. Now…if he could just remember what Heather had done. Oh, yes, those cold ring toys he had kept finding in the refrigerator. "I think ice helps to numb it."

The daddy looked at Griffin's glass hopefully. But Griffin, not having been driven mad by hours of this, still retained enough good sense to realize that an ice cube was one of the millions of things babies could choke on.

He transferred his glass to the other hand to remove temptation from the father, whose eyes were starting to look a little crazed. He remembered that feeling, when you would trade your soul for a few minutes of quiet—

except that apparently no one was interested in taking the deal.

"Sometimes just rubbing your knuckle against their gums can give some relief," he suggested. "And there's some kind of lotion stuff you can buy at the drugstore."

The daddy was obviously so desperate he'd try anything. He rubbed the edge of his index finger across the baby's tiny mouth. The crying faded instantly.

"Wow," the young man said, looking at Griffin with awed gratitude. "You're good at this baby thing."

Griffin smiled. "Not really," he said, remembering Heather's gentle ivory fingers smoothing matted hair from Stewbert's damp brow. "But I'm lucky. I know someone who is."

"My wife's good at it, too. But she's so tired today." The young man sighed and stood, not removing his finger from his daughter's mouth. "Hey, listen, I'm Doug. Thanks a lot. If I can fix this by myself, it will really impress my wife. She thinks I'm hopeless."

"Nobody's hopeless," Griffin said slowly, wondering if that could be true. Wanting it to be true. "Believe me, Doug. If I can do it, anybody can."

The young man smiled. "I knew you must have kids. How many?"

"None." Griffin stood up. "But I am just about to go home and fix that. Assuming, God help me, that it's not too late."

"Too late?" Doug looked concerned. "Why would it be too late?"

"Because I'm a moron, that's why. I'm an unmitigated fool and—"

Griffin stopped, wondering what on earth had come over him. Not only was he spilling his guts to a complete stranger...he also thought he saw Heather Delaney walking toward him, dressed in a flowered bikini, with a soft, transparent green skirt wrapped around her hips and a yellow hibiscus in her hair.

Right. Heather Delaney with a hibiscus in her hair.

He'd finally gone completely crazy, that was the only explanation. Still, he couldn't take his eyes off the woman, who would probably notice it soon and call the police. He'd never spent the night in jail before. At least that would solve the monotony of cookie-cutter hotel rooms.

But she walked like Heather, with that special combination of sex and elegance that made his knees weak. She was ivory skinned, rare on this island of sun-worshippers. Her hair shone like cinnamon glitter.

Something deep in the pit of Griffin's stomach began to pulse out a beat of primitive recognition.

It was Heather. It was.

"Hey, are you okay?" Doug sounded worried.

"I'm fine," Griffin said softly. "In fact, I think I'm about to be the happiest man on this island."

Doug frowned, then followed Griffin's gaze. Heather was still gliding toward them. She had begun to smile.

Doug laughed, light finally dawning. "Oh, I see. So I guess the answer is no, it's not too late."

"I sincerely hope you're right," Griffin said without

taking his eyes from Heather. He was afraid she might disappear if he so much as blinked. "I don't mean to be rude, Doug, but with any kind of luck the next few minutes are going to require a little privacy."

"Gotcha." Doug disappeared with a fascinated smile at Heather, who was now only a few feet away from Griffin.

She was, hands down, the most beautiful sight Griffin had ever seen. More beautiful than a golden October in Firefly Glen, a luna moth in Peru, or a roseate spoonbill over the Everglades—though those were three of the most stunning visions of his photographer's life. She made his heart pound harder than an earthquake, a charging lion, a war—though he had seen them all.

And with a flash of sudden awareness, Griffin understood that he was finished traveling forever. Without Heather, nothing would ever be exciting again. And, with her, nothing could ever be dull.

She came so close he could smell her. Then she tilted her lovely gaze at him and smiled.

"Well, as I live and breathe," she said, her voice husky, as sultry as surf rolling in over pebbled beaches. "If it isn't Playboy Cahill."

He almost couldn't speak. He didn't have a single clever one-liner at his disposal. It was as if he had dropped his bag of tricks from weakened fingers, and everything glib was running out like sand.

"Heather," he said simply. His voice was hoarse. "I can't believe it's really you."

She came another inch closer.

"Maybe," she said gently, "if you touched me, you'd be sure."

Something ungovernable was rising within him. It felt like something he had believed dead. It felt a lot like hope.

He tried to smile. "If I touch you, sweetheart, I'll be lost."

"Wouldn't that be only fair?" She gazed at him thoughtfully. "After all, I am here, away from everything I thought defined me. I'm here on this island with only one thing to trust—the way I feel about you."

"And what is that?" His throat was dry. "What do you feel?"

"Love," she said.

Her pale cheeks were flushed, and her eyes were bright with a fever he recognized. "I love you, Griffin. I always have. I followed you here to ask you to forgive me. I was a fool. I don't care if you want me for ten minutes or ten years. Just want me. Please say you still want me."

The wind blew a strand of silky auburn hair across her porcelain cheek. He reached up and eased it away.

"I want you," he said quietly. "But what about what *you* want? What about the better life you said you deserved? The better man you said could give it to you?"

She closed her eyes, sighing. When she opened them again, they were as clear and green as the ocean.

"I wish I had fallen in love with him," she said. "With a quiet family man who wanted to spend his life in Firefly Glen, at Spring House with me, with our baby in his arms.''

She shook her head. ''But I didn't. God help me, I fell in love with you.''

''Heather—''

''Please,'' she said, ''let me explain. I have thought it through very carefully, Griffin. If I married that 'better' man, it would be the most horrible farce. I would hate him, and myself, before the wedding cake was stale. And even worse—if I had another man's child.'' She took a ragged breath. ''I would spend my life searching his eyes, in vain, for some small sign of you.''

He tightened his throat, the very thought a hot knife in his gut. Another man's child...

She made a weak attempt at a laugh. ''So you have to agree, don't you? I'm not sacrificing myself by coming to you like this. I'm *saving* myself, and I'm saving that poor, unsuspecting fellow, too.''

''God, Heather...''

He reached out then and gathered her into his arms. She came willingly, folding herself against him without any lingering trace of resistance. She meant it, he thought, humbled. He was the most unworthy, superficial, cheating bastard on the planet. He had broken her heart once, and he'd almost broken it again. But somehow, in spite of everything she loved him. She was willing to give up her dreams for him.

But, for once in his self-indulgent life, he was going to do the right thing. He was going to refuse the offer.

He bent his head, letting his cheek rub the sun-warmed silk of her hair. "That may be the most generous offer anyone has ever made," he said. "But I can't let you do it."

She twisted in his arms, but he held her tight.

"Shh," he whispered, the way he might have soothed Stewbert when he cried. "I don't know anything about marriage. Not about happy marriage, anyhow. My parents destroyed each other, inch by inch, over twenty horrible years. That's all I've ever experienced. So you see, you were right. The very thought of marriage terrifies me."

"I know," she said. "But I don't care. You don't have to—"

"I won't let you do this. You deserve everything you ever dreamed of, sweetheart. You deserve a wedding, a home, a baby."

She made a soft sound of frustrated distress. "You're not listening," she said.

"No. *You're* not." He put his hands on her cheeks and lifted her frantic face to his. "I believe with my whole heart that you deserve a better man, Heather. So I will just have to become one." He smiled. "Maybe you can teach me."

She stared at him, tears half-shed and trembling on her eyelids. She frowned, shaking her head, seemingly without even realizing it. "I don't understand," she said.

"I'm asking you to marry me. I'm asking you to take all that amazing, generous love you have inside and teach me to be a good husband.'' He kissed the edge of her mouth. ''And then, when you're sure I'm worthy, you can teach me to be a good father.''

Her breath was coming fast. ''You don't have to do this,'' she said raggedly. ''That's why I came, so that you'd know you don't have to—''

''But I *do* have to.'' He kissed the other side of her mouth. ''I have to marry you because I can't live without you. When I stood up just now, I was coming home to ask you, to beg you, to be my wife.''

''Oh, Griffin…'' She swallowed, and the tears finally fell.

''If that's my answer,'' he said, smiling, ''it's a little ambiguous. I could use a simple yes or no.'' He kissed her nose. ''Of the two, a simple yes would actually be preferable.''

''Yes,'' she said, smiling through her tears. ''The answer is simply yes.''

He kissed her, then, though he knew he should have waited. A dozen people were watching, probably some children among them, and if he lost control he was likely to get them thrown off this island for public indecency.

But he couldn't stop himself. She was his. His heart was spinning flaming cartwheels, and his whole damn body was on fire with wanting her.

He couldn't get her close enough. He drove his kiss hard, and she opened eagerly. He wrapped his hands around her waist, slid his fingers down the frothy nothingness of her skirt, into the tiny fabric of her bikini…

And encountered the dreaded pager.

He extracted it with a curse. ''Bloody hell,'' he said. ''You didn't. You didn't bring this damn thing *with* you?''

She smiled sheepishly, her lips slightly swollen and pink from the intensity of their kiss. ''It's just for emergencies. Adam's in charge, but in case something comes up, I couldn't exactly—''

''Emergencies!'' Griffin growled. ''If that hypochondriac Anna Mizell calls you one single time, I'll throw it into the ocean.''

''She won't.'' Heather settled herself back in Griffin's arms comfortably. ''She went out of town for a family wedding, though I had told her not to, and she went into labor there. Some doctor in Rochester delivered her baby two days ago. Mother and child are both fine.''

Griffin chuckled. ''I guess now you have to admit that it might possibly be okay to take a tiny vacation now and then. Apparently you're not completely indispensable.''

She wrapped her arms around his neck. ''Apparently not,'' she agreed.

''Except, of course, to me.'' He slid the pager back into its makeshift pouch. His fingers touched the satiny skin of her buttocks, and Griffin felt himself tightening. They'd better get into the hotel room fast. Or maybe there was some gigantic sand dune nearby…

''Yes,'' she said, nuzzling his neck as if she knew

he was in danger of disgracing himself and was devilishly enjoying the idea. ''Except to you.''

''Let's go inside,'' he said gruffly. ''I'm on the top floor. Do you have a room?''

She smiled. ''I'm on the first floor,'' she said proudly. ''Wasn't that smart of me?''

''Brilliant,'' he agreed. ''We'll use yours.''

He took her hand and started leading her toward the lobby. But then he had a sudden annoying thought. He turned and, slipping his hand down her bikini panties one more time, he extracted the pager again.

''I'll keep this,'' he said. ''I'll be damned if I'm going to have the wretched thing going off while I'm trying to make babies.''

She stopped in her tracks. ''Make babies? Why, Griffin Cahill. I thought you just said we were going to wait until I felt sure you were worthy.''

''Ah. See how very bad I am?'' Grinning, he pulled her close for another kiss. ''I lied to you already.''